DEAR MISS KOPP

BOOKS BY AMY STEWART

Fiction

Girl Waits with Gun

Lady Cop Makes Trouble

Miss Kopp's Midnight Confessions

Miss Kopp Just Won't Quit

Kopp Sisters on the March

Dear Miss Kopp

Nonfiction

From the Ground Up: The Story of a First Garden

The Earth Moved: On the Remarkable
Achievements of Earthworms

Flower Confidential: The Good, the Bad, and
the Beautiful in the Business of Flowers

Wicked Plants: The Weed That Killed Lincoln's Mother
& Other Botanical Atrocities

Wicked Bugs: The Louse That Conquered Napoleon's
Army & Other Diabolical Insects

The Drunken Botanist: The Plants That Create
the World's Great Drinks

DEAR MISS KOPP

Amy Stewart

Mariner Books
Houghton Mifflin Harcourt
Boston   New York   2020

For information about permission to reproduce selections
from this book, write to trade.permissions@hmhco.com or to
Permissions, Houghton Mifflin Harcourt Publishing Company,
3 Park Avenue, 19th Floor, New York, New York 10016.

hmhbooks.com

Library of Congress Cataloging-in-Publication Data
Names: Stewart, Amy, author.
Title: Dear Miss Kopp / Amy Stewart.
Description: Boston : Houghton Mifflin Harcourt, 2020. |
Series: A Kopp sisters novel ; 6
Identifiers: LCCN 2019057826 (print) | LCCN 2019057827 (ebook) |
ISBN 9780358093121 (trade paperback) |
ISBN 9780358093107 (hardcover) | ISBN 9780358093015 (ebook)
Subjects: GSAFD: Historical fiction. | Mystery fiction.
Classification: LCC PS3619.T49343 D43 2020 (print) |
LCC PS3619.T49343 (ebook) | DDC 813/.6—dc23
LC record available at https://lccn.loc.gov/2019057826
LC ebook record available at https://lccn.loc.gov/2019057827

Printed in the United States of America
DOC 10 9 8 7 6 5 4 3 2 1

To
Maud Cauchois
and
Franck Besch

DEAR MISS KOPP

NORMA

Langres, France

CONSTANCE TO NORMA

May 2, 1918

Dear Norma,

You're a terrible correspondent and there's no excuse for it. Fleurette and I are left stateside while you march off to France. We had a few decent letters when you were in Paris and a passable selection when you arrived at your secret location, but lately you're sending us nothing but an occasional "I am well" to let us know that you're alive. Are words also being rationed overseas, even short ones?

I'm beginning to suspect that you wrote a year's worth of brief, perfunctory letters already—did you do them on the ship?—and now you simply select one to fit the circumstances.

It's true, isn't it? That sounds just like something you'd do. To wit:

Yours of a month ago read in its entirety: "All is well here and the meals are decent. Work continues apace."

Two weeks ago we were treated to: "Health is good. Food ordinary but adequate. Work proceeds as expected."

Yesterday the postman oughtn't to have bothered, so light were his duties. "Am well. Expect the same for you."

Really, Norma! Not even a mention of the decent, ordinary, adequate meals this time?

It's bad enough that our letters take weeks or even months to reach each other. Can't you put something in them that's worth the wait?

For the better part of 1917, when you were still here in New Jersey, we were treated to almost daily dispatches from Fort Monmouth. You seemed to have no difficulty in recounting names, personalities, conversations, arguments (mostly there were arguments, as I recall, but somehow the Army decided to keep you anyway), and, if anything, excessively detailed descriptions of the military's pigeon messenger program, its small triumphs and all too frequent setbacks. Why, then, is it so difficult to put down a line or two now that you're working on the very same program in France?

Meanwhile, here I am in a boarding-house with twenty other women. A letter from overseas is an occasion: we all gather around the parlor in the evenings to read them aloud. Just last week, Kit in 3F had a letter from her brother about a French mutt his unit picked up. He even drew a picture of the dog. I've heard tales of dances with officers (not that I expect you to dance with an officer), pitiable descriptions of wounded men coming out of surgery and asking how many limbs remained, and accounts of air raids that would set your hair aflame.

Pages, Norma! Pages and pages they write. The soldiers, the nurses, the ambulance drivers—every one of them has something to say about the war, except you.

I know that your work with the carrier pigeons is of great importance and must be cloaked in secrecy. But once—just once—give the censor something to do! Let him go to work on a four-pager. As it is, he hardly need hold your envelope up to the light to see that it contains nothing of interest to the Germans (or to your family, for that matter). He can probably tell by weighing it how little ink has been spilled.

We've never been apart in our lives, and there you are, half a world away. Couldn't you paint a picture of the sort of place you've been sent, or give some general idea of the goings-on?

If nothing else, I hope you'll take seriously my suggestion to keep a diary, and to make a record of anything that wouldn't be allowed past the censors. I put three note-books in your trunk when you left, and I'll send you more if you like. I'm convinced that if you don't write something down for us to read when you return, you'll come home and say that you single-handedly won the war and there's nothing else to tell. Well, there is quite a bit to tell, so get to it.

Yours,

Constance (and Fleurette, if she were here, but she hardly ever is)

NORMA TO CONSTANCE

June 6, 1918

Dear Constance (and Fleurette, if she can be found),

I suppose you're feeling puny down there in the parlor at night, when the others are reading their letters. I hate to think what sort of people you're living among, but if a letter from France is all they have to prop themselves up, I suggest you let them cling to their small triumphs and get on with your own work, or have you run out of saboteurs to chase?

I'm in a village in France that I cannot name, doing work I'm not allowed to describe, with the aim of defeating the Germans, which you already knew. What more is there to say?

Food is nourishing, bed is clean and dry, the war goes on.

As ever,

Norma

P.S. Aggie has read your letter and my reply. She became quite stern and demanded that I write a minimum of three pages next week. She's like a schoolmistress, only more fearsome.

P.P.S. Now I suppose you'll be wanting to know who Aggie is.

NORMA TO CONSTANCE

June 15, 1918

Dear Constance,

Your package of May 5 arrived in good condition. Aggie wants to write the thank-you letter herself and I will let her, but she says that I must do the introductions first, and make some sort of improvement on my previous correspondence.

Agnes Bell (Aggie, she insists on it) is a nurse stationed at the American hospital here. She comes from Columbus, Ohio, where, after her parents died, she was raised by a grandfather who is now quite elderly and has no interest in her (and didn't take much interest when she was younger). Her older brothers, who are known to her only by rumor, were placed in care elsewhere, most likely reformatories, and cannot be found. She hasn't any family to write to herself, which is why she takes such interest in your letters.

Aggie and I are billeted at a hotel that has been entirely requisitioned for women. It offers thirty rooms, which means sixty women, and if you think that sounds cozy and cheerful, you would be mistaken. What little the hotel had in the way of plumbing and lighting is excessively burdened by the demands of sixty American women, plus a few Canadians. (The British have made their own arrangements at the other end of town.) There's nothing in the way of a hot bath, only a bucket of water and a bar of soap in a frigid water closet. Even that is only to be enjoyed once a week according to a schedule posted on the door.

We have no parlor in which to gather as you do (not that I would gather in a parlor, with a war on), as even the lobby has been sectioned off and turned into lodging.

Aggie and I share a room, if you can call it that. It's really the corner of an attic with a few boards knocked together to serve as walls, so cold in winter that we often thought we'd be better off outside under a nice soft blanket of snow. With summer coming on, it's already stifling up here.

You might wonder why we're living at a hotel, and you would not be the only one. The Army made no provisions whatsoever for the women who have been called into service. I suppose it never occurred to them that hospitals would have need of nurses. Even in the Signal Corps, with women running the switchboards, no one thought to build a female barracks or provide anything in the way of uniforms or supplies. It's fallen to the YWCA to simply turn up wherever we happen to be sent, and to do for us in any way they can. Otherwise it seems to have been the Army's idea that we'd simply live on air.

This is why women tend to be billeted at hotels or tucked into a widow's spare room while the men are far more usefully housed in barracks alongside their place of work. In another village "somewhere in France," the girls on the switchboard are walking a mile and a half to work. Here in my particular "somewhere," the men are quartered at the fort while I live three miles away, in town, which makes for a walk of an hour if one strolls along as if to a picnic, or forty minutes at a good march. I arrive in thirty-five.

About my own duties I can say almost nothing. Aggie wants me to tell you about the village instead. I hardly think a Baedeker's guide makes for suitable war-time correspondence, but she's quite vocal on this point, and we do live in close quarters.

In spite of my best efforts to be sent to the front, I'm stationed in a village well away from the fighting. It isn't because I'm a woman, or it isn't only that: the canteen girls, after all, come through town with stories of hiding in a cave all night with the German shells whistling and bursting overhead. Somehow it's all right for them but I'm ordered to stay behind. The trouble is that it's impossible for me, being so far removed from the action, to have any idea if our program is seeing any success at all. But this is where they've put us and this is where we shall stay.

By "we" I mean about ten thousand Americans. Almost every training school of any consequence is here, including mine. We've doubled if not tripled the population of the place, and that doesn't count the refugees, the British and Canadian units, or the endless train-loads of injured men arriving at one of the hospitals here.

As you can imagine, we have quite overwhelmed this tiny village. I'm sure you can picture the sort of place it is: one of those old hilltop settlements with a stone wall around it, first established by the Gauls but then—inevitably—seized by the Romans, who made those improvements for which they are rightfully famous: bridges and buttresses, a system of water-ways, and carved channels for sewage. Such marvels of the ancient world are still enjoyed by the villagers today—or they were, until our boys came in and put a stop to it.

This was, in other words, quite a primitive place before the war. Now, courtesy of the United States Army, the sewers have been put underground where they belong, the entire village electrified, and the roads macadamized, so that our automo-biles (whose tires are far more delicate than horses' hooves, yet for reasons never adequately explained we send the autos into war) may pass over them.

Village life remains as unchanged as can be under the circumstances. A man comes once a week and drops a load of coal into the town square, which the villagers scurry out to collect according to some system never explained to me. Amid the rationing there is still a market day on Thursday, where one can find turnips in abundance, mounds of a soft round cheese covered in mold, and rabbits for stewing, that being the only meat not in short supply. Church services run more often than the trains in Pennsylvania Station, owing to the number of saints and so forth whose days must be observed. For this they gather in a drafty and dark cathedral that has served them in this manner for some eight hundred years.

Otherwise, the villagers live very much indoors, behind walls of ochre-colored stone and heavy wooden doors with enormous iron hinges forged during the Crusades. Their windows are similarly shuttered, as they abhor the outdoor air and fear it is poisonous. The mustard gas coming off the soldiers' uniforms does nothing to dissuade them of this notion. For roofing material they prefer chestnut shingles, weathered white, or red clay tiles in the tradition of the Spanish, held together with moss, lichen, and coal-dust.

There, now you have it. The candle is nearly gone, so I must close. If you're going to continue to insist on letters of this length, send some of those good tallow candles — but wait until summer is over or I'll get nothing but a puddle at the bottom of the box.

As ever,

Norma

P.S. I've had a letter from one of the girls at the Sicomac Dairy, written as a school assignment, I gather. (Is every child in America being told to write a letter to someone in France?) It sounds as though the dairy is being run entirely by the girls now, and that they have it well in hand and are making good use of our barn and fields while we're away. Have you been out to have a look at the house itself? It isn't good to let it remain boarded and locked. You ought to go out once a month to give it an airing and make sure the roof and gutters are in good repair.

P.P.S. Of course I don't keep a diary, it's strictly forbidden as it could fall into Boche hands. I do, however, maintain a log-book, which consists only of records of our activities and minutes of meetings. I write the minutes myself to avoid the sorts of mishaps and misunderstandings that occur with alarming frequency around here. The notes will be helpful as I've just had a letter from General Murray, who is stuck stateside and wants to know how our program is being run without him. I intend to give him an earful.

(ENCLOSED) AGGIE TO CONSTANCE

Dear Constance,

Norma shared your package with me and I absolutely begged to write a note to thank you. We appreciate the hand cream more than you can possibly know. My fingers get horribly chapped and raw by the end of the day. We will use tallow, petroleum jelly, anything! That it smells of roses is reason enough to keep it under lock and key—no one here has anything so fine. And please don't apologize for the stockings—the sturdier and woollier, the better. Silk wouldn't last an hour.

I want you to know how much your gifts mean to us, so if you'll pardon the gruesome details, I'll tell you that your package arrived at the end of an absolutely murderous day at the hospital. A fresh wave of wounded came in just yesterday, many of them gassed so badly that they'd been coughing uncontrollably for days. Some of them can't eat on account of their throats being absolutely ruined, and they arrive shockingly malnourished as a result.

The worst, though, are the men with truly devastating wounds that have received no attention beyond a hasty field dressing. Those bandages are, of course, muddy and soaked through in blood by the time they get here. Changing them is an ordeal that nothing in nursing school could've prepared me for. Three times yesterday I had to sit on a man's chest to stop him from bucking and fighting while the doctors peeled away the old bandages. To have to wrestle with a grown man like that, while he's in such screaming agony—well, a year ago, I never could've imagined I'd have the nerve.

But we must summon up the nerve! And then, when we go home at night (if we are able to go home at night, often we stay on duty for a day or two at a time), we are an absolute puddle, every one of us. That's why it means so much to see a friendly face waiting for us—your sister's face, in my case— and to have a package from home. That you are able to find any small luxury at all to send—well, I just can't tell you how it lifts me up. Norma left your dear parcel on my pillow last night, and when I finally crawled into bed after midnight, I admit that the tenderness of her gesture—and yours—made me cry a little. It's all right, though—a good cry settles me down, and after that I went right to sleep, and clutched your gifts all night long.

Most of all, though, I wanted to thank you for loaning me your sister. It is a hardship and a sacrifice to send our loved ones overseas. The war is unbearable, but Norma helps me to bear it.

She told me that your sister-in-law, Bessie, knows how to

make everything better with a cake. Now, when I have a difficult day at the hospital, Norma does the same for me. (Well,
she doesn't bake a cake, but she can procure one from the
baker down the street. Not an entire cake—those go to the
generals!—but a slice.)

What a blessing she is! A bit of cake works wonders, but
so does she.

I suppose you know that Norma is having her own difficulties with her work. I asked her if I couldn't just say a little
about what has been happening at the fort, and what a trying time she's having with that awful Captain Buscall, but she
won't allow it.

I told her that we ought to write it down and let the censor cross it out if he must. She insists, however, that it isn't
just the censor—it's Army regulations. Her work is of a secretive nature, and she fears the worst if the Huns find out what
she's up to. Still, I know she wishes she had her sisters here to
lend a sympathetic ear. I'm a poor substitute, but I do my best.
Fortunately, she's now corresponding with her former commander, General Murray, who sounds like a much more sensible man than the fellow in charge here. Perhaps he'll know
what to do.

I have my own work tonight, as we have an Army auditor
visiting the hospital in a few weeks and I'm poring over my
record-books to make sure they're in order. Please give my best
to Fleurette, Francis, Bessie, and the children. I feel as though
I know each and every one of you through your letters.

I am trying to learn my French phrases, so I will close with
Tendrement—
Aggie

June 18, 1918

Dear General Murray,

Yours of June 5 received last night. It was the first letter I've had by military courier. I've seen the man go by, but he's never stopped at the women's billet before. Do you know that he carries his letters in a sinkable pouch? We will leave no military correspondence for the Germans—if the ship is attacked, our letters go to the bottom of the ocean.

I was glad to hear that you've kept up your training duties at Fort Monmouth, but disappointed to learn that the hearing loss is worse. I still maintain that it was no reason to sideline you from the war. Half the men returning from the front complain of such ringing in their ears that we wonder if they'll ever hear properly again. They manage, and so could you. But as you say, the Army ordains and we obey.

As to your request that I report back on the troubles we're having with the pigeon program, I wouldn't mind at all. I appreciate that it's beyond your powers to intervene, and I wouldn't ask it of you. But you're right that the pigeon unit will continue beyond this war and (I shudder to think it) into the next. With that in mind, there is value in learning from our mistakes—and the mistakes are many, as you will see. A first-hand account, put down in the moment and not influenced by afterthoughts and second-guessing, could in fact be of use someday.

To begin, I'll tell you this: When I arrived, I was horrified to see that our unit had set things up entirely backwards and had no idea how to proceed. The trainees were on the verge of adopting the British method, which would've been a disaster, or, worse, the French method, which would've sunk the entire enterprise. You can be sure that I told them so on my first day on duty. Would you believe that not a single one of them seemed to hear a word I said, after I'd come all this way to say it?

Worse still, they took such great satisfaction in reciting back to me the orders they'd been given, in spite of the fact that those orders have led to any number of horrors: rotten and contaminated feed, a fungal outbreak, cankers, lice, and (predictably, as a result of all this) feather-picking. We wouldn't send a man to the front in that condition, and we can't send a pigeon, either.

If the men had been told nothing at all, I wouldn't blame them for the situation. As it is, they were given the wrong orders, carried them out with blind loyalty, and ignored the appalling results in front of them. For that I do place blame. I'd send them all home and run the place myself if it were within my power to do so.

But I'm not in command, Captain Buscall is. It would be a gross violation of protocol for me to give my unvarnished opinion of him, but it is strictly accurate to say that the man had never so much as fed a bread crumb to a pigeon before he took charge of our unit.

I hope that gives a general picture. More detailed reports will be forthcoming.

Yours in service,

Norma C. Kopp

AGGIE TO CONSTANCE

June 25, 1918

Dear Constance,

I hope you don't mind if I continue to write to you. I know how eager you are to hear something of Norma's work, and even she concedes that this is a story that shouldn't bother the censor. It has very little to do with war-work, but might tell you something of how the villagers adapt to suddenly having to live among thousands of foreign soldiers. I did try to persuade Norma to write it out herself, but her version of events made no sense whatsoever and I took over the pen.

Your sister works in tight quarters, at an ancient stone fort that the French have not entirely relinquished to the Americans. I've not seen it myself, but it sounds like a frightful old medieval shambles of a place, with wooden beams either half-rotted or half-burned, or both, carved with the names of soldiers who have occupied it over the centuries. In some of the old stone rooms—dungeons, really, are what they sound like—men stationed there eons ago made little marks to count the days as they passed. It's even surrounded by a moat and drawbridge. Honestly, it sounds horrible, but for some reason the French are quite proud of it and insisted on occupying it themselves as soon as the Americans expressed an interest.

Did the Americans leave politely, and find themselves another old ruin to inhabit? No, they did not. The Army simply took over the grounds surrounding the fort, built wooden barracks for the troops, and started constructing dovecotes and pigeon transport carts and all the other equipment required for the training program that Norma was sent here to put into place. This upset the French a great deal, as the fort's old stone buildings had been cleverly hidden from view through years of building up mounds around them and letting vines cover the roofs. Now the new barracks stand in plain sight, but honestly, it doesn't matter. Anyone flying over this town would see barracks everywhere. We've built an entire avenue of them just outside the old Roman gate. You should see it—it's practically a second village.

Back to the fort: At any given time, there are a hundred or so soldiers assigned to the pigeon unit. Most consider it light duty and complain that their time is wasted on bird-keeping. Nonetheless, everyone is expected to finish a ten-day rotation, and some are assigned to stay longer to do general maintenance and chores. That means that two or three times a month, Norma is presented with a new class of bored and list-less Signal Corps trainees who want nothing more than to return to town, where they might enjoy a late-night beer, paved streets to walk, and nurses with whom to keep company.

A requirement of the course is to load a cart with pigeons and to hitch it up to a weary-looking old horse conscripted from a nearby farm. Half the men are told to take the cart ten miles out into the countryside to release the pigeons, with messages tied to their legs, while the other half remain at the fort to receive the messages.

As Norma believes that those receiving the birds need more instruction than those releasing them, she generally stays behind. However, she recently learned that her students were not riding ten miles away as instructed. They were instead traveling only a mile, to a village even smaller than the one we occupy. It's not even a village, really—just a cluster of buildings where two roads converge, with a half-dozen farmhouses beyond.

Here's what was happening, in this most uncosmopolitan setting: The enterprising daughter of a pig farmer started running an impromptu café out of her father's barn, offering cigarettes and home-made wine to any American who happened by. She could see Norma's students coming, in their high-sided pigeon cart, from a good distance away, along the little lane that descends into the village. By the time they arrived, she'd have put out chairs and tables, a little glass cup of cigarettes, and a bottle of her father's wine. Her father, away in the fields all day, never saw the café society his daughter had formed, but the neighbors knew.

Word reached the girl's father soon enough. Yesterday he presented himself at the gates of the fort, with a hefty package of bacon wrapped in brown paper as a peace offering, and a polite but terse request that the soldiers find another *porcher*'s daughter to visit.

Apparently the commanders of Norma's unit were not particularly bothered by it and in fact proposed a walk down to this particular village themselves, to investigate the situation and perhaps gain a fuller understanding of the farmer's daughter who can turn a pig barn into a café.

Norma, however, was furious. It can't be easy for her, as the only woman. As you can imagine, the men don't see why they should take orders from her. I do know what that's like. At the hospital, we have male orderlies who won't listen to a nurse, even though she has medical training and he does not! It's endlessly frustrating and causes needless delays and unnecessary errors. In Norma's case, she feels like they're making a mockery of a program that she has, in one way or another, worked a lifetime to perfect.

Now, as a consequence of this latest mishap, she accompanies all of her students on their pigeon runs, whether they like it or not (and they don't). She punished the offenders by requiring them to clean the dovecotes, and to undertake the endless repairs to the lofts that are necessary to keep out the very determined French rats, who adore the pigeons' grain and have nothing better to do than to spend their nights gnawing through the wooden walls to get to it. The repairs are only temporary buttresses against the rats, but with metal in short supply, there is nothing to do but to constantly replace the chewed-up boards. It gives her great pleasure to inflict this chore on her errant students.

I must confess some sympathy for the soldiers. If a pig barn is to be their only entertainment, I say to let them have it. More than that, though, I admire the pluck of the farmer's daughter, who contrived to bring a spark of life to what must otherwise be, for her, a lonely existence.

Every one of these young men has lost friends and brothers already, and none of them can say with certainty that they'll ever see home again. Perhaps they deserve their merriment — but not on Norma's watch!

Tendrement —
Aggie

P.S. As you can see, we have blue envelopes now for letters home, with the idea that they are not inspected as closely. I hope this one goes through.

NORMA TO GENERAL MURRAY

June 28, 1918

Dear General Murray,

I'm writing with news of a rather alarming meeting I just had with Captain Buscall. You may form your own assessment of him from my notes of our discussion, held in advance of the arrival of Colonel Hartman, who will be here next month to inspect and review our operation.

About these notes: When I first arrived at Fort de la Bonnelle, Captain Buscall mistook me for his secretary and asked me to take minutes of his meetings. You can be sure I corrected him without delay. I do nonetheless keep my own records of my meetings with him. This he objects to, for reasons I cannot fathom, as he was the one who wanted me taking notes in the first place.

Nonetheless, I will copy below my transcript of this week's meeting. Disregard the business about the pig farmer's daughter. It was an error in trainee oversight on my part that won't be repeated.

BUSCALL: Miss Kopp! I see you've been out with the boys
   to call on the pig farmer's daughter. Did you send her my
   regards?
KOPP: We send our trainees on a northern route now, toward Chaumont.
BUSCALL: That girl's going to get lonely.
KOPP: You asked to see me, sir?
BUSCALL: Yes. The pigeons aren't working out at the
   front.

KOPP: Beg pardon?

BUSCALL: I can't even begin to name all the problems we've had with them out there. I think we ought to —

KOPP: If you wouldn't mind naming them anyway, the rest of us might not know what they are.

BUSCALL (after much unnecessary sighing and shuffling of papers): Very well, here it is. Only half the pigeons released at the front returned to their loft. The rest, for all we know, were intercepted by the Germans and their messages read.

KOPP: The messages are in code, so the Germans don't matter. Were they fed according to the schedule?

BUSCALL: The Germans or the pigeons?

KOPP: (Question appeared to be frivolous in nature, not answered.)

BUSCALL: It really isn't necessary to write down every word. This is what even the Army would consider an informal discussion.

KOPP: The pigeons must be kept hungry if they are to return to their loft under difficult conditions. That is why, as you recall, we went to the trouble to test seven different feeding schedules and choose the one with the best results.

BUSCALL (looking at ceiling, appearing not to recall the feeding schedules, in spite of numerous briefings, recorded on previous pages of this very log-book): It's possible that you worked on that project on your own, Miss Kopp.

KOPP: And then I typed out the correct schedule and had it printed for distribution. Are the men at the front capable of reading instructions, or shall we resort to drawing pictures?

BUSCALL: That wasn't the only problem.

KOPP: It's also possible that they released the males and females together.

BUSCALL: What?

KOPP: Didn't you think to ask?

(Buscall shifts around in his chair but makes no reply.)

KOPP: A male and female, released together, will not return to the loft but will go off to mate. They must be starved for both food and companionship if they are to return faithfully home.

BUSCALL: I've been starved for food and companionship since I left Fort Monmouth, but nobody's letting me return home.

KOPP: (This, too, seemed a frivolous remark and not in need of a reply.)

BUSCALL: You definitely don't have to write down every word.

KOPP: Then we'll assume they ignored my instructions on that point as well. I believe this explains the problem of birds failing to return. What are the other complaints?

BUSCALL: Do there have to be any others?

KOPP: You said the problems were numerous, but you've only enumerated one, that of the pigeons failing to return. If you've been given a list, I'd like to hear it.

BUSCALL (more sighing and sifting of papers): Let's see. Pigeons dropped from aeroplanes were stripped of feathers.

KOPP: As we have no aviation school nearby, we were unable to make adequate tests under my supervision. I'm sure you'll recall that we wrote away to Issoudun, and the pilots there ran tests for us. The results were unambiguous.

(Kopp waits for Buscall to recall the results. He does not.)

KOPP: Seventy miles per hour. The planes must be slowed to seventy miles per hour for a successful pigeon drop. Did they slow the planes?

(Kopp awaits response but receives none.)

KOPP: I suppose no one knows or has bothered to inquire about the speed of the planes. Are there any other complaints, or do the too-numerous problems stop at two?

BUSCALL: It says here that the rats ate the pigeons' rations.

KOPP: In the trenches?

BUSCALL: Beg pardon?

KOPP: The rats eating the rations. Is it happening in the trenches, or back at the loft?

BUSCALL: In the trenches, miss. You just can't imagine what it's like out there.

KOPP: I shouldn't have to imagine, if you'd send me to the front so I could see for myself.

BUSCALL (shrugs): Orders, miss.

KOPP: Is that all?

BUSCALL: Colonel Hartman's had enough. He wants the program shut down. You can go over to Chaumont and work a switchboard if you like, but we're getting out of the bird business.

KOPP: I've already solved every problem you named, which is why I was sent here. The men simply aren't fol-

lowing instructions. I'll explain it to Colonel Hartman
when he's here next month.

BUSCALL: Colonels don't generally want things explained
to them.

KOPP: He can tell me that himself.

(end of meeting)

General Murray, you can see for yourself what I'm up
against. If I had any sort of authority at all, I'd have all of this
turned around and running the way you and I intended.

As it is, Colonel Hartman is due here in a month. I only
hope he's a man who can listen to reason. That would make
him a rarity around this place.

Yours in service,

Norma C. Kopp

NORMA TO GENERAL MURRAY

July 2, 1918

Dear General Murray,

I have further evidence regarding the improper and inadequate deployment of pigeons to the front. My source is a reli-
able one: a soldier just in from the trenches.

This morning I stopped at the hospital where my bunk-
mate, Aggie, works, to deliver one of her record-books. (She
has charge of supplies and medicines at the hospital.) She'd
left the book in our room after sitting up half the night to go
over her sums and make sure nothing was amiss before the
auditor began his review of her work. I knew she'd be frantic

when she realized it was missing, but wouldn't be allowed to run home and retrieve it.

The hospital, by the way, is nothing like what you might picture from your vantage point in New Jersey. By the time the Americans arrived here last fall, the only buildings left for us to commandeer for a hospital were the *école maternelle* and, next door, the *école de filles*. (The children have been sent home and nobody's having babies right now anyway, so it's just as well.) But imagine using a children's school for a hospital! It's entirely inadequate. The British have taken all the good buildings. This is our punishment for delaying so long in going into the war. I certainly hope President Wilson has been made to see the error in his decision.

Nonetheless, what we have for a hospital is a pair of two-story stone buildings, put up only ten or fifteen years ago but in the traditional style, with the local stone, a slate mansard roof, and carved scrollwork around the entrance. On the second floor are tall windows, where I often see a flock of pigeons gathered on the ledges. Aggie tells me that when she opens the shutters on a warm day, the birds venture inside for a taste of an infirm soldier's lunch. They (the pigeons) seem to be descended from old French military stock from the last century. They're far too sociable and inquisitive to make good messengers, so I haven't bothered to capture one.

The hospital is guarded by a pair of young men from Wisconsin who serve no purpose, as they allow anyone inside. When I arrived this morning, I was permitted to walk right in, as they tend to assume that any woman in uniform is a nurse. There are too many uniforms to keep track of here, between the Army nurses, the YMCA and YWCA canteen workers, the

Red Cross, and the British, Canadian, and Australian counterparts of all of these. Anyone with an armband and insignia might plausibly work for one or another of them.

My next obstacle was Betty Sanger, one of our Signal Corps operators, who is also billeted at my hotel. She runs the hospital switchboard and has been put in the untenable position of serving as a kind of informal greeter, which is wholly unsuited to her talents and training, but the Army puts us where it wants us and we don't say a word about it, do we?

I didn't want to hand over the record-book and risk it going astray. Betty promised to track down Aggie for me, but just then, a train-load of wounded men were carried in, still encrusted in filth from the trenches and wearing the most ghastly bandages from the field hospital. I'd never seen such a mess. She quite naturally had to see to them. I was made to wait.

I tucked myself into a seat in the corner with a book—I always bring a book, if I might have to wait, and as you know, so much of war-work involves waiting—but soon found myself face-to-face with an American private, laid out on a stretcher parked directly in front of me. He introduced himself as Forrest Pike.

"Good day, sir," I said to him.

"I'm no sir, I'm a private. Call me Forrest, nurse."

"I'm no nurse," I told him, but didn't offer my name. It's best not to strike up an acquaintanceship with a wounded soldier. They expect you to visit, and then you do, and one day you turn up and they've gone gangrenous and there's nothing to say after that.

Forrest held up a bandaged hand. "Lost a finger," he announced, grinning. "Care to guess which one?"

"Not particularly," I told him, and leaned around his stretcher to see if Betty had found Aggie. She had not.

"Well, you don't need to worry," Forrest said. "It's only a pinky. I can handle Emma Gee without it. They'll fix me up and send me back to the front."

"As they should," I said. "We're expected to give our all, not just our pinkies."

He liked that. "That's just what my sergeant said to me. They should make you a sergeant, miss."

"I hold the rank of lieutenant, but not the title." I never miss an opportunity to remind anyone associated with the military of this fact, even a private.

"Is that right? Do they have lady captains here, and lady majors?"

I looked around again for Betty, but she remained occupied with the wounded coming in. The injured are packed into railcars, practically stacked like cord-wood, and it's no small feat to ferry them up the hill from the station and into the hospital. There's a funicular, but it is both too compact and too leisurely for war-time duty.

With nothing else to do but wait, I told Private Pike about the pigeon program and our training school just outside of town.

He grew quite excited at that and said, "Is that right? Do you mean to say that you're the one who sent those birds out to us?"

Betty returned at that moment and waved me over, but I

didn't move. This was just the information I'd been looking for. "How many have you had?"

Forrest lay back and held up his bandaged hand, as if to count, which I suppose he meant in jest but it's impossible to know.

"A dozen or so. There was a white one in the last batch —he was especially friendly, like he'd been raised by hand—"

That was King, one of mine. "He had been," I told him. "Did he have a little scar on top of his head?"

"Now, how did you know that?"

That poor bird had been pecked by the others and left for dead, but I don't like to tell a wounded soldier a story like that. "Doesn't matter. How did they do?"

"Do? Well, I wanted to keep that white feller for a pet, he was so friendly and knew so many tricks—"

"He would shake your hand," I said.

"Yes! Did you teach him that?"

Now, General Murray, you have probably already guessed at what happened here. I raised this one myself, after the others pecked at him. The wound on his head was wide open, as big as the end of your thumb. It's a wonder he survived. For two weeks he lived in my room at night, sleeping in a little box right next to me in bed, under the covers, because he needed the warmth if he was to survive. I carried him through the streets of the village and out to the fort with me every day, and back home again at night, until he was well.

By the time he recovered, he'd developed this little trick of shaking hands. He liked to reach out with one leg and wrap his splayed toes around a finger as if in greeting. I didn't

teach it to him—you know I don't go in for tricks and entertainments—but it is the custom of the men in this village to
shake hands when they met, even if only passing briefly in
the street. A man can't run an errand without giving a dozen
handshakes along the way. I suppose King saw the men doing
it and took to it.

I didn't tell Forrest Pike any of that. I just let him talk.

He said, "Well, I liked him, but the fellas wouldn't let me
keep him. They found a lady in the village who said she'd need
an even dozen to make a pie. The French do have a way with
birds."

He said it with such appreciation! Reverence, even!

Well, I told him in no uncertain terms that the bird in question could have saved his life, had he not baked it into a pie.

"How's that, nurse? Lieutenant, I mean. You never did give
me your name. Most of the girls give their name and an address where I can write."

It hardly need be said that I'm not about to carry on a correspondence with a soldier, particularly one who ate a military
asset for dinner.

"The next time you receive a shipment of pigeons at the
front, read the instructions," I told him.

"Instructions?" Forrest asked. "There wasn't so much as a
card enclosed. We didn't know who to thank."

Well, there you have it. My birds were sent to the front
with no orders at all. Imagine the men in the trenches, receiving a basket of birds like a package from home! It's no wonder
they ate them.

Colonel Hartman is due any day now. I expect he'll put a

stop to this nonsense and get our program back on track, the way it was meant to be.

As ever,
Norma

NORMA TO CONSTANCE

July 8, 1918

Dear Constance,

The war moves at double time, but our letters travel at a crawl. As I sit to write this, I'm guessing that the letter I sent you a month ago has only just sailed into New York Harbor.

You might accuse me of being maddeningly vague in what I am about to say, but if I put down too much more it would only get struck out by the censor, to whom I send my greetings and commendations. At least someone can be counted upon to do his job properly.

The most I can tell you is that things are unraveling. Nothing about my program has gone the way I expected it to. Everything we so painstakingly built in New Jersey has been taken apart. There seems to be little I can do about it, for as you know, I have no real authority and am being treated like a member of the Ladies Auxiliary. This in spite of the fact that I wear the uniform, am subject to a chain of command, and, most important, am not free to leave—even if I wanted to, and I don't.

What bothers me is not my own position but that of our program. It's treated as a frivolity, as a nineteenth-century relic, put here to appease the old generals like our friend Gen.

Murray back in New Jersey, but having no relevance in today's war. Nothing could be further from the truth—but the young men running things over here have never been to war and have no appreciation for the tried and true. If it's new and electric-powered, they believe it will defeat the Germans through its sheer novelty. If that were the case, we could show them a moving picture and be done with it.

And I hardly need tell you that when compared to the machines, guns, and aeroplanes, my program costs almost nothing. If it saved only one life, it would be worth it. But what if it saves millions?

Aggie would want me to write more of our everyday lives, the village, the countryside . . . but I'm in no mood tonight. Meals are adequate, bed is clean, and so on. Send socks at any opportunity.

As ever,
Norma

NORMA TO GENERAL MURRAY

July 15, 1918

Dear General Murray,

I hardly know how to begin.

What follows is an account of my meeting with Colonel Hartman, which took place this morning. The minutes are incomplete due to the meeting having already commenced when I arrived, in spite of my turning up fifteen minutes early.

I don't know what was discussed before I walked in, but it

was obvious that a decision had already been made and I was merely to be told of it and sent on my way.

I'll put my records here and you can judge for yourself.

BUSCALL: Oh, here she is. I was just telling Bob — Colonel Hartman here — about that business with the pig farmer's daughter.

KOPP: It's been taken care of, and the offenders punished.

HARTMAN: Well, don't punish them too much. It's not exactly Gay Par-ee out here.

KOPP: I don't believe we've been introduced.

BUSCALL (clears throat): Colonel Hartman, Miss Kopp here was recruited by General Murray back in New Jersey to work on our pigeon program in Fort Monmouth. Then they shipped her over here like all the other birds.

HARTMAN (slaps Captain Buscall on the back): You mean she didn't fly?

KOPP: I traveled in standard accommodations. The birds went in steerage.

HARTMAN: Of course you did. And how do you find France, Miss Kopp? Have you picked up a word of French since you've been here? I hear the ladies do better with languages than the fellows do. I can't make out a word they're saying.

KOPP: *Je parle très bien français car ma mère et ma grandmère le parlaient à la maison.*

HARTMAN: Oh — well, you do all right then, don't you?

KOPP: (No reply as none seemed necessary.)

BUSCALL: Miss Kopp likes to record our meetings in her

note-book. I've told her it's only an informal discussion, but she puts it all down anyway, every word.

HARTMAN: My wife keeps a diary. Locks it in a drawer, as if an Army colonel has time to go snooping through a lady's things.

KOPP: I understand there have been some difficulties with the deployment of pigeons at the front, owing to the fact that the men weren't given proper instructions, in spite of our having printed a manual for this very purpose.

HARTMAN: An Army manual, published out of this fort? That would take months to get approved, and I haven't even seen it yet.

KOPP: Captain Buscall has had it for months.

BUSCALL: I'm a busy man, Miss Kopp. Do you see all the papers on this desk? If we could bury the Huns in paperwork, we'd have won the war by now.

HARTMAN: What you need is a secretary. We should get a girl in here to sort you out. Say, I wonder if Miss Kopp would like to—

KOPP: Nonetheless, the pigeon manual is written, and it's a substantial improvement over the British manual, which the Army was on the verge of adopting word for word, to say nothing of the belles-lettres the French tried to pass off as some sort of instructional text.

HARTMAN: That's just fine, Miss Kopp, but the pigeons are too much damn trouble, if you'll pardon my language. It takes a week to acclimate them to a new loft. We don't have a week at the front. They can only fly by day, and even then only if there's no fog or gas. Speaking of gas, it's enough of a chore for my men to carry their own gas masks, much less those damned rubber contraptions to cover the pigeon baskets. We simply cannot be thinking about a basket of birds during a gas attack.

KOPP: I've already designed a better—

HARTMAN (interrupting): It's not just the gas. They get muddy in the trenches and then they can't fly. You've no idea what the trenches are like, Miss Kopp.

KOPP: No, because I'm not allowed—

HARTMAN (interrupting again): You're damned right you're not allowed. The trenches are no place for a lady, or a bunch of birds in a cage. You've seen what the men look like when they come in. Covered in mud from head to toe, trench foot so bad they can't walk, and eaten up with cooties besides. No, it's a mess out there, and the birds are only making it worse.

KOPP: But without any telephone wires in the trenches—

HARTMAN (interrupting again): Without any telephone wires, we send runners.

KOPP: A runner could be killed, and they can travel only a few miles per hour, while a bird—

HARTMAN (interrupting yet again): A runner could be killed, and they are. That's war.

KOPP: And it's far more trouble to keep a runner fed and looked after in the trenches, as compared to a pigeon.

HARTMAN (pushing back his chair, requiring all to rise): Here's my order. Carry on with the program, but don't send us another bird. I'm not shipping any of you home. I'd never get Pershing to allow an able-bodied man to leave in the middle of this mess. I can't reassign all of you, either. I'd have to write too many damn reports. So you're to proceed as usual. Raise your birds, train them, whatever else you do here. Just don't send any out.

KOPP: Why would we bother if they're not going to be of any use?

HARTMAN: It's been fifteen months since President Wilson ordered us into this war, but the offensive has only just begun. Do you know why? Because General Pershing wanted us to be ready. Entirely ready. He didn't want to send a hundred men at a time with no decisive path to victory. He figured that the Brits and the French could hold off the Huns for another year while we got ready, and that's what happened—except for this pigeon nonsense. You had a year to get it operational, and it isn't. It's too late now. Everything's moving too quickly. Pershing intends to be home for Christmas. We're moving on.

KOPP: But what if we—

HARTMAN (interrupting again): Keep this program operational, and I mean fully operational. If Pershing orders a cart-load of pigeons a month from now, then by God you'd better have a cart ready to ship.

KOPP: We have a dozen carts ready to ship today, and a manual to go with them.

BUSCALL: The meeting's concluded, Miss Kopp. You may finish your notes outside.

(end of meeting)

There you have it. I don't suppose word of this decision will reach you through any other channel, as it appears to be something that both Captain Buscall and Colonel Hartman intend to keep quiet. We're to pretend to carry on a military mission when in fact we're doing nothing but raising birds for our own amusement. I could've stayed home and done that, had I wished to. Instead, I thought I'd come all this way to serve a useful role in a vital Army communications program. That it could be so carelessly tossed away is unfathomable.

As you might imagine, I cannot countenance sending our men into battle without the communication equipment they require. The meeting may be concluded, but our program is not.

I trust you will keep this in confidence and await my next report. Must close as I have a great deal of work to do in light of these developments.

Yours in service,
Norma C. Kopp

CONSTANCE TO NORMA

July 18, 1918

Dear Norma,

It was so good to have a letter from you at last, and from Aggie! The mail's been exceptionally slow lately. None of the girls in the parlor have had a letter in weeks. It's torture for some of them, wondering what's become of their brothers and beaus. They do take comfort in the fact that news of a death seems to reach our shores much faster than a note from a soldier who is alive and well. As long as they hear nothing, they believe their men to be safe.

I had been telling myself all along that you wouldn't be allowed near the trenches, and as such I shouldn't worry— although now that I think about it, maybe they should send you to the front. One good scolding from you and the Germans would surrender. Nonetheless, do continue to write at any opportunity, and reassure me that you're well away from the shelling and the gas.

I worry also over these hints of problems with your program. It can't be easy, keeping everything running the way you'd like in the chaos of war. The Army must have its own way of doing things, and I suspect that isn't always in perfect alignment with how you'd want it done. I wish you could tell me all about it, but I know you can't. Still, say as much as you can, and let me guess at the rest.

As for my own work—Mr. Bielaski keeps me busy, but there simply isn't as much life-and-death, chase-them-down-and-arrest-them-in-the-nick-of-time investigative work left for the Bureau to do any more. The more competent German saboteurs—the ones setting fires at munition plants and sinking ships—seem to have fled the country once we entered the war. Our best guess is that they feared execution as enemy spies. Whatever the reason, they're mostly operating in Mexico now, where we can't get to them.

If you read the American papers, you might have some idea of the work I and my fellow agents are doing. Slacker raids, of course, although I've yet to meet a man who wants to avoid military service. They're all too eager to go. We are also obliged to investigate propagandist publications, a job that consists entirely of reading newspapers. You'd be perfect for it.

But mostly, I've been assigned to exactly the sort of anti-unionist espionage that I find distasteful. The factory owners are convinced that if their workers strike, it undermines the war effort. They've managed to bring the War Department around to this way of thinking, and have convinced them to dispatch government agents like me to quell uprisings. So I spend my days lurking around factories and listening for rumblings of union organizing among the women.

But, Norma, they are entirely right to organize! You wouldn't believe the filth and noise in some of these places, and the way every little mistake is deducted from a worker's paycheck, until she takes home hardly anything at all. To the extent that the girls complain about their employers, they're entirely justified. For instance, they prefer clean toilets, and an opportunity to use them, but they get neither. I was sent in last week to spy on a fuse line, and the place was so filthy and noisy that I nearly led a riot myself.

You asked about the farm. I have been out to take a look around. You needn't worry about the house. You're right that the girls are running the dairy now. They're bringing the cows over to graze in our fields, they're in and out of our barn every day, and they eat their lunches on our front porch. I think they enjoy getting away from their mothers and having a little piece of the business that they can manage on their own. Don't worry—if they noticed even a cracked pane of glass, they'd tell me. They did say that they missed seeing your pigeons around and didn't believe me when I said they'd been deployed to France.

Fleurette has left for another tour with May Ward. I don't suppose she's written to you. I'm lucky to get a postcard myself. I know she writes to Helen—I run into her sometimes in

Paterson, and she's always had a letter from Fleurette when I have not. I suspect Helen knows quite a bit more about what she's up to than I do.

I know you consider it frivolous for her to sing and dance her way through the war, but a little entertainment does lift the spirits of the men getting ready to go overseas.

What you might not see from your vantage point is that the waiting is absolutely miserable for the men in training. On one hand, they're desperately eager to join the others in France, and to get in the middle of the action. On the other hand, they're terrified of going and wonder if they'll ever touch American soil again. If a night of entertainment relieves their cares for a few hours, that's a useful service—as useful as sewing uniforms and rolling bandages, which is what she'd be doing otherwise.

And there's no shortage of Army camps. She seems determined to visit every one of them and will have seen more of the country by the time the war ends than we ever will. She recently sent a panoramic postcard of Camp Cody, in New Mexico, where thirty thousand men live in the most desolate sand-strewn landscape. Imagine an endless run of white pyramid-shaped tents—so many that they vanish into the horizon—punctuated all too infrequently by water towers that couldn't possibly satisfy the thirst of so many men. The rows of long, low wooden barracks likewise march so far into the distance that they disappear. Where they found the lumber to build them I can't guess, because there isn't a tree to be seen anywhere.

In addition to sandstorms and scorpions, the men contend with the occasional German, sneaking up from Mexico by way of El Paso to have a look at the enemy. Our agents down there have a nice collection of them now, all stewing in a military jail and refusing to say a word against the Kaiser.

Speaking of our agents, and the Germans—a munitions plant in Syracuse was almost entirely destroyed in an explosion recently. Fifty men died and of course all those explosives —just waiting to be sent overseas—went up in flames. It's a horrible tragedy and a massive blow to our side. I'm told they manufactured a quarter of the dynamite we ship to France.

Because it's in the papers, I'm at liberty to tell you that Mr. Bielaski sent me, along with a few other agents, up to Syracuse for a few days to investigate. There's no evidence so far of German meddling. It only takes one spark, and a building goes up. That can happen by accident no matter how much care they take. Nonetheless, the mood at the Bureau has grown tense over it. We saw so many attacks of this sort carried out by the Germans on our soil last year, and we were always too late to stop it. Now we're in the highest state of alarm over the possibility that they've rebuilt their network and resumed their attacks. Every fire, every train derailment, every outbreak of smallpox or anthrax is treated with suspicion and investigated as a possible act of sabotage.

We're so eager to hear from you again, so send us a word when you can. Bessie's been wanting to bake a treat for you, but fears it wouldn't survive an ocean voyage. There's something called a trench cake made with raisins, brown sugar, and a stick of something-or-other that we're meant to believe takes the place of butter and eggs. They seem to make it to France all right, according to the girls in the parlor. Could you use one of those?

We're always told to send more durable foodstuffs overseas
— hard candy, for instance, or coffee, along with tobacco and
razors. I doubt razors and tobacco hold much appeal to you,
except for bartering purposes. Please know that we're happy to
send anything at all that might be of use, however trivial — you
have only to ask.

Give our best to Aggie, and the birds.

Yours —

Constance

CONSTANCE TO FLEURETTE

July 20, 1918

F —

Would you look at this! Apparently the way to get a letter from
Norma is to order her to write one and to assign a topic. I
could do with a little less architecture and French history and
a bit more in the way of current events, but I'll take it. At least
I've shamed her into writing longer letters.

Can you imagine Norma in a place like that? I can only assume that she holds the entire village in a state of terror, and
that the Army has been made to regret its association with her.

Regardless, this is the most correspondence we've had in
months. I believe this roommate of hers is a good influence. As
long as we hear from one or the other of them, I'm satisfied.

I hope this finds you well. I'm building quite a collection
of postcards of the Army camps, so do keep sending them. It's
amazing how they all look the same. I didn't know we had such
vast, flat, treeless spaces in America, all conveniently situated

along rail lines, but apparently there are several dozen at least, and you'll see them all before the war's over.

Yours,

C.

FLEURETTE TO CONSTANCE

July 25, 1918

C—

For your collection, a postcard from Camp Travis, in Texas. Horrified to learn that Norma now keeps written records to help her win arguments with her superiors. Is there any chance of her leaving that habit in France? I suppose we ought to have warned the Army about her—I can only imagine her issuing orders to a general. She wouldn't do that, would she?

And is it really a fort, in the sense of an ancient stone edifice with a moat around it in the countryside? I can't quite picture such a thing, but I suppose if I had to, Norma would be patrolling it like an alligator, snapping at invaders.

Yours,

F.

FLEURETTE

Camp Pike, Little Rock, Arkansas

CONSTANCE TO FLEURETTE

July 28, 1918

F—

Such a celebration over Soissons! Did they ring the bells in
San Antonio? It was bedlam here, with the factory whistles
going all at once, the fire station sounding its alarms, the
church bells ringing, motor cars honking their horns, street-
car bells jangling, and even a little music from a marching
band. There are a few naysayers who insist that Pershing re-
claiming that bit of territory and taking four thousand prisoners should not be interpreted as a sign of victory to come,
but we can't help but cheer and ring our bells, we're all so
desperate for encouraging news. People were crying and kissing in the streets—can you imagine how it must've been in
Paris?

I'll be away for a few days, owing to some trouble with a
brewery in Pennsylvania. The brewers are all German, and as
such the War Department loves to listen in. I'm to ingratiate

myself to the wives and keep one ear attuned to the men's conversations. For once, Mr. Bielaski doesn't want me to change my name or pretend I don't know what they're saying. The idea is that I'll present myself as a nice German lady this time, and see how far I get.

Bessie had me over for Sunday dinner on a Friday, because I'll be gone over the week-end. There was no dessert, as just last week she put everything she had into a cake for Norma and Aggie. It was her own version of a pineapple upside-down cake, made with fruit that she very cleverly dried and candied before our own days of rationing. She's been hoarding the coconut as well (how she manages to keep her hands out of it, day after day, is beyond me—I would've eaten it on cereal if I'd had it in my pantry), and found that it worked as a sweetener.

It was otherwise, she claims, "just a plain cake" made with an assortment of what passes for flour these days, and a good portion of Sav-An-Eg, which is meant to take the place of eggs in a recipe, although no one would ever mistake it for the real thing. Regardless, you know that Bessie works a wonder with what she has. This was her first time with this recipe, and she's anxious to know how it travels. She hopes the extra lemon juice preserves it. We might not know for a month or two, as the mail is just crawling over from France these days.

Bessie wants to know if they're feeding you anything more than Army rations. If it wasn't for her, I'd waste away on boarding-house fare.

Yours,
C.

FLEURETTE TO CONSTANCE

August 5, 1918

C—

Your letter landed just before we left Camp Travis. I'm off to Little Rock next. The food at the camps is dreadful but at least there's plenty of it. Tell Bessie I expect her to feed me every day for a week when I'm home next.

There's nothing new to report here. Camp is muddy. We trudge around in boots now, and carry our slippers. Our costumes are twice as dirty, and we spend our days on laundry and the scrubbing out of stains. Isn't it glamorous?

Yours,

F.

FLEURETTE TO HELEN STEWART

August 7, 1918

Dearest Helen,

It was our rotten luck to be held over in San Antonio for two more nights, the trains out of town being too crowded for Mrs. Ward's liking. The consolation prize for waiting around so long was the last-minute arrival of not one, but two of your letters! That's one advantage to staying put for a week. You and I might have something like a proper conversation via the mails for once.

Mrs. Ward's objection to the crowded trains, by the way, was not entirely unreasonable. We would've had to stand the whole way, or take the seats the boys offer us and be gracious

43

about it, but even then, we end up crammed together, our bags in our laps and our feet getting trampled, and nothing to look at but the belt-loops of the men crushed in all around us. Truly, you can hardly breathe. Usually the men are jolly and beg us to sing a song, but sometimes they're awfully somber and we feel like fools, riding along to the next camp to put on another silly show, while they prepare to face the enemy.

It's generous of you to imagine that I'm out serving my country. It hardly feels that way to me. You, my darling, are making a far greater sacrifice by taking charge of all those little brothers of yours while your father toils away in some surgery in France. They never would've let him go otherwise—a widower with dependent children would've been strictly unwelcome in our Army, even if he is a doctor. You remember how desperately my brother wanted to go, but at the first hint of a wife and children (not to mention his advanced age—43! The Army would require a geriatric ward!), they sent him straight back to Hawthorne.

What I'm doing doesn't amount to anything. The camps are not exactly starved for entertainment. Every orchestra, every circus act, every comedic troupe—they are all gainfully employed in trotting from camp to camp, singing and dancing and high-stepping in front of the largest audiences most of them have ever seen. There are never any worries about selling tickets: the men are practically required to attend. If only Broadway worked the same, every mediocre act from Poughkeepsie would be guaranteed a full house.

I'm just not sure that by putting on our little show, we do a thing to lighten their burdens or relieve their cares. So many of these boys are marking time—another evening in the auditorium, another day, another week, another month—and then they're off to France, to live in a water-logged trench and shoot at Germans. We're marking time also—four nights in Arkansas, then a day to get to Kansas, then another week down the road somewhere, and what does it add up to?

If I sound like I'm complaining of the tedium, it's not that, exactly. It's the feeling that something enormous and consequential is happening Over There—and we are here, shuffling from place to place, singing our ditties while the fighting goes on.

I STARTED THIS letter from the train station back in San Antonio. It being impossible to write on the train, I put it away until evening. We're settled now at Camp Pike, just outside Little Rock. I'll be here for only four days, so there's not much use in writing to me, but I enclose the address anyway.

May Ward has thrown another fit and refuses to stay at the YWCA's Hostess House. She's hopelessly attached to the way things used to be and can't give up her old habits. She likes a good downtown hotel, a room with a telephone (and a man on the other end of the line who brings up a tray of drinks whenever she calls for it), and a hot bath at any time of the day or night. Oh, and she doesn't mind a crowded lobby, where she might appear in an evening dress and act surprised when someone chases after her for an autograph.

Nothing of the sort is on offer at the Hostess House. You can imagine exactly what species of place it is: a hastily knocked-together rooming house, with a great central room for cards, games, and a library of moldering old donated books.

Bedrooms the size of a closet, fitted with two bunks each, and a bathroom down the hall that's always occupied. Breakfast cheerfully served at six, tea and bits of something dry and stale at three, etc.

At the Hostess House we are chaperoned, but not in the hardened "I know what you're up to" style of Mrs. Ironsides, that lady hired to tour with us in the old days. She was at least a worthy adversary. Here we're looked after in the far more ir-ritating "I shall shower you with motherly affection and watch-fulness" of a Mrs. Brady (or whatever she's called, there's one of her at every camp). There's something quite deliberate and self-conscious in the way they carry out their matronly duties, almost as if they're auditioning for a part.

What galls me about Mrs. Brady—and again, I refer gen-erally to all the Mrs. Bradys, not only this one in particular —is her earnest belief that we girls are just as anxious to be sheltered from the menace posed by five thousand khaki-clad men living in tents as she is to shelter us from it. She's for-ever *reassuring* us that we are as protected and looked after as we ever were at home—as if any of us want looking after any more.

Here was the scene when we arrived:

Mrs. Brady came bustling out to the porch and called, "La-dies! Welcome. You'll want to take the afternoon to get set-tled."

There wasn't much settling for us to do as there was no room in which to do it. For porters we had three weary old men who'd found new occupations for themselves in the shuttling of visitors from train station to camp and back. They had al-ready dragged and kicked our trunks down the hall and pushed them into the aforementioned closet-sized rooms. There was no hope of having anything pressed or blocked or even hung decently on a hanger, so we saw no need to unpack.

"Oh, we're quite settled. I believe we're at our liberty," Eliza proposed. She tries this gambit at every camp, and it has never once won us the least bit of liberty.

It wasn't going to work on Mrs. Brady, either. "Oh, then you'll want to write your letters home, and tell them where you've landed. We put out writing-paper at two, and the post-man comes at three, and then you girls can help me with the tea, and . . ."

That was when May Ward rebelled. You would've thought she was covered in fleas, the way she jerked about and itched at the very idea of letters and tea. She'd had only the tiniest brandy and soda before we left for the train station that morning, which put her roughly three brandies and sodas behind schedule.

As Mrs. Brady was unlikely to put out a seltzer-bottle and sliced lemons on a tray any time soon, May ventured to ask, "Mightn't I take a glass of ice cubes off to my room, and a lump of sugar, if you can spare one?"

The sugar, added to the afternoon's drinks, comprises Mrs. Ward's only nourishment until her after-theater supper.

Mrs. Brady—suspecting nothing, as near as I could tell—said breezily, "We do without the conveniences of ice and such things, just as the boys will in France, but sit down right here and let me fetch you a glass of water. I believe you're to share a room with our Gwennie—"

At that May slumped into a chair, as if overcome, and said faintly, "But we wired ahead and requested a single room."

Mrs. Brady, already on her way to the kitchen for a glass of clear and untainted water, didn't even bother to turn around.

"We're full to the rafters tonight," she called, "and you'll adore Gwennie. She's a water-colorist, if you can imagine that. Ask to see her sketches!"

May looked perfectly stricken at the idea. She collected her hat, tucked her pocketbook under her arm, and smiled weakly at all of us. She didn't have to tell us where she was going. Some man lingering outside with an automobile (there's always a man lingering about with an auto when the great May Ward needs one, don't ask me how she does it) would spirit her off to the nearest hotel, which is probably an hour away. Once tucked into a comfortable suite, she'll get caught up on her brandies and sodas and make tearful, unimaginably expensive telephone calls home to Freeman, after which she'll be an hour late for her thirty-minute call, if she turns up at all.

I, on the other hand, write my letters, and Mrs. Brady approves. Give those little red-headed boys a kiss from me, and here's one for you, too.

Affectionately,

Fleurette

FLEURETTE TO HELEN

August 8, 1918

Dearest Helen,

I'm writing to you at the end of what I can only hope is the most disastrous twenty-four hours of my so-called war-time service. It ended with one of us being released from "girl jail" with a case of cooties to remember it by, another one of us banned indefinitely from the stage, and the remaining six so scared of meeting the same fate that they're considering running off to the nearest convent.

Which one am I? I don't have cooties, I'll tell you that.

Last night began exactly as I predicted. May Ward did not return for her thirty-minute call, nor was she present when the show was to have begun. We've kept a crowd waiting for as long as an hour before without any difficulties, but this time the stage-hands and camp commanders and other powers that be were entirely unwilling to delay. The soldiers had been brought in—rather perfunctorily, I thought, no eager crowd, this—and were growing restless. None of them were particularly starved for the sight of a lady, either, as there are ladies on stage almost every night here.

When five minutes had passed with no movement of the curtain, the men in the audience started to wander out. That is apparently their right—so much for strict military order—but the parties in charge didn't like it and told us to go ahead with our show before we lost any more.

The trouble was that we weren't just missing our cherished leader. We were also missing Bernice.

How could we have lost one entire chorus girl, you ask? It's easier than you might think. The auditorium here at Camp Pike is equipped with three small changing-rooms. May Ward and Her Eight Dresden Dolls should, as you've no doubt calculated, allocate three girls to each room, except that Mrs. Ward requires her own room and won't let any of us use hers —even if she's on stage, even if she's out signing autographs, and even if she's absent entirely.

That leaves two rooms for the eight of us, and three costume changes a night. We tend to run back and forth in a panic, searching for lost stockings and begging to borrow a hairpin. You can see how any of us might think that if we were in one room, Bernice could be in the other.

And where would she have gone, and when? The theater's only just across the way from the Hostess House. We aren't allowed to wander the camp on our own and, anyway, it's nothing but mud topped with muddy wooden walkways. The boys in khaki make for nice scenery, but Bernice is the oldest and wisest of us all. She wouldn't be so captivated by them that she'd strike out on her own.

Regardless—there we were. No May Ward, no Bernice, and a stage manager tapping his little foot with all the impatience of a train conductor whose passengers are too bumbling and slow-witted to disembark according to his time-table.

What could we do but put on our show? We didn't want to report Bernice missing and set off a camp-wide alarm. Thinking she might be ill, or detained at the Hostess House over some other calamity, Charlotte ran back to look for her while the rest of us went on with our first number. There isn't a song in our program that Mrs. Ward hasn't missed at least once, so we know how to manage. One of us takes her part, the chorus rearranges itself, and the show goes on.

Eliza took Mrs. Ward's place for the first number. (There's no more singing of "The Bird on Nellie's Hat"—all they want any more is "Off for France" and "Pack Up Your Troubles.") At the end of it, Charlotte reappeared and let it be known that Bernice wasn't to be found at the Hostess House.

The girls agreed—with hardly more than a whisper and

a nod to each other as we cavorted around on stage between songs—that they would all dash off together to decide what to do about Bernice, and leave me on stage by myself to sing a solo.

This, I am sorry to say, is where my share of the trouble began.

There's nothing unusual about one of us singing a solo. Sometimes it has to be done to pull off a costume change. The solos, of course, go to May Ward when she's here, but when she performs one of her disappearing acts, the privilege might fall to any one of us.

What I should've done was to lead the boys in a round of "My Old Kentucky Home" or some other number that they can all holler along to. It makes the interlude go faster and takes the strain off my voice.

But there was something about the piano player last night. He was too good for an Army camp, and too good for the likes of us, so spirited and—well, I don't know how else to say it— frisky, if you know what I mean. I just knew he wanted to have a little fun.

And so did I. Every eye in the place was on me. Oh, Helen, forgive me for loving that as immodestly as I did! I was as drunk as Mrs. Ward probably was at that moment, only I was drunk on the gaze of seven hundred men in khaki.

I walked across that stage like I owned every man in the room. I leaned over to the piano player, counted off, and burst out with the first line of "There'll Be a Hot Time in the Old Town Tonight." It didn't take him more than a measure to catch up with me. The next thing you know, the two of us were making some magic happen.

I don't have to tell you how that feels! Do you remember that night, way back when we were students at Mrs. Hanson's, and you and I sang "She Pushed Me into the Parlour" as a duet and ran all over the stage, throwing props around and making the audience laugh so hard they cried?

It was like that, only these men weren't laughing. They were falling head over heels.

I sang, *You must be my man, or I'll have no man at all* . . .

. . . and oh, Helen, I sang that line like it has never been sung! The longing in every pair of eyes—I could live off that. I wouldn't need bread or water, if I had an audience clamoring for me like that every night.

It's wicked of me to talk like this, but you must understand just how it was, so you'll know why May Ward threw such a fit.

Because May Ward, I discovered later, had turned up after all. She strolled right down the center aisle, just as I started singing. I didn't see her, what with the boys all jumping off their benches in their eagerness to have a better look at the dazzling Fleurette Kopp.

If I had seen her, I wouldn't have been able to sing that song like I did. On this tour, the stage belongs to May Ward. We're her accessories. We're there to make her look her best, and we all know it. When any of us are given a solo, we perform in the most straightforward manner, delivering our lines but never giving our hearts out to the audience.

It's something you'll understand, Helen, because you've been on the stage. You can give them everything—more than you knew you had, even—and they will give it right back to you, a hundred times over. Or you can simply stand on your mark, a flat-footed mortal, and do your lines.

Usually, we just do our lines. But May Ward saw me give my whole heart to the audience, and take theirs in return, and it infuriated her.

After my number, all the girls returned to the stage except for Charlotte and Eliza, who had been sent to search for Bernice. (By this time I'd almost forgotten about poor Bernice, and perhaps you had too, but hers was the more dreadful night, as you'll soon learn.)

We continued on as usual. Mrs. Ward never did make it to the stage—and remember, I didn't yet know that she was even in the theater. The rest of us put on a better-than-average performance after that, because the men were—well, let me just say that the men were warmed up. We all felt it.

After curtain call, we ran backstage to learn what had become of our Bernice, only to be met by a spiteful, incoherent May Ward. She'd dispensed with the soda but stuck with the brandy, and would've been entirely incapable of changing into a costume and joining us on stage. By the time she wheeled round to face me—and I knew, all at once, what she'd seen and exactly what she thought of it—she could hardly stand up. Nonetheless she took a swing at me and did manage a good hard slap across my cheek.

It was nothing I couldn't bear. In fact, I was on such a high that I was ready to forgive her for it and to look after her the way I always do when she gets like this. She isn't usually a mean drunk—she's weepy and wobbly, and in need of cold compresses and appeals to her vanity. I've sat with her many a night, repairing the gorgeous gowns she treats like garbage, and feeding her aspirins and flattery.

But not last night! She spat out pure venom, and it was all aimed at me.

I won't even write down the words she used, for fear you'll leave this letter sitting around and one of the boys will read it. Just imagine every way that a woman can be degraded, and what parts of the anatomy might be involved, and the manner in which she might be paid for such an act, and how one's own mother might be implicated, too, and you have the gist of it.

She finished with this: "I want you out of my chorus! Pack your things, and go on back to Jersey. Don't you dare drag that filth on my stage again."

The girls knew better than to stand up for me. There's no talking to Mrs. Ward when she gets like this. We all agreed, by silent assent, to wait until morning to find out what, if anything, she remembered of the evening.

Fortunately, she was by then ready to drop. She took another swig from the little bottle tucked into her bosom and we let her. Sweet oblivion, carry her away! It did, soon enough.

As she was not officially in residence at the Hostess House, we couldn't take her there. Fortunately, the man who'd driven her from her hotel was waiting around behind the auditorium with his trusty machine. We simply put her back from whence she'd come, pooled our coins to tip the fellow, and sent the two of them on their way.

That difficulty solved, at least temporarily, we were anxious to find out if Charlotte and Eliza had tracked down our mysteriously departed Bernice. For once we were glad of a chaperone, who kept the eager lads away and conducted us directly back to the Hostess House. (How I would've loved an evening with the eager lads, but Mrs. Ward had spoiled everything and by then we were starting to panic over Bernice.)

Charlotte was waiting for us in the room that she and I shared. We all crammed inside and did our best to speak in whispers.

Bernice, we learned, had been apprehended by one of those Protective Committee women. Just before we'd all left the Hostess House for the evening, she'd stepped out on her own, snuck around back, and lit a cigarette. As she was already in costume and looking quite lovely, she naturally attracted the attention of a few boys in khaki, who stopped to chat for only a minute or two—just long enough to share a cigarette!—and it was in that condition that Mrs. Jailhouse found her.

What you must understand is that these Protective Committee ladies aren't like ordinary matrons. This isn't Constance, issuing warnings and doling out demerits. These women are positively zealous. They serve a mission that they believe to be of military importance, which is to exact punishment and imprisonment upon the girls of this country in the name of moral hygiene.

Did you know that we pose a threat to the troops, and that we weaken their morals and inflict upon them crippling social diseases that make it impossible for them to defeat the Kaiser?

Well, that's how they see it. I know all about it, because Constance complains ceaselessly about the doings of the Committee on Protective Work for Girls whenever I'm in Paterson. These ladies have been given unlimited authority, handed down directly from Washington, to lock girls away if they show any signs of degeneracy. And by lock away, I mean just that—

put them into a detention home or a state home, for the duration of the war, or longer if it suits.

And apparently, it suited Mrs. Jailhouse (I can't be bothered with her name, I hate her so) to reach into that pleasant scrum of khaki and extract Bernice, dragging her by the collar —really!—through camp, and into an automobile, where she would have been taken to some horrible old place on the outskirts of town—had the automobile not blown a tire!

It was our good luck—the only good luck of the night—that Mrs. Jailhouse had no means of repairing the tire. Bernice was then dragged to Mrs. Jailhouse's little office at the other end of camp. If you wonder why Bernice didn't just run off—well, where was she to go? As she saw it, she was in an Army camp, surrounded by several thousand soldiers. How far would she get, if Mrs. Jailhouse put out an alarm? There was nothing to do but to see it through. At least, that was her way of looking at it. I'm not sure I would've done the same.

If you're wondering how Charlotte and Eliza ever found out what had happened, just know that the boys in this camp are heroic in ways both large and small. When Bernice was so cruelly torn away from her newly found friends, they followed along at a discreet distance, and I suppose one of them might've run ahead and had something to do with that punctured tire.

Another of the boys waited around behind the auditorium to tell us what had become of Bernice. When Charlotte and Eliza left in the middle of the performance to look for her, he was waiting there to tell them that Bernice was being held in Mrs. Jailhouse's office. (Billy is his name, if you want to include him in your prayers.) Once they understood the situation, they decided that Eliza, being older, should handle Mrs. Jailhouse alone. (Eliza is twenty-five, and Bernice twenty-seven—can you imagine locking a woman of that age in a girls' detention house?)

What sort of battle of wits ensued between Eliza and Mrs. Jailhouse? We didn't yet know. Charlotte told us everything that she had heard, and we were left to wait for Eliza to return and tell the rest. Fortunately, it was only another hour before both Eliza and Bernice tapped at Charlotte's window and crawled inside. (Curfew had long passed.)

Now we could learn the rest of it. Eliza, having been told by Billy where to find Bernice, went right up to Mrs. Jailhouse's office, rapped on the door, and insisted that Bernice be released. She made it plain that she and Bernice were career women, free to travel and earn their living as they pleased, and not entirely unfamiliar with the workings of the legal system.

"If Bernice has broken the law," she said to Mrs. Jailhouse, "would you be so kind as to summon a police officer, and put something in the way of official charges against her? That way, I can follow her along to jail, wire my attorney, and put up her bail."

"I was the one to put her under arrest," sputtered Mrs. Jailhouse.

"Oh!" gasped Eliza. "Beg pardon. One of our girls has a lady police officer for a sister. She carries a badge. I suppose you do, too?"

"I don't need a badge," Mrs. Jailhouse bristled. "I'm chair of the Committee—"

"But what if you aren't?" Eliza asked (quite sensibly, I thought). "What if you're just—well, just anyone? You can't simply deprive a grown woman of her liberty on the strength of your committee chairmanship. We absolutely must send for the police and ask them to settle this."

"The police know full well—" Mrs. Jailhouse put in, but Eliza pressed on.

"I'm sure they can tell us all about the crime of smoking a cigarette in the presence of Army men. I suppose it's a new law, just passed in Arkansas? I wonder if there's been anything about it in the papers? Speaking of the papers, we might call in a reporter, too."

Eliza continued in this manner until Mrs. Jailhouse was simply ready to drop from exhaustion. It was eventually agreed upon by both parties that Bernice was, in legal fact, free to walk out of Mrs. Jailhouse's office under her own power, and that future violations of camp rules by visiting performers might better be handled by a stern warning or eviction from camp—the latter being preferred by both Eliza and Bernice, who were by then thoroughly sick of Camp Pike.

I've never written such a long letter in my life, but you had to have the whole evening at once, not in installments! Besides, I'm too keyed up to sleep.

I'll put this out now for the morning mail, and you'll just have to wait and wonder, as I am, about Mrs. Ward's state of mind toward me come the dawn.

Yours aff—
Fleurette

P.S. The cooties! I almost forgot about them. Would
   you believe that in the short time Mrs. Jailhouse
   had Bernice in her possession, she wrapped her

in a horrible infested blanket and made her wait on a nasty old bunk outfitted with the most terrible chicken feather pillow? Poor Bernice was already scratching at the back of her neck when she came home. We had to smuggle the petroleum ointment out of Mrs. Brady's cupboard, for fear of being charged extra rent for all the unapproved six-legged visitors.

P.P.S. We're off to Camp Funston, in Kansas, next week. If you write to me quickly at the enclosed address, I might just meet up with your letter when I'm there.

FLEURETTE TO HELEN

August 12, 1918

Dearest Helen,

You must've dashed that letter off the minute you received mine, because it was waiting for me at Camp Funston, which is the next stop on this utterly mad tour.

To answer your first and most pressing question: May Ward had, in fact, forgotten about my little solo performance by morning. The trouble is that she remained dimly aware that she'd taken a dislike to me—only she couldn't recall why—the result being that she ignores me now, and treats me with more than the usual disdain. I'm doing more seamstressing than singing, which is always the sign that I've fallen out of favor. At least she hasn't sent me home. I take that as a victory.

Oh, and she never even knew about the trouble with Bernice. We managed to leave Camp Pike free of scandal—and free of cooties, thanks to a Herculean effort with a comb and a jar of ointment.

You keep asking if I've fallen in love yet, and I tell you, I refuse to do it! I can't bear to have a sweet young man go off to France with my heart tucked into his jacket, only to have it (and him) blown to bits in the trenches. You might think it morbid of me to put it like that, but they bring it up first, and then we're left with the task of consoling them. It wears on a girl.

Just last night there was a pale and frightened-looking young man sitting off by himself at the little party they threw for us at the Hostess House. The way these affairs go is that they clear all the chairs and tables and games away from the great-room, to make way for dancing. After our concert, we're expected to remain in costume and to dance and sing and be gay for another couple of hours, just when we'd all like to disappear into our rooms and soak our feet.

But how can we think about our feet, with a war on? You see how it is.

The men are invited according to a lottery system. We're promised no more than five men to every girl, but of course it never works out that way and each one of us is simply mobbed. We don't dare hope for anything so civilized as a dance card —the boys cut in at will, and you might dance with ten of them before a song's over. They wear the most enormous boots and step all over you—for once, I envy Constance and those sensible leather clodhoppers she wears. She'd probably kick a dancing partner right back and teach him a lesson. But we don't dare. Our slippers get ruined, and we laugh and try to be pretty about it.

Anyway, this poor soul was off by himself, pretending to look at the magazines, but obviously wishing he didn't have to take part in the gaiety. My neck, by then, had a permanent crick in it from looking up at my dancing partners — whether by luck or design, they were all simply gigantic, and made tiresome jokes about "the weather down there" — so I was ready for any excuse to sit out a song or two. I sat right down next to him.

At first, the boy talked to me because he had to, not because he wanted to. (Did you know that there is such a thing as a soldier who's immune to my charm?) He gave his name — George Simon — and told me that he'd come from some other little town down the road I'd never heard of. Camp Funston itself is bigger than any city he's ever visited in his life.

"I wonder what you'll make of Paris," I said, but this was precisely the wrong subject to introduce, for he only looked more miserable and said:

"I'll find out soon enough. We're shipping out next week."

Oh, Helen, I never know what to say! Do I wish them well, or do I commiserate? Don't ask me why, but I thought to make light of it a little, so I said, "Is that how you won a ticket to the dance? Is it to be nothing but parties and dancing until you leave?"

But I was only making it worse, and he let me know it. With eyes already tortured and far away, he said, "Today we had to apply for our war insurance, and write down the names of everyone who depends upon us for support, so they could figure how much to take out of our pay."

"Is that what they do?" I said. "I never knew how it worked." We were by then quite comfortable in our corner together. I expected someone to pull me back to the dance floor at any minute, but so far we'd been left alone.

George nodded. "You might put down your mother, if she's a widow, or your wife if you have one."

Of course I wanted to know who he'd written down, but I couldn't think how to ask. "Who will receive your war insurance?" makes the prospect of death on the battlefield sound like a business transaction. I thought it best to wait, and let him talk.

At last he said, "I told them I didn't want it. There's an aunt who raised me, but we didn't part on the best of terms. She has a son of her own, anyway. Let him support her."

It sounds cruel when I write it down like that, but he was more dejected than angry. The song changed just then and I thought he might ask me to dance, but instead he said, "Tell me something about yourself. Where do you live, and how did you come into this way of life, going around the country and singing like you do?"

I told him, and I tried to make it sound lively and gay so he'd think of something other than war insurance. I told him that my own mother had died, and that I'd been raised by my sisters who were old and dull like an aunt might be—and he smiled at that. I told him all about Constance, and how she'd become a lady police officer and been written about in newspapers all over the country, and how she was doing secret war-work that I wasn't supposed to know about, except that she tells me more than she should, and I knew it had to do with hunting for German saboteurs.

He chided me a bit and said that she didn't sound old and dull at all. He wanted to know how she'd gotten into that line of work, so I told him about the man who'd threatened to kidnap me, and how she stopped him. It did sound thrilling, the way I put it to him.

And I told him about you, and how we auditioned together for May Ward's troupe, and about how I'd already been going around the country with Mrs. Ward before the war. I made it sound quite a bit more glamorous than it ever was.

He loved to hear about all of it, and he asked a hundred questions. He seemed happy to think about anything else, if only for an evening. I'd only just started to tell him about Norma and her pigeons—and you should've seen the way he lit up when I mentioned those pigeons, I can't imagine why—when the music ended, and the lights came up.

At the prospect of parting he looked positively crushed. He's one of those men who looks like a child in his uniform—skinny shoulders, a gap in the collar, and a belt cinched tight and high around his waist because his pants would simply drop right off without it. He's not at all square of jaw and broad of chest—he's just the opposite. Who knows what France will do to him?

He stood to say good-bye, and I just looked at him, trying to memorize him. I had the funniest idea that I would see him when he returned, and that I would compare the picture in my mind to the man who would someday appear before me. What a strange notion—but no stranger than the realization that you might spend an evening with a man, and tell him everything about your life, then never see him again.

At a moment like this a man usually asks for an address, and a picture. They all want to write home to a girl.

But he didn't ask for any of that. He only said, "I didn't want to come tonight. That business with the war insurance had me thinking that they were asking me to bet against myself, and I didn't like the odds. But then my luck changed, because I met you. Good-night, Miss Kopp."

Before I could say a word, he was gone! I admit that a little piece of my heart went out the door with him. It's hard not to love them, just a bit, when they talk to you like that.

You tell me that you're living vicariously through my accounts of life in the Army camps, but you could get out yourself once in a while, you know. I'm sure your little brothers would be happy to watch a parade or see the training exercises. If you want a soldier of your own to write to, just step outside without a hat. They can't resist red hair. Charlotte talked me into a henna rinse, but you can hardly see it unless I'm out in the sunshine. I can't say I'd give a Scottish girl like you any competition.

We're here for a week, if you want to risk another letter.

Much love to you and the boys—

Fleurette

FLEURETTE TO HELEN

August 18, 1918

Oh Helen, Oh Helen, Oh Helen—

You will think I've completely lost my mind, and perhaps I have. Do you remember that sweet sad George Simon I cornered at a dance? He turned up again yesterday, just before he was to leave Camp Funston for points east. We aren't allowed visitors here at the Hostess House (isn't it funny that a place called Hostess doesn't welcome visitors, but never mind —our virtue is unassailed, and that's the main thing), but it was a lazy sunny afternoon and all eight of May Ward's Dresden Dolls were lolling about on the porch. We made a very pretty picture. Everyone in camp could walk by and have a word with us, and they did.

George looked as nervous as a debutante when he approached. You can only imagine how I felt—had I unwittingly entered into an understanding with the young man? Had he been given Reason to Entertain Certain Expectations? Really, there was a knot of dread in my throat as he made his way down the road. (This place is like a city, you understand, a treeless city of tents and wooden barracks and bare dirt roads between, crowded day and night with soldiers running off to their exercises.) I waited stoically to learn my fate.

He carried something quite large in one hand, but it was covered by a blanket and I couldn't guess what it was. When he walked up to the porch, I grinned and waved, but he only stood awkwardly, obviously wanting to ask if there was someplace private we could talk but not knowing how.

I didn't know how, either, as the entire point of the place is to keep chorus girls and soldiers apart from one another. But I rose nonetheless and walked down to the very end of the porch, where I could dangle my feet off the edge as one would at a dock on the lake. Surely the deck-railing between us would stand for propriety.

He came around and set his queer package down, then said, in such a huff—I could tell he was bursting to get it out of him, whatever it was—"Did you say your sister knows something about birds?"

NORMA? He wanted to talk about NORMA? It has never once happened, in all my years on this sweet Earth, that any young man has come running over to speak to me of Norma.

Nonetheless, I took it with grace. I said, "She would be the first to tell you that she knows everything about birds. She's been raising and training her messenger pigeons since the day I was born, and now she's over in France, showing the Army how to do it."

That set him back on his heels. "Do you mean to say she's enlisted? She's a real girl soldier?"

"Something like that," I said. I was already bored with the conversation. At least he wasn't asking to marry me. Perhaps he wanted to marry Norma—what a relief that would be to all of us!

"Would you like to write to her?" I offered. "I'll give you her address."

"No, I just—" He looked down at the package on the ground next to him. "You come from a family that knows something about birds. I just wanted to make sure of that."

"Oh, I wouldn't say that the entire family—" But it was too late. He pulled the covering off and revealed that he'd been carrying a bird-cage—and the cage held the most magnificent green parrot you've ever seen.

Oh Helen, oh Helen, if you could see her, you would know

how captivated I am. She wears the most astonishing emerald-green plumage, with a little yellow cap, and red tips at the ends of her wings like ruby bracelets, and orange eyes, and—oh, she's simply magnificent. She sat on the perch inside that cage with perfect composure, blinking at me through one eye and keeping the other eye trained on her surroundings, like the bright, alert girl she is.

George was staring at me so intently that I thought he might faint from the effort. "They won't let me take her to France," he said.

"No, I don't suppose they would," I said. I put a finger out to the bars of the cage, and that darling bird kissed it— well, she hasn't any lips, so she can't kiss, exactly, but she took my finger very gently into her beak, as if getting to know it, and then she let it go. It was quite elegant, the way she handled me.

"I can't leave her with my aunt, either," George said. "She hates birds. Thinks they're filthy. She said that if I left her at home, she'd open the cage and let her fly away."

"No!" I cried. "She can't be turned loose in a cornfield in Kansas! She belongs—well, in a conservatory, or an orangery. Where have you kept her all this time? Surely they don't allow birds at Camp Funston, either."

"One of the lieutenants rents a cottage in town. His wife wanted company, so they've been keeping her."

At that the bird let out a very pretty whistle—and would you believe it? It was an absolutely perfect high C. She's a soprano, like me!

"Does she sing?" I asked.

"Not yet," he said. "She's only just grown. But the lieutenant's wife plays the Victrola for her and she whistles along."

"Then she'll have a nice life until you come back for her," I said.

"But they can't keep her, either," he said. "They're being moved down to Camp Travis, and they have a baby on the way. This was only ever meant to be temporary. I want you to have her, Miss Kopp. You and your sister who knows all about birds. She'll be looked after, no matter what happens to me. I can tell you've taken a liking to her. Not everybody does."

Oh, who couldn't love an exotic bird with such chic feathers and a high, clear voice? I felt a kinship with her instantly. She was just so perfectly put together and seemed entirely composed, even as her fate hung by a thread.

Of course I put up all the usual arguments: I'm traveling for another month, at least, and we expect to be extended after that, and the Hostess Houses aren't exactly welcoming to avian visitors, and, besides, it's no life for a bird, going from city to city. How would I even carry her on the train? Mrs. Ward isn't about to buy an extra ticket for her cage.

But he wouldn't hear any of it. He had a feeling about me, he claimed. (Thank goodness it wasn't that other kind of feeling, although when did I start inspiring in men the desire to make a zoo keeper of me rather than a wife?) He just knew that I would appreciate his parrot, and be a good companion to her, and when he heard me mention Norma and her pigeons, it seemed to him like a sign from above.

He wasn't going to let me refuse, Helen, and oh, I confess,

I didn't try very hard! I never had any interest in a cat or a dog, although they ran around our farm from time to time, and I certainly never wanted anything to do with Norma's pigeons. We always had cows or goats or chickens, and once we even raised a pig—but you'd best not get attached to any of them, and I wouldn't have wanted to, anyway.

But this extravagant creature! She is something else again. She looks right at me and I do believe she understands something about me, and I about her. Would she wear a hat, I wonder, if I made one for her? I suspect she might.

The long and short of it is that Laura lives with me now. Oh, yes, her name is Laura. When he told me that, I decided at once to give her a new name—Esmerelda, perhaps, or Octavia—but then he said that he'd named her after his dearly departed mother, the only woman he ever loved, and what could I do? Laura she is, and Laura she shall remain.

Laura comes with a rather large brass cage and a smaller carrying-case so that she can sit on my lap on train rides. She's perched atop her cage right now in my cramped little room at the Hostess House, watching me and whistling now and then as I write.

Charlotte has the upper bunk and finds the whole situation droll. She wants to teach Laura to climb a ladder, but I've declared that Laura has enough adjusting to do without being taught silly tricks.

The ladies at the Hostess House don't know about Laura yet. There will be trouble when they do. Fortunately, we leave for Camp Grant tomorrow. I'll write again from our next perch. (See, I'm already thinking like a bird!)

Oh, don't be mad and tell me I'm irresponsible, I love her too much already—

and you—

Fleurette

FLEURETTE TO NORMA

August 19, 1918

Dear Norma,

I hope this letter finds you well and that you've made a success of things in France. I'm sorry I haven't written before, but I can't think what would possibly interest you about my tour through these training camps, except to tell you that we are shipping men out by the thousands and they had better be ready for you and your pigeons.

It's because of the pigeons that I write. I have come into the possession of a parrot. It's only temporary until the man who raised her returns from France. I would appreciate any advice you could give on the care, feeding, and training of a barely grown Amazonian parrot.

I've been told to feed her fruit and vegetables and soggy bread, and seed when I can get it. She has a blanket to cover her cage at night, which keeps her both warm and quiet. I worry about taking her from place to place, but I'm not due home for another month. If I hadn't agreed to take her, she would've gone to an awful aunt who intended to just open her cage and let her fly away.

Any advice on the treatment of avian ailments would be

welcome as well, although she seems perfectly fit at the moment. I've never had to care for any sort of creature at all apart from myself, and I just don't know what I'd do if she were to become ill or inconvenienced in any way. Write to me at Constance's, and she can forward it on.

Give the Germans what they deserve—I know you will—

votre sœur—

Fleurette

FLEURETTE TO CONSTANCE

August 19, 1918

C—

Here's another address for you as we depart for Camp Grant in Illinois. Were your ears burning? I was telling a soldier about you a few nights ago, and the work you do (in the most general of terms, of course, not wanting to give away any government secrets). He was quite impressed to hear that you used to carry a gun and make arrests just like a policeman. I told him about how you marched into Mr. Bielaski's office at the Bureau of Investigation last year and demanded a job when one didn't exist. He could hardly believe that such a tactic worked. When I think about it, I can hardly believe it, either.

I hope you're off on some thrilling case, intercepting bombs or spotting submarines sneaking up the Passaic River. Do you suppose they come up the rivers? You probably couldn't tell me if they did.

My contribution to the war effort this week (apart from

singing and dancing) was to sell tickets to a baseball game to benefit the Tobacco Fund. I went to Junction City with a couple of the girls, all of us in costume and causing quite a stir. We sold every ticket we had and returned with nearly a hundred dollars to put toward the cause of keeping the soldiers supplied with cigarettes. I wonder if Norma ever sees the packages they send over.

Speaking of Norma, you'll be pleased to know that I wrote her a letter and you didn't even have to tell me to do it. Give my love to Bessie and Francis and the children—

Yours,

F.

CONSTANCE

Paterson, New Jersey

August 20, 1918

Dear Mr. Bielaski,

You will have had Agent Gifford's report on last night's raid by now, but I told him I'd prefer to write up the part about the girls myself. We did turn up one promising lead that I intend to pursue.

With a pair of New York City police officers we raided the St. Regis restaurant at 440 West Forty-Sixth, on a charge of running a disreputable house in the basement. An inebriated German had been picked up in the alley the night before, and gave the impression that the place was frequented by his countrymen. The prospect of a clandestine enemy clubhouse was reason enough for the police to invite us along.

As per usual, the police went in the front door, flashing their badges and terrifying the patrons. The manager, Charles Farwell, did his best to interfere with the police and got himself arrested in the process. Meanwhile, Agent Gifford and I took the alley entrance. I slipped in first, headed straight downstairs to the basement, and quieted the girls ahead of a rather boisterous entrance by the police.

It was a small operation, just fifteen girls, but frequented by Germans, along the lines of Martha Held's old place. You remember how she worked it: Irish girls and German beer, and plenty of quiet corners for thugs and ne'er-do-wells to pass on messages and plan their next explosion at the docks. This was just that sort of place, but less inviting: instead of wallpaper and tufted settees, there was only a dingy room outfitted with what scraps of furnishings the restaurant upstairs might cast off, and behind that, a narrow hall lined with what I can only describe as stalls. They were too small to qualify as rooms under any definition. The walls were nothing but bare lathe, stuffed here and there with horsehair, and for doors they had tattered old moth-eaten curtains.

To my everlasting relief, less than half the rooms were occupied, and the inhabitants all at least partially clothed. I sent the men out into the waiting embrace of the two officers and Agent Gifford, and I herded all the girls into the very rear of the basement, which was outfitted with a dingy sink, a toilet, and a mirror.

"If you're going to haul us off to jail," said a girl I later identified as Ginny Monroe, age twenty-two, "take us now before the shift change at the precinct house. The boys on night shift know how to get us in and out before the sun comes up."

I wasn't at all interested in taking them to jail, but I didn't tell them that. Instead I asked, *"Spricht einer von Ihnen deutsch?"* and was met with blank stares. For good measure I added, *"Sie bekommen einen Dollar, wenn Sie es tun."* The promise of a dollar if they admit to speaking German usually wins me a raised eyebrow from anyone who understands what I'm saying. In this case, though, I'm quite certain that none of them picked up a word of it. They looked to be Irish and Scottish, mostly, fair-skinned and red-headed. They were thin to the point of half-starved. Through the scraps of muslin and lace they wore to entertain their customers, I could count their ribs.

"Do you ever hear a man speak German around the place?" I asked them. I was by now sitting on the floor with them, so they could look me in the eye.

They turned to one another, as if making up their minds about what to say, and then Miss Monroe shrugged and spoke for the group. "The Germans seem to like us," she said, "and they're cleaner than the Italians."

It would suit me just fine not to know which class of customer is cleaner than another. I said, "We're fighting the Huns overseas. I don't want you offering them comfort at home. What can you tell me about any of them—their activities, their associates, their whereabouts? What do they talk about amongst themselves? Do you hear them making any plans? Any talk of poisons or dynamite?"

Again the girls shrugged, and again Miss Monroe spoke for them. "It's all in German. To be honest, miss, that's what we like about them. They don't bother us with their talk."

"Do they ever exchange anything amongst themselves? Papers, packages?"

"All the time" came the answer.

"And what do you suppose we'll find on them tonight?" I

asked. The girls didn't have any idea. I could hear the officers in the other room, shouting at the men in the way that people tend to shout at foreigners in a vain attempt to make themselves understood. Agent Gifford tried twice to quiet the police, and to remind them that the German-speaking lady agent would be along in a minute to interrogate the men.

I searched the ladies myself and watched them dress to make sure they weren't hiding anything. Then I handed each of them my customary list of doctors, churches, and charity houses, and marched them out into the night so that I could turn my attention to the men.

The fellows, as Agent Gifford no doubt told you, seemed long on ambition but short on execution. They'd gathered up some weapons and a small amount of gun cotton but didn't appear to have a plan to use them. They might've dabbled in forged passports and anti-war propaganda, but as far as I could tell, they hadn't been doing much lately apart from drinking beer and bothering the girls.

We nonetheless searched the men and then searched all the rooms. That yielded little more than ticket stubs, matchbooks, some crumpled German newspapers, and a few scribbled notes that don't amount to much.

One of them did carry a slip of paper with the address of the Hudson Printing Company, in Paterson, written on it. He refused to say why he had the address, but he looked awfully shifty about it. As I happen to live nearby, I told Agent Gifford I would take this one myself. The proprietor is Andrew Wilmington. Do you have anything on him?

Yours very truly,
Constance Kopp

BIELASKI TO CONSTANCE

August 22, 1918

Dear Miss Kopp,

I appreciate, as always, the lively report. We had a look into our files concerning Andrew Wilmington. British citizen, immigrated in 1914, never been in any trouble to our knowledge, but he deserves a closer look. I suggest you find yourself a position with the company under our customary arrangement. As printing is his business, keep an eye out for propaganda, seditious publications, document forgeries, etc.

As per usual, if you turn anything up, take no action and report back. Cable if arrests are to be made and I'll send our boys in.

Yours very truly,
A. Bruce Bielaski

CONSTANCE TO NORMA

August 24, 1918

Dear Norma,

I've only just received Aggie's letter about the wayward soldiers and the pig farmer's daughter. She is a literary sensation in Mrs. Spinella's parlor. I'm sorry to say it, Norma, but we're a bit disappointed that you put a stop to the soldiers visiting the little café in the pig barn. We just know that there's further intrigue to be had there, if only you could turn your back long enough to let it happen.

How I wish I could tell you the particulars of the assignments I'm given, the cases I'm pursuing, and the small victories we can claim. But I'm not allowed to utter a word beyond the most general statements, even to my family, even to the girls here at the boarding-house. (Fleurette, when she's home, finds out more than she should—I don't know how she gets it out of me.)

Suffice it to say that I'm once again crawling around in the dark and disreputable corners of our city and those nearby. The other agents call it the "sight-seeing tour of the underworld" because we only glance at most criminal enterprises and then move on. For a souvenir we might pick up an odd scrap that leads to an investigation, but we leave the rest for the local police.

I've picked up one such scrap, and it's my good fortune that it'll keep me in Paterson for a while. Beyond that I can't say.

Do you remember, back in Hackensack, how Judge Seufert enjoyed the reports I wrote on my probationers? He seemed to value them more as literary entertainments than official filings, but I was always happy to oblige, as it seemed to raise his estimation of me. I think he appreciated that I was frank in my opinions and spared no detail, because it gave him some confidence that he had the full story.

The same has come to be true of Mr. Bielaski. It frustrates him to no end that he's now tied down to a desk in Washington, reading memoranda, while the rest of us chase down the enemy. The other agents, it seems, dash off only the briefest of notes and tend to omit crucial details. I began as the others did, with no-nonsense reports of only a sentence or two. But I've gradually started to write for him something more in the line of what I did for Judge Seufert, quoting conversations as best I can recall them, adding a few lines of descriptive prose to better paint a picture, and, as you might expect, injecting my opinions.

In reply to my most recent letter, he thanked me for my "lively reports." In return, his letters have grown more forthcoming. I suspect he tells me more than he does any other agent.

All this correspondence makes for longer nights, but what else have I to do? Fleurette is off with May Ward for weeks at a time and I'm lucky to have a postcard. Bessie and Francis are busy with their own lives (and Francis has taken up League work, I'm sorry to say—more about that another time), and of course you're "somewhere in France" and I have to beg you for so much as a paragraph. (Although your letter-writing has picked up quite a bit lately, and I do appreciate hearing from Aggie.) I share all your letters with Bessie and Francis, who send their best.

Fleurette has moved on to Camp Grant in Illinois. She complains of mud and boredom. I suspect there's quite a bit more going on, but she doesn't tell me about it.

I suppose we ought to get used to knowing less and less about what Fleurette's up to. Do you think she'll come back to her family at all, *après la guerre*? I know there isn't any point in thinking about what comes next for the three of us, but I can't help it. Any conversation around here meanders over to that question eventually. I know that someday we'll wake up, and the war will be over, and the world we knew before will be unrecognizable. But what will our lives look like, the three of us?

I don't mean for you to answer that question, and I know

you won't, anyway. You'll keep your nose to the grindstone as you always do.

Last Sunday I helped Bessie with a book drive at the library. There's an effort under way to collect two million books to ship overseas, and to supply the training camps here. Fleurette says the camp libraries are just terrible. The books are handled so much that they fall apart, the soldiers pass them around and never return them, and there simply isn't enough of what the boys like to read. They want to be entertained—they'll fight over any Zane Grey, or Jack London, and they're happy to have Kipling or O. Henry. A few of them are quite earnest and want to read anything on engines and tanks, road-building, mechanics, warfare, or European history. They tear a new *Popular Mechanics* or *Saturday Evening Post* absolutely to shreds.

Bessie heard that in the hospitals overseas, the books given to the men in quarantine have to be burned after. That inspired her to go on a magazine drive in her neighborhood, thinking it better to burn a magazine than a book. Now her neighbors are taking extra subscriptions just to donate to the hospitals. A bit of reading material must be quite a comfort for men who spend weeks in bed, with nothing else for diversion.

I wonder, do any of our books ever make it to Aggie's hospital? Do the men have enough to read, and could we send anything just for them?

We're all thinking of you. Write when you can. The censor has struck out a few lines here and there, but (don't tell General Pershing!) it's actually quite easy to hold the paper up to the light and make out what you've written. So please, proceed!

    Yours,

    Constance

CONSTANCE TO BIELASKI

August 27, 1918

Dear Mr. Bielaski,

I've made arrangements to start work at Hudson Printing Company using, as you called it, the usual method. What follows is my report thus far:

Andrew Wilmington is a mild-mannered British transplant who runs a printing concern specializing in advertising calendars, business stationery, receipt-books, and the like. He employs but one secretary, a Miss Anne Bradshaw, of New Hope, Pennsylvania. She's been in his employ for fourteen months and lives in a respectable boarding-house very similar to mine. She keeps to herself and has had no trouble with the police.

To secure a position with the company, I followed Miss Bradshaw home at the close of business. I approached her when she stopped at the entrance to her boarding-house to hunt for her key.

I find it best not to dance around the subject. I showed her my badge and told her at once that I worked for the Bureau of Investigation and that I needed to speak to her regarding urgent government business.

"Is it a poster you want printed or a booklet?" she asked.

"If it's a poster, you ought to go over to Hamilton Press. We're not equipped for it."

"It does concern the print shop," I said, "but please do let me come inside and tell you about it. Or we can go to my office if you prefer." (I haven't any kind of office, as you well know, but it doesn't matter. No one ever wants to go to a government agent's office. That's why it makes such a useful fiction.)

After considering her options, Miss Bradshaw invited me in. I found myself in the foyer of a rooming house exactly like my own: the boarders' parlor to the right, a business office and private sitting-room for the landlady to the left, a staircase straight ahead, and behind the stairs, the kitchen, which smelled, as all boarding-house kitchens do, of the morning's wilted banana peels and the evening's thin stew.

It was a fish stew this time. "I'd almost forgotten it was Meatless Tuesday," I said. This was my way of showing Miss Bradshaw that I was a kindred spirit.

She took my remark in the manner intended and laughed. "I don't mind going without the meat. It's the Wheatless Wednesdays that bring my spirits down."

"There is something restorative in a dinner roll," I said, "or a basket of them."

Miss Bradshaw and I were now on the friendliest of terms. "I suppose it isn't a matter to discuss in the parlor," she said. "You can come up to my room if you don't inspect it too closely."

"I won't inspect it at all," I said. "I live just as you do, over on Chestnut."

"Have you lived there long?" she asked.

She was by this time leading the way up the stairs, to the

second floor, where four bedrooms were arranged around a little hallway and a shared bath.

"Since the start of the war," I said. "I've one sister in France
and another touring with a vaudeville act that goes around
singing at the training camps. We had to close up our place in
the country, with all of us away."

"That's a shame," she said. "My parents live out in the
country, in Pennsylvania."

"What brought you here?" I asked.

"I thought I'd look for war-work in New York, but everyone
was applying at once and I seemed to just miss every promising
opportunity. I couldn't wait—I had to take the first position offered, and it happened to be here in Paterson."

"I might have something better for you if you're interested," I said.

She was, of course. I've found that it pays to take a little
time, and allow the idea to come forth naturally. There's a ten-
dency among agents to begin with threats and intimidation,
but how does that serve us? A bit of gentle maneuvering, along
the lines of what I've just put down, is almost effortless and
takes not a minute longer.

Miss Bradshaw's broom closet–sized room was outfitted almost exactly like my own. She'd been given the standard-issue
brass bed, a bureau, a wash-stand, and a dim old mirror nailed
to the wall. In the custom of all entertaining done in furnished
rooms, Miss Bradshaw offered me the bed and she perched on
her trunk, which was tucked into the corner and undoubtedly
held all her worldly possessions.

I looked around for some patriotic display and was relieved

to see a bouquet of flag ribbons wrapped around the doorknob. Nodding at it, I said, "I know you'd do anything you can to help us win the war, isn't that right?"

"Yes, of course," she said. (I always phrase my questions in such a way that they find it impossible to say no.)

"Here's the difficulty," I said. "We aren't entirely sure that Mr. Wilmington feels the same."

At that she sat up very straight and looked at me with alarm. "Oh, you can't possibly mean that he's a traitor," she said. "I've known him for over a year. There's never been a hint—"

"No, there wouldn't be," I said, "because if there had been a hint, you would've told the authorities, wouldn't you?"

I'm sure Miss Bradshaw had never even imagined such a scenario, and it seemed entirely plausible to me that she'd never been given any reason to. Nonetheless, she said, quite insistently, "Naturally, I would've gone directly to the police, but I've had no cause to. Am I in some sort of trouble myself over this?"

"Not at all," I said. "You seem to me to be of sound judgment and good character. I only require your co-operation for a few weeks' time. I'm to take your place at the print shop and have a look around myself. I'm a trained agent, you see, and although the possibility is remote, I might just notice something that you would've overlooked. If you're willing to help, you'll be rewarded handsomely, and you can return to your post just as soon as my assignment is complete."

"And what's to become of Mr. Wilmington?" she asked— half out of concern for his well-being and half, I suspect, out of morbid curiosity over the fate of a suspected traitor.

"Nothing at all, if he's above suspicion," I told her. "He'll never even know he was under investigation."

I neglected to mention the possibility that I might arrest him. Perhaps Miss Bradshaw assumed as much, and her thoughts had returned to her own fate. "What am I to do, while you're at my desk?" she asked.

"I can offer you steady work at the War Department as a stenographer. You'd be serving your country and earning a wage. When my work is done, you may return to Mr. Wilmington, or stay at the War Department, as you prefer."

"But how do I know he'll take me back, once I've left?"

"You're to request a temporary absence. We must settle on a story that you don't mind telling. Perhaps your mother is ill and you must return home for a few weeks. Or it could be an illness of your own, if you're a good actress. Maybe you require a small operation? It's up to you, really. You're the one who must tell a persuasive story."

She smiled at that. We were co-conspirators now. "I hate to wish ill health on my mother, but I suppose I'd have the easiest time convincing him of that. He knows nothing about my parents."

"That's fine, then," I said. "Your mother's fallen ill and you must rush to her side. You expect to be back in three weeks. She might take a turn for the worse, but don't even suggest that."

"Yes, let's not think of it," Miss Bradshaw said, already looking a little worried about her mother.

"We want him to believe that yours is but a brief leave-taking, most easily filled with the replacement you suggest. Even if the new girl is a disaster, she'll be gone quickly."

"And you're to be the new girl?"

"Precisely. Shall I be your cousin or one of the girls here at the boarding-house?"

Now she was enjoying herself! She grinned playfully at me, cocked her head to the side, and said, "We look nothing alike, but cousins often don't. He knows where I live, so if I tell him you room here, you'd have that much more pretending to do."

He knows where she lives? I didn't like the sound of that. "There's a Mrs. Wilmington, is there not?"

She caught my meaning right away and shook her head vigorously. "Oh, I didn't mean to suggest—no, no, it's nothing of the sort. He often asks me to run little errands for him after work. He doesn't want to send me too far out of my way, so . . ."

She'd grown flustered, trying to explain it, but I didn't think she was lying. The landlady wouldn't allow a male visitor regardless. "He wanted to know where you live so he could send you on errands along your route."

"Yes, that's it," she said, relieved.

That's all there was to it. We arranged to meet the following evening so that she could brief me on the particulars of my new position, and I could brief her on her new role at the War Department. More as I know it.

I see the American Protective League men ran another slacker raid in Paterson last night. They sent forty men off to jail, leaving a real mess for the police to sort out. Every one of them was registered for service—they just didn't have their papers with them. You should know that these raids are testing the patience of the police here, who are already stretched thin with so many of their men in France. Their view is that the League is made up of overzealous office men frustrated that they're too old for the draft. (I should know, my brother is one of them. If you get a report from a Francis Kopp of Hawthorne, you'll know you have half the Kopp siblings reporting to you.)

Yours very truly,

Constance A. Kopp

BIELASKI TO CONSTANCE

August 29, 1918

Dear Miss Kopp,

Afraid you're right about the League men. This business of citizens spying on citizens started small but came on strong, like a bout of tapeworms. At first we had a few upright and trustworthy men offering their automobiles and their business connections in any way that might serve the nation. Now they're holding recruiting fairs, issuing membership cards, and swearing in new members every week. I hate to turn down the manpower, but they're unruly.

Never mind, though—that mess is mine to worry about. You keep your eye on this Wilmington. I like the sound of the Bradshaw girl. You ought to watch out for girls like that. If she's quick-witted, discreet, and self-reliant, she'd make a promising agent. I wouldn't mind bringing on a few more lady recruits if they're up to your standards.

I will write to Mrs. Bailey at the War Department regarding Miss Bradshaw's assignment. Look for a copy for your own files.

Yours very truly,

A. Bruce Bielaski

BIELASKI TO MRS. BAILEY

August 29, 1918

Dear Mrs. Bailey,

I'm sending you a Miss Bradshaw, lately of Paterson, New Jersey, for any secretarial post you might have available. She has been temporarily removed from her current place of employment due to a sensitive matter under investigation by the Bureau. She can return to her old position within a few weeks if she chooses, but you may wish to keep her on. We regard her as trustworthy and professional and expect you will too.

Yours very truly,

A. Bruce Bielaski

cc: Constance A. Kopp

CONSTANCE TO BIELASKI

September 2, 1918

Dear Mr. Bielaski,

I've installed myself at the Hudson Printing Company. The place consists of a red brick warehouse fronted by a cramped office of the usual type: high dingy windows, a metal door with a name-plate, and an old coal-stove for heat. A dozen men work in the print shop. The office is staffed by Mr. Wilmington himself, a man at the counter named Sam Archer, and a secretary.

Now I've taken the secretarial post. On my first day I presented myself promptly at nine o'clock, under an assumed name. (Winifred Sedgewick, chosen from the New York City directory by my sister Fleurette the last time she was in town. She picks ten names at once, and this was the next on the list.)

I walked in and found myself in a shabby little foyer. The walls are plastered in samples, which in this case means invoice blanks and fire alarm calendars. The only furnishings are a single wooden chair whose cushion has long been discarded, a garish electrical light dangling overhead, and a floor of chipped tiles. Behind the narrow counter is a rack where the print jobs wait to be retrieved, and behind that a secretary's desk. The door to the owner's office sits just out of sight so that no customer can see, from the counter, whether the man in charge is in.

I'm sorry to say that I proved to be quite a disappointment to Mr. Wilmington and Sam Archer, both of whom are too old for the draft and regard it as a consolation prize that they might enjoy the comforts of a warm office and a pretty secretary while the young men have their adventures in the trenches.

"Miss . . . Miss Sedgewick?" asked Mr. Archer when I introduced myself, perhaps hoping he'd heard me wrong.

"Yes," I said. "I'm Miss Bradshaw's cousin."

Hearing me announced, Mr. Wilmington emerged from his office. If he is in fact a traitor or a spy, he is as bland as they

come: a narrow face and a high forehead, hair of an indeterminate beige, ink-stained fingers, and rumpled gray tweeds
nearly worn through at the elbows.

His expression and his voice are so mild that he didn't register shock the way Mr. Archer did. Instead he marshalled his
good British manners and welcomed me properly.

"Miss Sedgewick, of course," he said, "and right on time.
We were terribly sorry to hear about Miss Bradshaw's mother.
I take it she's your aunt?"

"My very favorite aunt," I said. "I pray for her quick recovery."

"As do we," he said, rather fervently. "There's a desk for
you here"—he stepped aside, a little awkwardly, to wave me
toward the desk I'd already spotted—"and I believe you'll find
things in order. Miss Bradshaw said you'd worked in printing
before?"

"Advertising, mostly." The less said about my invented past
as a secretary, the better. That seemed to satisfy him.

"Well. I'll leave you the morning to get settled. Can you
work a telephone?"

"Certainly," I said.

"That's fine. Tell them I'm out, unless it's my wife or
Thomas Edison. On second thought, I only want to speak to
Mr. Edison."

He smiled eagerly: it was apparently a joke he enjoyed. Mr.
Archer laughed on cue.

Miss Bradshaw kept meticulous records and left everything
in perfect order, so there was little to do but to step in and take
up her system of filing, ledger entries, correspondence, and so

forth. It's not terribly difficult work, which leaves me plenty of time for ferreting out bomb-makers, spies, and Bolsheviks.

Operations seem unremarkable so far. Sam Archer stays busy behind the counter, taking in a steady stream of orders for any sort of printed good a company might require, from crate labels to packing slips. He is visited by clerks and delivery boys, none of whom have done a thing to raise my suspicions. Mr. Wilmington works at his correspondence and goes back to the shop every hour or two with some question for the printer.

The men in the print shop are all American-born and (like your League men) eager to serve but sidelined for one reason or another. What comes off the presses is so mundane it would put you to sleep. If you're having difficulties in that area, let me know and I'll send you a batch.

Yesterday I volunteered to man the counter for an hour while Sam sorted out a botched order back in the print shop. I went through every package awaiting pick-up and scoured all the boxes and bags under the counter for anything of a suspicious nature—a note, a diagram, a German flag (I'm kidding about the German flag)—and saw nothing. I have been walking through the print shop every day, on the flimsiest of pretenses, and likewise find nothing there to be out of order.

At night I've taken to strolling by at odd hours to look for any signs of activity within, thinking that perhaps a surreptitious print run at two in the morning is what I'm meant to find. The shop is always closed, the windows dark, with no tell-tale hum of machinery within.

I've only one more trick up my sleeve, and that is to read

the correspondence that Mr. Wilmington sends out himself. While I type his business letters, he does write out a few notes by hand. None are addressed to private residences: they're all being sent to business concerns in New Jersey, Pennsylvania, and New York and seem to me to be ordinary correspondence that he, for whatever reason, prefers to handle himself.

Commencing tomorrow, I'll take his letters to the post office on my lunch break. Fortunately, I live nearby, so I can bring them straight back to my room and steam them open. I have enough acetone and copper arsenate but haven't another drop of fusel oil. Is there an alternative that might be easier to find in Paterson? The chemists seem to have run short on everything a Bureau agent requires to do her job.

Yours very truly,
Constance A. Kopp

BIELASKI TO CONSTANCE

September 4, 1918

Dear Miss Kopp,

You'll have to go in to New York for fusel oil. Robertson's on Lexington still serves as our chemist. Tell him you're one of Bielaski's men and he'll hand you everything you need out the back door and won't charge you for it.

Yours very truly,
A. Bruce Bielaski

P.S. My secretary asked me to change this to "one of Bielaski's ladies," but that sounds all wrong,

and Robertson will know what you mean regardless.

P.S.S. Speaking of ladies, I had a good report about
that Miss Bradshaw. She might not want to return to the print shop when your job is completed.
Have a word with her.

CONSTANCE TO NORMA

September 5, 1918

Dear Norma,

Yours of July 8 just turned up, looking as though it had walked
across the Sahara to get here. We all grumble endlessly about
lost and delayed letters, but in the middle of war, no one can
stop to organize a better postal system. We will take what we
can get.

I was quite stricken to hear that your program is "unraveling" and that no one seems to recognize the necessity of it. I
would offer to go and speak to General Murray myself, but you
say that you are writing to him directly. I trust that you will tell
him all that you have told me.

As two months have already passed, there's little I could
say that would do you any immediate good. I can only tell you
what Sheriff Heath used to say to me: We can only do our part.
We cannot, as individuals, put a stop to crime or mayhem or
even war. (Especially war.) We won't, in any final sense, ever
win. There will always be a police department, or a sheriff's
office, or an Army and Navy, because there will always be another criminal, another battle, another belligerent nation. All

we can do is to get up every day and to stand on the side of justice and fairness. In this war, we are all standing on the side of a free Europe and a free world.

You will do your duty to the best of your ability. I know you will. Others might not come around to your point of view. They often don't. But what matters is that we are all fighting toward the same end.

I wish I could be of more use! I hope to have a batch of letters from you any day now that tells me that you've put everything right again. You haven't telegrammed to say that you're returning on the next ship, so I can only hope that you've found a way out of your predicament.

I just returned from Sunday dinner with Bessie and Francis and the children. The meal was, as always, a war-time conjuring trick. I don't know how she makes half of a baked ham stretch all week, even when she isn't feeding her ravenous sister-in-law. This time she even came into a bit of sirloin, bartered through the kind of elaborate network that springs up among housewives in trying times. Thanks to our laying hens (it was smart of you to install them in her backyard, and you were right, the neighbors don't complain as long as they get their share of eggs), she's able to swap eggs with Mrs. Foster, two doors down, whose uncle has an apple orchard. With the fruit she earns on that exchange, she keeps a bit for the family and barters the rest with Mrs. Quackenbush across the street, whose son is a butcher and supplies Bessie with ham-bones and the butt-ends from his best cuts.

In this way she assembles a bit of this and a bit of that, bakes it all with noodles and cabbage like you used to do, and covers the whole of it in mashed potatoes, cheese, bread crumbs, and whatever else she can put together. I'm pretty sure there was a crust of stale corn flakes tonight, which sounds appalling but was, in fact, a minor culinary triumph.

Did you know that we're now saving nut-shells and fruit pits for gas mask filters? Frankie Jr. has joined the local collection committee. He goes up and down the street every Tuesday to pick up from the neighbors. Francis wants to impart upon him a sense of his duty. You see in the two of them the frustrated efforts of sidelined men: Frankie Jr., still just a boy, and Francis too old, at 43. Both of them wish desperately for a uniform and an obligation. Frankie has found a sense of purpose in his weekly rounds (Bessie embroidered a flag on his cap, and he wears it like a uniform), and Francis finds his purpose in his League activities.

It's a good thing that neither of us can talk too much about our work, because I fear we might come to fisticuffs. He's part of that crowd of Paterson businessmen intent upon ferreting out anti-American leanings on the part of any new arrival, or even the son of an immigrant, which is of course precisely what he is—what all of us are. I hadn't noticed, before the war, how far he'd gone in turning his back on Mother's Austrian roots, but now that I think on it, I can see the ways he's scrubbed himself of anything that isn't entirely American.

For instance, have you ever heard him speak a word of German? He understood Mother perfectly, but he always answered in English, didn't he? And when he and Bessie moved to Hawthorne and filled their bungalow with new oak furniture, straight from the department store, I thought he was simply embracing the "new" and the "now," but I wonder if he just wanted nothing to do with those old carved chairs and bureaus, bearing the finger-prints and wax polish of a century's worth of Viennese grandmothers. He wanted to sit on an American chair, milled from American oak in a factory just over in Pennsylvania. And he never liked it, did he, when Bessie tried to make Mother's dumplings or even those little sugar-dusted cookies she used to bake when we were children.

Nothing of the Old World appeals to him, in short. I always thought that he merely wanted to look ahead, and to see himself as a man of the twentieth century and of this country. Now I wonder if he didn't see something dirty, something shady and suspicious, in Mother's old ways—if he didn't so much step into the new as he rejected the old. It's a wonder he hasn't changed his name from Kopp to King and tried to pass his heritage off as British.

For that matter, it's a wonder he hasn't changed his age. If Francis hadn't grown so jowly and stout in the last few years, he might've tried to pass himself off for a younger man and run off to war anyway. (Bessie would never stand for it, of course, not with two children at home who depend upon him, but I wouldn't put it past him to try.)

What I mean to say is that I see a bitterness in him now. For so many men the war seems to provide a ready-made sense of purpose where one was missing before. It's as if he has, for the first time, seen what his life was meant to be, and lost it before he ever took hold of it, due entirely to an accident of his birth-date. There's a vacancy behind his eyes that was never there before.

I don't mean to worry you. The war affects us all. The men left behind here are wounded in their own way, but it's nothing compared to what you see in France.

As for my own work, I'm in that watch-and-wait stage that might lead somewhere or it might not. I do hope I get a good arrest out of it. Mr. Bielaski, for all his fine qualities, still tells me that he'll "send in the boys" if arrests are to be made. He knows full well what I can do, but he's simply in the habit of sending the boys in to do it. Of course I'm not wishing for a saboteur with a suitcase full of dynamite, but I wouldn't mind an opportunity to toss someone into jail, just to remind him (and myself) that I can.

Yours,
Constance

CONSTANCE TO BIELASKI

September 9, 1918

Dear Mr. Bielaski,

Fusel oil in hand, letters steamed open per protocol, but it makes an awful stink. My landlady, the formidable Mrs. Spinella, complained about it even though I kept a window open. At times like this an agent really could use an office. Doesn't the Bureau have anything in downtown Paterson?

I found nothing unusual in the letters. Mr. Wilmington writes congenial notes in longhand to his most favored customers, those who've been with him the longest and given him the most business. I scrutinized the letters for code, passed them over a candle, and held them up to the light, but I see no indications of secret ink or hidden messages.

I was about to bring the whole operation to a close when an unusual package for Mrs. Wilmington arrived from England.

Mr. Wilmington was away on business overnight (he goes to Philadelphia to call on new prospects once a year), and Sam Archer, the counter man, was quite agitated about the unexpected delivery.

"Mrs. Wilmington doesn't like to wait," he told me. "If there's something here for her, she wants it brought over immediately. Mr. Wilmington carries them home himself."

"But he'll be back tomorrow night," I said. "Isn't that good enough?"

"Not at all." Mr. Archer makes a good counter man because he's meticulous about his counter, and anything having to do with receiving, delivering, or shipping. You could put him up for Postmaster General and you wouldn't be disappointed.

"I'll have to carry it over myself," he said, but he sounded displeased about it. It was a busy day behind the counter and he doesn't like to leave me in charge. (I should say in my defense that I've never mangled an order or mishandled a package.)

"It must be terribly important, if she's in such a rush to have it," I said.

At that he rolled his eyes. "It's nothing but a family keepsake. She used to get them all the time. Vases and figurines and the like. She's having them shipped over because she doesn't want them bombed in London. I thought they'd have run out of valuables by now."

"I'm sure it's the sentiment that matters," I said, trying to sound womanly about it. "Let me carry it over. They don't live far, do they?"

They don't, and Mr. Archer was happy to send me out with the package.

Once out of the office, I had to move quickly. I rushed home—ignoring Mrs. Spinella, who doesn't like to see her tenants home in the middle of the day when she's cleaning—and proceeded to pry apart the box. It was nothing but a flimsy wooden carton, nailed shut with tiny finishing nails. It took a bit of delicate work with a letter-opener, but I was able to pop them out without any sign of damage.

The sender had filled the carton with sawdust—what a mess that made, but never mind—and within the sawdust, wrapped in plain cloth sacking, was a ceramic figurine of a lady dancer, with a full ballroom skirt like our grandmothers might've worn. Although it lacked a maker's mark on the bottom—more about that in a minute—I suspect it wasn't of English manufacture. It looked German or Austrian to me. My mother, who was born in Vienna and immigrated with her parents at the age of sixteen, had such keepsakes in her curio cabinet, as did my grandmother.

More important than its origin, however, was the fact that it rattled when I shook it. Something was inside.

It wasn't a loose, hard rattle. The insides must've been similarly packed with sawdust or some other material. It was a slight, dull, muffled rattle—but there was no mistaking it.

And about the base of the figurine: the original base had been very carefully cut away and a new ceramic piece glued into place. I could see the seam around the edge, and I noticed a slight difference in the color of the glaze between the bottom and the sides of the base.

I could've broken it open, of course, and kept whatever was inside without Mrs. Wilmington ever being the wiser, but Sam Archer knew I had the package. I decided to put it all back together, deliver it, and learn what I could of Mrs. Wilmington. I nailed the carton shut and took it directly to her.

The Wilmingtons live in a rather elegant apartment building of the sort you might see in New York but rarely in New Jersey. Most shopkeepers and factory owners live in one of the more congenial neighborhoods away from downtown, where they can have a lawn and a tree with a swing dangling from it. But Mr. Wilmington says he prefers to live like a Londoner and walk to work. "I'd live above the shop if it were up to me," he once told me, "but Mrs. Wilmington thinks it's cheap and common. This is our compromise."

I bustled over to the place and was greeted by a trim, plainly dressed woman of about forty. I noticed right away something severe in her manner: hair back in a tight bun (hairstyles might not matter to you, but they tell me quite a bit, and Mrs. Wilmington's style suggested a woman not given to frivolity or vanity), and lips pressed together in a humorless greeting. She didn't seem inclined to let me in, but I took a step over the threshold as if I'd already been invited—it's best in our line of work, I've found, to behave as if one belongs—and she stood back to let me pass.

"Mr. Archer sent me," I said. "I'm Miss Sedgewick, the secretary, come to deliver a package that only just arrived."

"Put it down, then," she said. She offered nothing else by way of greeting, and why should she? I was of no consequence to her. A secretary is, in this way, the perfect cover. Nobody thinks twice about me.

The Wilmingtons' apartment is a portrait of London life before the war, or at least what I'd imagine London life to be. As I understand it, they left in the fall of 1914, presumably to seek a better situation for themselves before Germany advanced too far. They brought absolutely everything with them: gilt-edged mirrors and marble-topped bureaus, framed engravings of pastoral English countryside scenes of the sort a man in the printing business might collect, high-backed chairs and carved settees, and good Indian rugs. Beyond the sitting-room I caught a glimpse of Mr. Wilmington's study. Once again, it was the picture of an Englishman's retreat: a leather chair, a roll-top desk, and a pair of brass lamps.

There were no figurines on display. The lady dancer would not, as far as I could tell, be joining any companions.

Naturally I remained suspicious of the figurine, but I could nonetheless conjure up a reasonable explanation. Someone could've hidden jewelry inside of it, for instance, to avoid customs duties.

Then, just as I turned to leave, Mrs. Wilmington bent down to sweep aside a rug caught under the door. In doing so, she managed to pop a button loose on her blouse and cursed softly under her breath. I was standing just close enough to hear her say, *"Herrgott nochmal,"* which translates loosely from the German as "Oh, my Lord." It's something my mother would say if she was particularly exasperated.

Until that moment, the few words Mrs. Wilmington had spoken to me suggested no trace of a German accent, but now I had to be sure.

"I hope I haven't inconvenienced you," I said, as I stepped outside. (She was practically pushing me out the door.)

"It's no trouble," she said. That wasn't enough conversation for me to get a clear impression of her manner of speaking.

She was fingering the gap where the button had broken away. It was a flimsy shirtwaist with button-holes so poorly stitched that the fabric could tear easily. With that in mind I added, "I have a waist like that myself, and I had to do all the button-holes again. They just don't hold."

She smiled ever so slightly at that and said, "I should do the same, but I wouldn't know how. Mr. Wilmington complained from the day we were married that I couldn't so much as darn a sock. He wants me to take a class or hire a tutor."

There it was—just the slightest trace of German in that word, "tutor," under an otherwise perfect (to my ears) English accent. I'm not sure I would've noticed it had I not been listening for it.

"I don't like to sew myself," I said. I started to explain that I had a sister who handled all our seamstressing, but just as I did, I had an idea—which I'll explain later, if it proves necessary.

In that moment, there was nothing more I could do without inviting suspicion. I wished her a good day and returned at once to the office.

I've given you as full a picture of the situation as I can, with the idea that you might decide to keep me on here for another week or two while I continue my duties as secretary, but take an opportunity to investigate the wife.

Is it at all possible that we've been looking at the wrong Wilmington?

Yours very truly,

Constance Kopp

CONSTANCE TO NORMA

September 10, 1918

Dear Norma,

My work has taken an interesting turn. You won't be surprised to learn that I've uncovered something that only a woman might notice. (In fact, it was something that only a German-speaking woman might notice.) It might lead nowhere—we never know, when we set out on an investigation—but if I'm right, I will have succeeded once again in convincing my superiors on this point: The Bureau needs every sort of American. Men, women, of German extraction or French or Spanish, Catholic, Protestant, and so on.

I saw something—or, more specifically, I heard something—that might've gone unnoticed by another agent. How much does the Bureau miss—or any police department, for that matter—if every officer is just like the next?

You don't need to answer that. I only want to tell you that my quiet little case has just become unexpectedly lively.

I wonder how many letters you sent in August, and if they'll ever arrive, or if they're gone for good. It seems that every week we hear another awful story of mail being lost at sea. Just recently a German submarine sank a boat right off the New Jersey coast with forty thousand letters on board, plus another fifty sacks of parcel post. You'd be forgiven for writing only a line or two if you thought it was going to end up at the bottom of the Atlantic, but please don't let that stop you.

It's maddening not to know what you're up to over there, and to have the letters be so terribly behind when they do arrive. I pore over the newspapers every day for news of a village of the sort where you might be stationed, but of course it's impossible to guess. You could be anywhere. As long as you're not at the front, I just have to trust that you're safe.

Bessie has been going door-to-door in an effort to adopt French war orphans—not in the sense of bringing them here to New Jersey, of course. It's a type of charity by subscription, in which a family pledges to send ten cents a day to benefit the child of a fallen soldier, so that the child may be kept at home with its mother or relatives and not placed in an orphanage. Bessie says that Americans have "adopted" 85,000 French orphans so far, and by Christmas it is hoped that our nation will adopt another 250,000. I've taken on two myself. They give you the names of the children: I am responsible for little Armandine Jourdren, of Vincennes, and Charles Vilfeu, of Sarthe. I don't suppose a few dollars from an American does much to comfort a child whose father gave his life for France and for all the world, but when I'm absolutely staggered by the reports of bloodshed, the way I gather myself together is to think of Armandine and of Charles, and to imagine them asleep in their own beds, with someone to look after them.

Aggie must see the horrors of it first hand, every day. How is she faring at the hospital, and how are you getting on at the fort? I wish you could tell us more about it. You've made it clear that the men attached to your particular unit hadn't ever given messenger pigeons any serious thought before now. Have patience with them. (I know you won't, but absent any particulars, it's the only advice I can offer.)

Yours,
Constance

NORMA

Langres, France

August 1, 1918

Dear General Murray,

I've had a few days to put a new operation together and I can now report on my progress.

As you know, the pigeon program has, for all practical purposes, been put into mothballs, owing to a litany of failures on the part of certain officers, beginning with the failure to dispatch field manuals along with the pigeons, thus making it impossible for soldiers in the trenches to deploy them properly. Military resources are now being squandered on the care and feeding of birds that will not, unless conditions change, be put to any use at all in our fight against the Germans.

Under the circumstances, I'm left with little choice but to find alternative methods of deployment that are not strictly under the command of the United States Army Pigeon Service. I realize that this is highly irregular and that I take some risk in reporting it to you, but I will take you at your word when you say that you wish only to have as complete a picture as possible to improve the training program at Fort Monmouth. If, however, you believe yourself to be obliged to report my activities, please do so without delay. I stand ready to face the consequences.

I now spend my days at the fort doing what I'm ordered to do, which is to keep the pigeons fed and housed and in sufficient condition to fly a mission, should they be called to duty —although it has been made plain to me that they will not be.

But my nights are my own, and with the time I have to myself I am doing all that is in my power to return the pigeons to their original assignment, that of aiding our soldiers in defeating the enemy. To that end, over the last several evenings I have constructed the following:

Twelve (12) cylindrical pigeon carriers, each meant to accommodate an individual pigeon, fashioned from discarded wicker-work and fitted with a metal clasp and a leather carrying strap.
Twelve (12) rubber bags, cut and fitted to drape over the carrier in case of gas attack.
Twelve (12) metal feed canisters to protect against rot and rats.

I then packed these supplies, along with twelve of the program's best pigeons, into a crate and wheeled them to the train station to be distributed to those soldiers discharged from the American hospital and deemed fit to return to the front.

It must be noted that on the way, I encountered the town baker, Madame Bertrand, rushing back from the hospital with a cart piled high with crumpled flour sacking and bread-baskets. It was from her bakery, the Patisserie Confiserie, that I obtained the discarded baskets now in use as pigeon carriers. Madame Bertrand stopped to have a look at my handiwork and remarked that if I was capable of repairing wicker-work so tidily, I might repair hers rather than fish them out of the bin for my own use. I mention this only to make the point that the baskets are of a high quality, in spite of having been fashioned from ruined French wicker rather than anything supplied by the United States Army, which is no longer a party to this project.

I arrived at the train station just as the men from three units were being shipped back to the front, along with a railcar full of supplies. With all the loading and unloading, there was a great deal of chaos on the platform. This provided an opportunity to speak to the soldiers without attracting the attention of their commanders.

To a man they proved unreceptive to my message. Soldiers on their way to the front are a nervous and morose group: many in this batch had only just been released from the hospital and were not terribly eager to go back. Three young ladies from the YMCA canteen were on hand to offer up sandwiches and words of encouragement. A custom has developed among the canteen girls to adopt a soldier as a *filleul de guerre*, a war-time godson, which entails a promise to write letters, with no romantic entanglements. A few more *filleuls* were hastily adopted on the platform as the men paced and fretted.

Into this scene of misery I waded, and addressed the soldiers as follows: "I've come to give you a pigeon to carry with you to the front for the purpose of testing a new messaging program. There's a blank form attached to the bird's leg already. You have only to write your name and the time of release. They've all been fed and won't want anything for twenty-four hours. That should give you plenty of time to send one from the trenches."

I had not anticipated that any reminder that they'd be living in a trench within twenty-four hours would be enough to send the men into another nervous fit. "You don't know what it's like out there, miss," they each told me in turn. "I can't look after a bird."

Again I explained that the birds were no trouble to look after and came equipped with their own rations. That only got them talking about Army rations and how they'd miss the treats the canteen girls brought over to the hospital every day.

"Only the Brits use pigeons," another told me, "and we don't take orders from the Crown. General Pershing likes his telephones."

Efforts to persuade them that a message sent by pigeon might help save a life or win the war were met with disbelief and incredulity. When the train pulled away, I was left with a dozen birds in baskets, having failed to convince a single soldier to take up the experiment.

It's no wonder the program as we had implemented it previously failed, as the men are entirely consumed with their own immediate needs and unable to grasp the strategic importance of messenger pigeons to the Army's overall mission, that of defeating the Germans and liberating Europe from tyranny.

I'm forced to conclude that the commanders won't order the use of the birds, nor will the men take them willingly. However, this is by no means the end of the project.

Another train departs next week. There will be pigeons on board that train.

Yours in service,

Norma C. Kopp

AGGIE TO CONSTANCE

August 7, 1918

Dear Constance,

I want to tell you about a kindness your sister extended to a soldier. She has warned me not to say a thing about her work, but I think that if you (or the censor, hello, Mr. Censor) read this carefully, you will find not one line that gives anything away.

A few weeks ago, she met a soldier named Forrest Pike who was in the hospital for what, I'm sad to say, passes for a minor injury around here. He lost a finger, when most men lose so much more. He's quite healthy, otherwise, and has been bored during his recuperation. Nonetheless we must keep him here until his wound closes completely. There's no possibility of a fresh bandage in the trenches, and we don't want him back with an infection.

I begged Norma to go and visit him, but she genuinely didn't see the reason why. She said she hadn't anything to say to him. I explained that all the men are so lonely, and happy for any company at all. Forrest himself told me that the sight of American girls makes him want to get up and fight again.

Do you know what Norma said to that? "They should fight because they're ordered to. They're soldiers. If pretty girls were required to keep an army going, Pershing would've sent for a battalion of them. In fact, I believe he'd like the troops to spend a little less time looking at girls. That's why he doesn't let them go to Paris any more."

(If you haven't heard—and why would this be in the papers, anyway?—the troops are no longer allowed Paris leave and go instead to a new encampment in the countryside, where the YMCA girls fry doughnuts, organize dances, and play cards with the boys. It's meant to be more wholesome than the sinful streets of Paris, and more of a proper rest. The soldiers don't complain, at least they don't complain to us. I've been told by dozens of them that they'd rather see a girl from Wisconsin than a Parisian dancer any day. I've decided to believe them. We all have our little lies that we cling to in war-time.)

Back to Norma: I told her that Forrest has been asking about her. He's interested in those pigeons of hers. He used to keep canaries, he told me, and he wouldn't mind having a bird for company again, especially if it was hand-raised the way the last one was.

Norma insisted that her pigeons were no more pets than they were pie filling, and said that he wouldn't be allowed to keep a bird in the hospital anyway.

"Oh, he knows that," I told her. "He wants to take one to the front. We're sending him back on Tuesday."

Norma won't let me say too much about her . . . let's use the word "predicament" . . . but suffice it to say that only a few days ago, she very much wanted to hand out pigeons to soldiers returning to the front. Apparently she wasn't able to convince anyone to take a bird, and now she's working on another plan that she's keeping secret even from me.

Somehow, though, I managed to convince her to return to the scene of her most recent failure and to give Forrest Pike a pigeon that she raised herself, an exceptionally good flyer with a friendly disposition. She named it Mon Chou because of me. I found it so confusing, at first, that the French would call someone they loved "my cabbage" as a term of affection. You hear it every time a lady walks down the street with a baby. Everyone stops and coos, *"Mon chou, mon chou."* Finally Norma told me that the villagers are most likely thinking of a *chou à la crème,* a cream puff. It makes much more sense to call a baby "my little cream puff" than "my little cabbage," although just thinking about it does make one hungry for cream puffs, which even Madame Bertrand cannot conjure just now.

The point is that Norma happened to be ready to name a pigeon on the very day she explained to me the difference between cabbages and cream puffs, so Mon Chou was the name this little bird received.

Yesterday, when Forrest Pike was to depart, we went down to the station together to see him off and to deliver Mon Chou to him. I often go to kiss the soldiers good-bye. It means the world to them, poor souls. Norma didn't seem interested in kissing any of them, but she did shake a few hands, and the men accepted that good-naturedly.

I happened to be carrying Norma's pigeon in a basket as I made the rounds. You should've seen how many men were jealous that I'd brought a bird only for Forrest. They're just so eager for any little keepsake! They probably would've accepted a basket of mud-pies if I'd handed them out with a smile.

We found Forrest already on board, looking mournfully out

a window, but he hopped off when he saw us on the platform. He took Norma's pigeon basket with all the excitement of a child opening his Christmas stocking.

"What happens if he gets loose?" Forrest wanted to know. "He won't go to headquarters and tell on me, will he?"

"He'll fly right back here," Norma assured him. "It's the only home he's ever known."

"But that could be two hundred miles! Maybe more." Poor Forrest didn't know where, precisely, he was being sent. It must all seem a million miles away from the safety and comfort of our little village.

Norma told him that she's sent her birds five hundred miles away, and they came straight back within a day or two.

Forrest whistled. "They must really want to get home. I'd fly all night too, if I thought it would get me home."

"But not until your job was done," Norma said. (She's not terribly sympathetic to longings for home, your sister.)

Anyway, she handed over a month's worth of rations and a little booklet she'd painstakingly typed herself, with all of her instructions in it. I can't imagine a booklet lasting a day in the trenches, but Forrest took it politely nonetheless. He really is a very sweet young man, quick with a joke and eager to please.

"Does the bird eat cooties?" he asked. "If he does, he'll get fat in the trenches."

"Ground beetles and grubs, more like," Norma said. "If you do send him back, write me a note with the date and time of release, and your location if you can give it. At least I'll know how far and fast he flew."

"Happy to. But I'd rather keep him with me, if it's all the same to you."

"You might as well," Norma told him. "All my best flyers are sitting around in their loft, getting fat and lazy. At least Mon Chou will see the front."

That's all I can report for now. I'm sure you're breathless for the next thrilling installment. If we get word from either Forrest or Mon Chou, I'll write to you immediately!

Tendrement—

Aggie

AGGIE TO CONSTANCE

August 10, 1918

Dear Constance,

Your sister nearly wept when she opened your box and found Bessie's trench cake inside. (I'm going to call it a raisin cake, because "trench cake" sounds so unappetizing, and this is delicious.) You can't imagine what these packages from home mean to all of us. It is as if we're opening a portal into the dear familiar world we left behind.

Norma is reading over my shoulder and insists that she was not "nearly weeping." I'm quite certain I heard a sniff. She claims she was merely inspecting the cake for mold. (Is she this argumentative at home?) She found no mold, in case you're wondering. It traveled quite well.

Please give our love and thanks to Bessie. We've shared her cake all around and are the most popular girls at the Hôtel de la Poste tonight. Thanks also for the "practical necessities" you enclosed. I would hate for you to know what a foul and grubby bunch we are, because you might not want to associate with us at all. Suffice it to say that soap is every bit as much a luxury as sugar, and that sweetly scented talc will make us all a little easier to be around. I didn't share it with everyone in the hotel, because it would've been gone in a minute, but I did dole some out to the other girls who use our bathroom. They send their appreciation as well.

Norma won't let me say a thing about what's been happening at the fort. Please don't worry, it's nothing she won't survive, but just know that she's having the most trying time and the cake arrived when we needed it most. In fact, after what happened at the train station with Forrest Pike a few days ago, she's come up with a new plan to win the war (I'm only exaggerating a little), and I have a role to play again. Naturally I agreed to do anything I could to help, if only to cheer her up. You know Norma much better than I do, and you must know that "cheerful" isn't a word that aptly describes her on the best of days. But when she has a definite mission, something that involves plans and lists and bouts of skilled labor and technical expertise, she is, in her own way, happy. She was just that way tonight, telling me the intricacies of her plan and the many steps ahead as she puts her ideas into action. I hope to report back soon on our success.

I'm handing the pencil to your sister now and insisting that she think of something she's allowed to write about. She says she's already told you everything there is to know about this place. But in the note Bessie enclosed with the cake, she asked what we have in the way of bakeries here. In fact, there is a

story to tell about our town baker. I've made it Norma's responsibility to tell it.

Tendrement —

Aggie

NORMA TO CONSTANCE

August 10, 1918

Dear Constance,

Very well, I'll tell you about the baker, as Aggie gives me no
choice. But don't speak of her as the town baker. She's never
been recognized as such and probably never will be.

The Patisserie Confiserie is located on the town square,
just around the corner from our hotel. Until recently, it was
owned by Monsieur Bertrand, the present baker's brother.

He died a month before we arrived, and the village has
not yet stopped mourning him. He was apparently the sort
of man who told jokes and sang songs to children and gave
away as much as he sold. It doesn't sound like any way to
run a business to me, but these small French villages like
their irregular little shops. To this day his portrait hangs in
a place of honor in the bakery, behind the counter. His sister
—I'll get to her in a minute—tried to take the portrait down,
claiming it grieved her to see his face every day, but the villagers nearly came after her with pitchforks and torches. She
was forced to leave it up.

From his picture I can tell you that he possessed a high, intelligent forehead, lined with wrinkles caused by laughter, and
a mouth that turned habitually up at the corners. He was ex-

ceptionally gaunt for a baker, a characteristic attributed to the fact that he was diabetic.

It is Aggie's belief that he was poorly treated for his diabetes. He avoided sweets except when he desperately needed them: if he was ever seen nodding off behind the counter, a customer would break a corner off a *tarte à la frangipane*, push it through his lips, and that would bring him around.

It was the diabetes that killed him. One evening he dropped off in his chair, and no one was there to resurrect him with sugar. (In case you're wondering how he had any sugar at all in war-time, Monsieur Bertrand was a notorious hoarder of hard-to-find ingredients. He brought in a supply of beet sugar and fruit preserves at the very beginning of the war, in anticipation of shortages. He was not about to let the village go without its treats.)

Since Monsieur Bertrand had never married nor had any children, his nearest living relation was his never-married sister, Madame Bertrand, who traveled from Toulouse when news of his death reached her.

Madame Bertrand is nothing like her brother. Where he was lean, she's round, with enormous dimpled arms and thick ankles that she soaks in cold water after lunch and in the evenings. Where he had only just started to go bald, she has had the misfortune of losing all the hair around her forehead, so that she is bald nearly to the top of her head. What hair remains she combs back in thick black strands and pins up in a flat bun, but this is, of course, wholly inadequate at concealing the truth.

She does own a wig, so dark and coarse that I've often wondered if it's made of horsehair. She detests the wig. It's hot, she says, and it itches and interferes with her work. The wig spends most of its time on a mannequin's head, high on a shelf alongside the flour canisters. In the time that I've known her, she's worn it only twice, when she heard that the generals were expected in town. The generals do not, as a rule, visit bakeries. She had however heard that General Pershing was partial to strawberry cream, so she had reason to hope.

As far as Aggie and I can tell, Madame Bertrand was greeted sympathetically, but not particularly warmly, by the villagers. She possesses a temperament exactly the opposite of her brother's, which is to say that she believes she is running a business, not a cabaret, and doesn't see any reason to tell a joke or sing a song or know a customer's name. She has no friends in town and seems disinclined to make any. A few of the baker's old chums have invited her to dinner, out of a sense of duty, but she always declines those invitations, claiming that she's far too busy getting her brother's shop in order (it seemed perfectly in order to the villagers) and learning his recipes (which would, the villagers acknowledged, take time).

However, in short order, she did learn to turn out cakes that nearly rivaled her brother's. When the villagers expressed surprise that she could master a brioche or a *flan pâtissier* so quickly, she merely brushed them away in disgust and reminded them that she and her deceased brother were both taught by the same mother.

I'm sure you're wondering how a bakery is allowed to turn out anything in the way of cakes and pies in war-time. Even Paris is doing without its *profiteroles* and its *éclairs*. Of course we're subject to the same rationing as the rest of the country. Her brother, as I said, hid quite a bit away in his cellar before the rationing began. Here in the countryside, there's always an informal trade in eggs, butter, and honey. There are preserves tucked away in cellars. There are sweet liqueurs in cabinets. One way or another, Monsieur Bertrand put his hands on what he needed, and his sister seems to do the same.

The trouble is that after serving the Americans, she rarely has anything at all left for the villagers. This town has been entirely commandeered by the United States Army for its training schools, and we have an appetite. The restaurants and hotels, serving American officers and visiting dignitaries, still expect their desserts and buy all that she can bake.

In this way, Madame Bertrand has come to be thought of as the official American military baker. She saves her best for the officers, and sells her scraps to the villagers. That's how I'm able to knock on her door, late at night, and persuade her to turn loose of one miserly slice of a *tarte aux fruits*. She tries to keep the Americans fed. We're the ones with a bit of money in our pockets, and sometimes an Army shipment of Karo Syrup to barter. (We've seen her carting boxes over to the post office, in which she packs cakes for a sister in Belgium— apparently Monsieur Bertrand had another sister he never told anyone about, and she, too, benefits from the secret stores of sugar while the villagers go without.)

Of course, there's still the bread. Madame Bertrand is obligated to bake the national bread, whose recipe is abhorrent to the French. It seems to contain quite a bit of rice flour in addition to wheat, and turns an unappetizing gray when baked. She supplies it to the hotels and the hospitals. The villagers line up mournfully for their ration, too (which they call *pain de Boche*, out of spite), and when they do, they both see and smell the treats she's turning out—but not for them. In this way their resentment grows. She won't even bake for a special occasion: not a wedding, not a birthday. The villagers are sent home with only their loaves of gray bread, while the Americans get madeleines.

That's why the villagers don't like her. That, and the fact that when she took over the shop, she fired her brother's sole employee, Fernand Luverne, who had been in his employ for twenty years and rented a room above the shop alongside Monsieur Bertrand's own apartment. No one looked kindly upon Madame Bertrand for putting Fernand out of both home and work at once. It's a small village and people take sides. Most everyone has sided against her.

As ever,
Norma

CONSTANCE TO NORMA AND AGGIE

August 11, 1918

Dear Norma and Aggie,

I was just over at Francis and Bessie's for dinner. All the talk is of war, and I confess I'd like to call a halt to it. I miss the old days, when world affairs rarely encroached upon our Sunday dinners. But even the children are swept up in it. Little Frankie (I'm not supposed to call him little, as he's now eleven) is, of course, fascinated by news of the war, and reads over his father's shoulder every night. They spread out maps and cover them with marks as the troops advance and retreat. That boy can draw a perfectly accurate picture of every aeroplane, rifle, and ship deployed in Europe's defense. He saw in the newspaper that we're sending a million horses to France, because apparently those autos you detest so much can't roll over the soggy, uneven ground around the trenches. He took a length of butcher's paper and tried to draw a million horses on the march. I'm not sure he managed more than a hundred, but it was an admirable effort.

Still, none of us can imagine everyday life in France. Your letters mean more to us than any newspaper article. Lorraine just turned thirteen—can you believe it?—and doesn't seem to know what to make of the war, or her place in it. But these dispatches from you give her the idea that women have a part to play. She doesn't seem to look at her aunt Constance as any kind of a role model, which is to say that she has no interest in wearing a badge or carrying a gun, and why should she? It isn't for everyone. But in your letters, she obviously finds something that interests her. Keep writing them, for that reason alone.

I can tell you something about a case I worked earlier this summer, now that it's going to trial and the papers have the story. I was sent over to the Curtiss North Elmwood plant in Buffalo to look into allegations of sabotage. What made the case unusual was that the man accused, David Rogovin, had been reported by two German men who worked alongside him. Mr. Bielaski seemed, at first, more alarmed about the Germans making the report than about the man they were reporting.

The Germans had never caused any trouble nor raised suspicion among the supervisors at the plant, but Mr. Bielaski wanted them interrogated in their native tongue to make sure that not a word was lost in translation. As German-speaking agents are something of a rarity, I was sent along with another man to make the inquiries.

The Germans, when I spoke to them, claimed to have been in the country for over ten years and to have no loyalty to the Kaiser. In fact, they were both eager and proud to work on the aeroplanes that would help bring an end to the war. I interviewed them for nearly an hour while my fellow agent, in disguise as a new man on the line, observed Mr. Rogovin as he went about his work. In no time at all he witnessed the act of sabotage.

Mr. Rogovin was hammering wood-screws into the aeroplane frames rather than screwing them.

It's impossible to believe that he didn't know better. When interrogated after his arrest, he denied everything and said that the two German men had it in for him, then claimed he'd lost his screwdriver, and then claimed that he didn't know the screws could be so easily pulled out. (He showed some surprise when the agent demonstrated for him, but his surprise rang false.) He later claimed he'd fallen into a fit of abstraction over worry for his ill child, and that made him careless, but when I visited the family, I found nothing the matter with any of them.

Is Mr. Rogovin an agent of Germany, or is he simply the worst carpenter this nation has ever seen? The trial might tell us. It just started yesterday.

What worries me more than the actions of a single carpenter is the difficulty the German men had in reporting the problem. They tell us that they tried to speak to the foreman but were unable to convince him to make a simple inspection of Mr. Rogovin's work. The foreman, of course, claims never to have heard a word about it. Every worker we interviewed had a different idea about how they might go about reporting shoddy work.

There's little we can do to intervene in how a factory conducts itself. At least we convinced the management to inspect every piece Mr. Rogovin had touched (he'd only been employed there a week), but imagine what would've happened if those aeroplanes had been sent up in the air!

With such a weak defense, I assume the man will be convicted. Typically in a case like this, they're given a fine they cannot possibly afford to pay, and sent to prison as a result.

Must close—I have an early day tomorrow. Fleurette is well and sends her postcards dutifully. She says that the men at camp are made to practice trench-digging, and that hundreds of them go out with picks into what once was a farmer's field, and dig trenches for miles, then fill them in again. They come back to the barracks covered in dirt, but grinning, because here we have laundry and showers. In France they'll simply go to bed grimy and wake up grimy, and they know it.

Yours,
Constance

NORMA TO GENERAL MURRAY

August 19, 1918

Dear General Murray,

It's astonishing that you received my letter of August 1 and I had your reply today. The courier tells me that the military service typically manages eleven days each way, but that's the average: the record so far is seven days.

I appreciate your assurances that these letters will be retained strictly for historical purposes and not acted upon. Please don't take offense when I say that it is my sincere belief that involving more commanders will not help us win this war, much less revive the pigeon program. Left to my own devices, I can put it right. But the Army is not in the habit of leaving anyone to her own devices.

Here, then, is an account of my progress thus far.

Pigeons issued before today: 1
Pigeons issued as of tonight: 24
Pigeons returned: 0

Owing to the difficulties encountered in issuing pigeons to soldiers departing for the front, I have deployed a new strategy, one involving an off-duty nurse presenting the birds as tokens of affection. While this is not an optimal manner of deployment, as it confuses a military asset with a sentimental gift, it has proven effective. As of this date, twenty-five of our top pigeons have been dispatched.

The new protocol works as follows:

Pigeons are placed in their customary carrier baskets, but adorned with patriotic ribbons in the manner of the sorts of small gifts and packages typically given by nurses and canteen girls to soldiers when they depart.

Pigeon communication instructions have been modified to encourage the soldiers to return the bird with a message for the giver of the "gift" (it is not a gift, it is a military asset, and this must be emphasized), but they are also reminded that should they find themselves in any sort of trouble, a pigeon may be dispatched to call for help. These instructions have been put into verse and written out in a woman's script, courtesy of Nurse Agnes Bell:

> *You're patched and plastered and right as rain*
> *But I couldn't put you on a train*
> *Without some token from the girl you love*
> *If it can't be my heart—please take a dove*

> *When you miss the old days and the times we had*
> *Write me a note, and make my heart glad*
> *Or if you're in distress, lost, or alone*
> *Put pencil to paper—then send this bird home!*

Let me assure you that I did raise numerous objections to the content of the poem, particularly the highly irregular labeling of pigeons as "doves," but Nurse Bell insisted that she had the greater experience in writing romantic poetry, having filled volumes with it as a girl. I had to admit that no one else involved with this project had ever written anything in the way of a line of poetic verse.

Also at the insistence of Nurse Bell, two dozen miniature madeleines were purchased from the Patisserie Confiserie, at considerable personal expense, and wrapped in tissue to be presented to the soldiers prior to the offer of the pigeon, on the theory (proffered by Nurse Bell) that a man who wouldn't accept a madeleine was even less likely to accept a pigeon.

Having obtained these supplies, Nurse Bell (after nearly

an hour lost to hair-styling, nose-powdering, and the trying-on of various scarves borrowed for the occasion) was dispatched to the train station to present her gifts. At Nurse Bell's insistence, I ferried the supplies in a wagon and kept them out of sight so as not to make it appear that a cart-load of parting gifts was simply to be off-loaded to every man on the platform.

Instead, Nurse Bell took one at a time (a madeleine and a pigeon) and approached each soldier individually, engaging him first in conversation, offering an address where he might write letters, and then presenting her gifts, first the sweet and then the bird. Not a single man refused to accept them, and in this manner, two dozen pigeons were dispatched to the front.

The deployment was deemed a success. The results are less certain. As considerable time and expense was involved, we will await the return of at least three pigeons before sending out the next batch.

I do wonder what use my methods could possibly be to you. I can hardly imagine a new training program at Fort Monmouth on the use of love-notes and lip-stick to deploy carrier pigeons. Then again, war itself is irregular and unpredictable. Our methods must be as well.

Yours in service,
Norma C. Kopp

AGGIE TO CONSTANCE

August 20, 1918

Dear Constance,

Norma forbids me from saying too much about the pigeon

scheme I alluded to in my last letter, but I will tell you this: A little charm goes a long way. She has the right idea about this pigeon program—I'm sure she does, after so many years of study—but perhaps she hadn't considered the best way to approach a lonely, love-sick soldier. They just want to speak to you, and to tell you something about themselves. They very much give the impression that they don't want to be forgotten, as if, by planting a little memory with one of us, they might live on.

For instance, do you remember me telling you about Private Forrest Pike, who took one of Norma's birds away with him? He wore a button on the front of his jacket that was ever so slightly thicker than the others. You'd never know to look at it. But then he pried it open and what do you suppose was inside? A tiny photograph—of his mother! He said he didn't have a girl at home (I can't believe that and told him so), but he and his mother are especially close, because he is the baby of the family, considerably younger than his older brothers and sisters, and for that reason spent most of his years alone with her.

So imagine that: a young man wearing his mother's portrait into battle. I told him I would never forget her face or his, and I won't.

Some of the men want a souvenir. When I went to the train station with Norma yesterday, a soldier handed me his mess kit and asked me to engrave my name on the top of it. I don't know if you've seen their kits: they're just little oval dishes made of tin with a lid attached. The metal's quite soft and the men make all manner of carvings: elaborate pictures, a list of all the places they've been stationed, and, in this soldier's case, the name of every girl he's kissed.

It was impossible to refuse either the engraving or the kiss, after he told me how he stares at those names in the trenches and remembers one sweet moment after another. I scribbled my name between a Betty and an Annie, and then . . . well, you should know that the little pot of lip-stick Fleurette sent along was put to use! I'm not ashamed to say that more than a few of the men boarded the train with red kisses on their cheeks. *C'est la guerre!*

> Tendrement—
> Aggie

NORMA TO GENERAL MURRAY

August 23, 1918

Dear General Murray,

I've had some early results from my pigeon deployment. What I've received so far is of little use to the program, but I will report it to you nonetheless.

Of the pigeons dispatched at the train station, two have returned with sentimental notes addressed to the nurse who distributed them. Neither included the date and time of release, nor the location, in spite of my instructions and the typewritten form with blanks provided.

Pigeons issued: 25
Pigeons returned: 2

U.S.A. 19079 UNNAMED, BLUE CHECK HEN
Dispatched: Unknown, not recorded
Arrived: August 22, 1918, 10:27
Origin: Unknown, not recorded
Time flown: Unknown
Distance flown: Unknown
Message:

This pigeon is longing for home, and so am I. Don't forget about your boy at the front.

U.S.A. 18 16757 "CUISY BILL," BLACK CHECK
GRIZZLE
Dispatched: Unknown, not recorded
Arrived: August 23, 1918, 18:14
Origin: Unknown, not recorded
Time flown: Unknown
Distance flown: Unknown
Message:

A hundred kisses is all I ask
I've only collected two
And so I wish for a gash or a scratch
So I can return to you

As you can see, twenty-three birds remain in the field. It is to be hoped that the soldiers will, in the future, consider their mission when completing the form.

Yours in service,
Norma C. Kopp

(NOTE DELIVERED TO HÔTEL DE LA POSTE)
CAPTAIN BUSCALL TO NORMA

August 25, 1918

Dear Miss Kopp,

It has come to my attention that twenty-five pigeons have been removed from the premises. I've dispatched Private Kearns with this note to collect you at home or church, wherever you may be found on a Sunday morning, and deliver you immediately to the fort. I'll be waiting. There is no need to bring your log-book.

Yours truly,
Captain Buscall

NORMA TO GENERAL MURRAY

August 25, 1918

Dear General Murray,

The new pigeon distribution program has been temporarily suspended owing to new restrictions on who may have access to the pigeons housed at the fort. I will write with more information when I have it.

Yours in service,
Norma C. Kopp

AGGIE TO CONSTANCE (UNSENT)

August 27, 1918

Dear Constance,

I'm writing this letter because if I don't tell someone what's happened to your sister, I might burst. We're always told not to write home about our troubles, because the letters take so long to get there and arrive all out of order. More than likely, whatever was bothering us will have been smoothed over by the time a letter travels to the States, and it will only cause you unnecessary worry.

But I've tried for two days not to put these words down. I simply can't hold back any longer.

Constance, your sister has been banished from the fort and removed from her post. She's been placed on disciplinary leave for a week, and told that when she returns, she's to be put on secretarial duty, where she might be "better supervised." Even worse, she's not to have anything to do with her pigeons—only paperwork.

To explain how this came about would take pages and pages, and I just don't have it in me tonight. But you know your sister. You can probably imagine it. She's had disagreements with her superiors from the day she arrived. It's been impossible for her to get the program working to her satisfaction. She has no friends that I know of at the fort, and therefore no one to speak up on her behalf. It's been a battle for her every day.

I'm sure she knows the best way to carry out the pigeon unit's mission—how could she not, after a lifetime devoted to the subject? But her superiors don't see it that way. They expect to give their orders, and to have those orders followed. That's how it is in the Army.

But Norma won't allow anyone to have authority over her. She knows how things ought to be done and considers it a waste of her time to entertain someone else's ideas.

She's more certain of herself than any woman I've ever met. I admire her for that. I only wish I could be more like her! I doubt myself every minute of the day. But I'm afraid she's paying a terrible price for—well, for the way she is, and it breaks my heart.

She's been off-duty for two days now and it's driving her absolutely mad. She's cleaned our tiny room from top to bottom, re-organized the bathroom we share with four other ladies (much to their disapproval), and was banished from the hotel pantry before she could turn that into a military commissary.

In the evening she has nothing to do—no reports to write, no plans to make, and no letters to send home, because what could she possibly say to you at a time like this?

It will absolutely crush her to go on secretarial duty, I know it will. And there's no way to keep her away from the pigeons. She's already talking about sneaking back to the fort tomorrow to gather up her equipment, so that she can recruit some of the French pigeons around town and start up a new breeding operation behind the hotel. I've begged her not to, but I'm at the hospital all day. What can I do to stop her?

I only wish you were here, because surely you would know what to say to make the situation right. This can't be the first time Norma's run up against opposition like this. She needs her family. She's more family to me than she knows—that's what happens to us in war-time, we become sisters overnight —but I'm not enough right now. I'm useless, in fact.

Norma's watching me write this. Any minute now she'll demand to know what I'm writing, or, worse, she'll snatch it away and read it. I'm going to put this away and hope that I come to my senses in the morning and decide not to mail it.

Avec grand chagrin—

Aggie

NORMA TO GENERAL MURRAY

August 28, 1918

Dear General Murray,

One of our birds has done its job. I only hope it isn't too late. My report is as follows.

The pigeon Mon Chou was issued to Private Forrest Pike on August 6 and arrived at Fort de la Bonnelle today in critical condition, having been shot through the chest, one eye blind, and one leg dangling by only a tendon.

Pigeons issued: 25
Pigeons returned: 3

U.S.A. 18 19657 "MON CHOU," BLACK CHECKER COCK
Dispatched: time not given, date believed to be
August 28

Arrived: August 28, 1918, 16:18
Origin: Vaulx-Vraucourt
Time flown: unknown
Distance flown: 250 miles
Message:

WE ARE ALONG THE ROAD TO NOREUIL OUR ARTIL-
LERY IS DROPPING A BARRAGE DIRECTLY ON US FOR
HEAVEN'S SAKE STOP IT

Owing to the urgency of the message, the following was
not transcribed verbatim, but I am recording it now, from
memory, to complete the record.

KOPP: This needs to go to headquarters immediately. Telephone it in.

BUSCALL: Miss Kopp, I gave you an order to stay at home
for one week. I also said that you're not to touch a single pigeon in the possession of the Signal Corps. Either I
need glasses or that's a bird under your arm.

KOPP: Read the message. It looks like friendly fire. If you
telephone to headquarters they can put it through.

BUSCALL: I'm not telephoning anything to headquarters,
and I want you out or I'll have you escorted out.

KOPP: It comes from a private named Forrest Pike. He
probably sent it over three hours ago. We might already
be too late.

BUSCALL: I don't see Pike's name on this. I don't see anyone's name on it. Where in God's name did you—

KOPP: It arrived just now. The bird's been shot and won't live the night. The men won't either, if you don't put the message through.

BUSCALL: That pigeon was shot and it kept flying?

KOPP: It's Mon Chou. One of my best. I gave it to Private Pike—

BUSCALL: I don't know which is worse, that you gave the pigeons names or that you handed them out without permission. Now, I warned you—

KOPP: Are you going to put the message through?

BUSCALL (studying it again): How do I know the Germans didn't send this? It's not in our code. I can't tell our boys to stop firing because a lady brought in a note.

KOPP: We're the pigeon messaging service. What do you expect us to do with messages?

BUSCALL: We put the messaging service in mothballs, don't you recall?

As you can imagine, I'd heard quite enough from Captain Buscall. I retrieved the message, commandeered an Army draft horse, and rode it to town. Upon my arrival I persuaded the hospital operator, a fine Signal Corps girl by the name of Betty Sanger, to transmit the message.

We await further news.

Yours in service,

Norma C. Kopp

AGGIE TO CONSTANCE AND FLEURETTE
(UNSENT)

August 31, 1918

Dear Constance and Fleurette,

Norma refuses to allow me to mail this letter, although she can't stop me from writing it. It's true that the censors wouldn't allow a word of it to go through. Instead I've asked her to keep it and deliver it personally to you *après la guerre,* so that you'll know something of the heroism and tragedy that occurred here.

A few weeks ago, Norma issued a pigeon, Mon Chou, to Private Forrest Pike, of Savannah, Georgia. He'd been sent to our hospital after having lost a finger, and suffered other minor wounds in battle. Because his injuries were not terribly serious, Private Pike won over the nurses with his good cheer and warm southern accent. He made friends easily and even befriended Norma.

Private Pike professed a love of birds, particularly canaries, and begged Norma for a pigeon that he could carry to the front. Although he said he wanted the bird for companionship and not to transmit messages, Mon Chou was nonetheless equipped with the standard military message tube and given a full measure of rations.

A few days ago, that bird returned to us, having nearly been shot out of the sky. The message, miraculously intact, told of U.S. artillery fire landing directly on its own troops, presumably mistaking them for Germans. It ended with this plea: "For Heaven's sake stop it."

Although Forrest didn't sign the message, we now know that he did send it.

As Norma was unable to convince her commander of either the urgency or the legitimacy of the message, she took a horse from Fort de la Bonnelle, entirely against orders, and rode it three miles to town. The American hospital sits just at the southern entrance and is practically the first building one encounters. Norma abandoned her horse at the hospital door and ran inside, where she said this to the first orderly she saw: "I need a nurse for this pigeon, and I need to see Betty."

Her fellow Signal Corps member Betty Sanger was usually stationed at the switchboard but had only just stepped away. Norma was quite exercised over her message and issued her demands at a louder than usual volume. She therefore attracted a crowd. Soon I heard the commotion and ran over myself.

The pigeon was tucked under her jacket and only barely alive. I took it from her and did what I could with antiseptic and bandages, but there's not even such a thing as an aspirin for a pigeon and I don't believe I was able to offer it much comfort at all. I'm sorry to say that the bird did not survive.

After a bit of a scramble, Betty was located. Unlike Norma's commander, Betty found the message entirely convincing. She told Norma, "I don't have to send it directly to the commanding officer at headquarters. I can send it to an operator in Chaumont who can simply report that she received it. Neither she nor I have to decide whether it's credible. Our business is only to relay the messages that come in."

Betty did exactly that: she relayed the message to another operator, and then—nothing. All we could do was wait.

Betty warned us that there might not be any response for some time. She was right. It was three days before we heard, via a friendly operator in Chaumont, what transpired.

We learned that Forrest Pike's unit—over two hundred men—had wandered off-course and found themselves on the other side of enemy lines. They were entirely surrounded by German troops. They hunkered down in a little hollow, hoping to wait out the Germans and sneak back to safety, but soon our troops began firing on the Germans. They didn't know about the Americans in their midst.

Forrest decided to launch his pigeon. I'm told it flew fast and high with both German and American gunfire in the air. The siege went on for some hours, until at last Mon Chou landed here. From the switchboard, the message was passed on to headquarters and then to the troops in the field. At last the barrage ceased. The men still had to undertake a dangerous escape along enemy lines, and we're told that several didn't survive. Among those killed was Forrest Pike, who insisted on being the last one out, only after the others had made it to safety.

Owing to the strength, bravery, and perseverance of Mon Chou, Private Pike, and Norma Kopp, 194 men survived.

Furthermore, the pigeon program has been revived. General Pershing took a personal interest in the success of Mon Chou's mission. Pigeons will be shipped to the front every week now. The mayor issued a proclamation to the Signal Corps, commending it for its service, but Norma has thus far refused to take time away from her duties to accept it. Her commander insists that she go. He has in fact ordered her to do so. Norma's stubbornness is very nearly a match for the authority of the United States Army, and I cannot guess which will prevail.

Either way, she's earned the respect of her commanders, and proven what her pigeons can do in battle. That means everything to her.

Tendrement—

Aggie

FLEURETTE

Camp Sherman, Ohio

CONSTANCE TO FLEURETTE

September 1, 1918

F—

As you seem to be in the same place for a few days, I'm for-warding you a batch of Norma's letters. By the way, I've started shipping some of your creams and lotions and powders over to France—not for Norma, who's never put anything fancier than hoof salve on her hands—but for Aggie, who tells us so much and appreciates any little gift. I hope you don't mind, and if you do, you can always come home and put a stop to it.

    C.

FLEURETTE TO CONSTANCE

September 3, 1918

C—

I would mind, if it were anyone but Aggie. The poor girl needs it more than I do. I suppose it's part of a nurse's duty to bestow a little red kiss on those soldiers' cheeks. They expect it here, too, of course, even though they're so far away from the front. They might only be departing for the latrine and they put on a sad face, like they might never see a pretty girl again.

Don't worry, though—the soldiers don't bother May Ward's Dresden Dolls. They aren't allowed to. These camps are zealously patrolled by matrons, who are determined to keep us apart. Aren't you glad you didn't end up as one of them for the duration of the war?

I keep trying to guess at the so-called difficulties Norma's having with her pigeon program, but what could it possibly be? No pigeon has ever dared to disobey Norma. It must be her commanders who aren't following instructions.

Off to Camp Sherman tomorrow. I'll send an address when I have it.

F.

FLEURETTE TO HELEN

September 4, 1918

Dearest Helen,

Let me tell you, it's quite something to travel with a parrot. It's just my luck that Mrs. Ward detests birds of all kinds. According to Bernice, who has toured with her the longest, she thinks them dirty, diseased, and parasite-ridden—which is starting to describe the girls in her chorus, if we can't have one night in a real city to take hot baths and do our laundry properly.

The point is that I'm obliged to hide Laura not just from the ladies at the Hostess House, but from May as well.

When we left this morning, I couldn't put her large bird-cage out with our luggage to be loaded onto the train, because Mrs. Ward would quite naturally want to know why I was hauling a cage around. I was instead obliged to pack it inside my trunk, which is, fortunately, enormous, but nonetheless it just barely fit. I had to fill the inside of the cage with my clothes. (That isn't quite the mess you might think it is: I keep Laura's cage scrupulously clean. I know that much from living with Norma and her pigeons all these years.)

I then carried Laura on board the train in her much smaller traveling cage, which George very thoughtfully provided for this purpose. She was tucked under a scarf, and since Mrs. Ward always sits apart from us, even when there's no first-class car, I had some hope that she wouldn't be spotted.

But wouldn't you know it—there wasn't another seat to be had anywhere else on the train. The boys had very generously given us several rows to ourselves and crowded into another car so we might have a moment's peace. After wandering the train in search of superior quarters, Mrs. Ward finally abandoned hope, and returned to settle down a few rows ahead of the rest of us.

In a lull in the conversation, as the train rocked to and fro on its way to Ohio, I lifted up the scarf to take a peek at Laura, and she whistled at me.

She didn't just whistle a note—she whistled the chorus to "Over There"! Just those two lines:

Over there, over there,
Send the word, send the word over there

It was a little fast—she doesn't keep time, this one—but it was perfectly in pitch. Mrs. Ward turned right around and looked back at us.

"Which one of you can whistle?" she called. (She was, as I said, a few rows ahead, and we were not alone in the car—there were some other weary-looking civilians, and a couple of rows of soldiers in the very back.)

All eyes turned on us at once. Bless those chorus girls, they kept my secret! Every one of them turned to look around as well, as if they, too, wanted to know who had whistled so nicely. Eventually we all looked back at May Ward and shrugged.

"Well, one of you should learn," she said, a little harshly, as if she'd only just recalled this particular shortcoming of ours. "I'd put it in the act."

I had by then draped the scarf back over Laura's cage. Fortunately, she stayed quiet the rest of the trip.

I had an easier time smuggling her into the Hostess House. Mrs. Ward had made arrangements in advance for her own hotel, and disembarked one stop ahead, in the little town outside of camp. When we arrived at our own accommodation, there were so many people turning up at once—not just us, but an entire girls' choir, come from Chicago—that I snuck right in with my bird tucked under my arm.

And she is *my* bird already, Helen! I've grown so attached to her. It's quite a feeling to have an exquisite little creature who is all your own, who goes everywhere with you and depends upon you for its very life. I suppose I don't have to tell you about that, when you have all those lovely little brothers to look after, but when I grew up, I was always the pet! Now I have a pet of my very own, someone to devote myself to—

And she's quite devoted to me! When I lift the blanket from her cage in the morning, she hops right up to the door, eager to step out onto my finger and look me over and run a strand of my hair through her beak. (It's really quite tender, the way she does it. You'll see.) She takes treats out of my hand with such satisfaction that I'm afraid I spoil her. Charlotte warns me that she'll grow quite fat if I keep sneaking crackers to her, but I can't help it—it's so delightful when she sees me coming with anything at all. She bobs her head up and down joyfully, and stretches her wings out with anticipation.

Earlier tonight, the girls' choir started up in the great-room, and with that racket for cover, I tried teaching Laura to whistle another song. She cocks her head to the side and listens with such interest—you can just tell that she possesses an exceptional musical gift.

She was able to eke out just a line of "The Bird on Nellie's Hat." Oh, it's the funniest line ever sung, coming from her! Charlotte and I couldn't get enough of it. By the end of the evening we had her taking my cue perfectly, so that when I sing,

Well, he don't know Nellie like I do

She answers right away with her whistle:

Said the saucy little bird on Nellie's hat.

Charlotte just loved it! She said, "I have to admit that she's marvelous!" and put her face down next to Laura's as if to give her a kiss. "I wonder what else she can do?"

At that very moment, Laura straightened herself up to her full height, took hold of Charlotte's bright red hairpin with her beak, and pulled it out! Charlotte's hair tumbled all around her shoulders, and the two of us were laughing so hard we could barely breathe. Laura quite graciously allowed Charlotte to have her hairpin back, and we now know to keep a close eye on little glistening, brightly colored objects in her presence.

I'm so sorry to give you news of nothing but my bird. I'm like one of those women who prattles on about her babies and forgets that no one is interested in other people's children. I suppose other people's birds are equally dull.

The mail-room was closed when we arrived, but I hope to find a letter from you waiting for me in the morning. My next letter, I promise, will be much less feathery.

Yours always—

Fleurette

FLEURETTE TO HELEN

September 5, 1918

Dear Helen,

Forgive the scrawl—I've only a minute to write this. Was out walking last night with Laura on my shoulder, still in costume. A soldier stopped to look at the bird—not at me! Nonetheless one of those committee ladies grabbed me and hauled me off —thinking the worst because of my dress and face-paint—I could not convince her that I stayed at Hostess House as a guest of the camp.

Am now in girls' detention. Charlotte has come to rescue

Laura but can't rescue me. I'll give her this note to mail & she will wire Constance for help.

Don't want to worry you but I knew you'd start to wonder if I didn't write—

I will be fine—the other girls here have it much worse—

Not at my best but kisses to you—

Fleurette

TELEGRAM FROM FLEURETTE TO CONSTANCE

September 5, 1918

AM LOCKED IN GIRLS DETENTION AT CAMP SHERMAN OHIO I AM ABSOLUTELY NOT AT FAULT BEHAVIOR ABOVE REPROACH JAILER IS MRS WINTERS PLEASE USE YOUR CONSIDERABLE POWERS TO SECURE MY RELEASE

CONSTANCE TO MAUDE MINER

September 5, 1918

Dear Miss Miner,

I thank you for taking my distressed telephone call in the middle of what sounded like important business. Per your instructions, I waited by the telephone all afternoon. I did receive a call from Mrs. Winters only moments ago. As you asked for a thorough record of what transpired, I took notes as we spoke.

MRS. WINTERS (after the usual greetings): It was highly irregular to have a call from Washington about any particular girl.

MISS KOPP: Fleurette is known personally to Miss Miner. I served as matron of a National Service School camp last year, under Miss Miner's leadership. She's thoroughly acquainted with the character of all three Kopp sisters.

MRS. WINTERS: Character doesn't come into it. This girl was out after hours, in provocative dress and face-paint, with an exotic bird on her shoulder.

MISS KOPP: I beg your pardon, did you say she carried a bird?

MRS. WINTERS: She was obviously trying to attract attention, and had already solicited the company of a young man.

MISS KOPP (trying vainly to contain my outrage at the implication behind the word "solicited"): Mrs. Winters, have you been able to confirm that Fleurette is a member of the traveling troupe known as May Ward and Her Eight Dresden Dolls, and that she is an invited guest of the camp, residing at the YWCA's Hostess House?

MRS. WINTERS: Yes, and I believe the rest of the Dolls were inside where they belonged, and appropriately dressed.

MISS KOPP: And were you able to confirm that Fleurette was merely wearing her stage-costume, and was perhaps on her way home from the evening's performance? I assume the bird was a theatrical prop. (Miss Miner: I don't know precisely the hour of Fleurette's transgression, or if she was in fact just leaving the theater. I was merely grasping at what I hoped was the truth.)

MRS. WINTERS: The circumstances don't excuse it. The effect on our young men is the same. She'd already lured one and would've left on the arms of a dozen if I hadn't intervened.

(Miss Miner, how does one even take the arms of a dozen men? I leave this to Mrs. Winters' active imagination.)

MISS KOPP: I know how difficult it is to judge each girl's motives. I worked as jail matron in Hackensack myself. There were good girls, caught in difficult circumstances, whom I could help. There were others beyond saving.

MRS. WINTERS: It's a fool's errand to even try to tell them apart. Nothing matters more than keeping our boys in fighting form. Mothers are willing to sacrifice their sons, if necessary. But they will not give up—

MISS KOPP (here I interjected): They will not give up their sons' honor, or their immortal souls. We've all read the same letters from mothers in the papers, Mrs. Winters. But Fleurette is not after anyone's immortal soul. She was only leaving her place of employment, wearing what is to her a professional uniform. May Ward is welcome at the camps because she offers wholesome entertainment. She wouldn't be allowed if she wasn't above reproach in every way. And I myself am a former deputy sheriff, now serving my country at the War Department. I can absolutely vouch for Fleurette's good conduct.

MRS. WINTERS: You could better vouch for her if you kept her at home. What of Fleurette's mother and her father?

MISS KOPP: We three sisters have only each other, and an older brother. Fleurette is twenty years of age, and perfectly capable of traveling in the company of her employer.

MRS. WINTERS (by now, Miss Miner, she was simply running out of steam): As I've said, it's highly irregular for our committee to have outside interference. Miss Miner might be our chairwoman, but she sits behind a desk in Washington. She can't rule on every individual girl's case. Why, I've had hundreds of girls through my detention house since our committee began. Does Miss Miner wish to hear each girl's special circumstance?

MISS KOPP (seeing the futility of continuing in this line): If you can see clear to releasing Fleurette so that she may be on her way with her troupe, I'm sure she won't give you another minute's trouble. I will come and collect her myself if necessary, although that would require that I explain the circumstances to my superior, Mr. Bielaski, who runs the Bureau of Investigation.

MRS. WINTERS (snappishly): Yes, I'm aware of Mr. Bielaski. That won't be necessary.

MISS KOPP: Then I'll look forward to a word from her when she's released. I thank you for your service to the country.

At that, Mrs. Winters rang off. I await a telegram from a newly liberated Fleurette. If I don't have one by morning, I'll set off for Camp Sherman myself.

I can't thank you enough for your intervention. You said on

the telephone that you'd come to have some misgivings about these local committees, and now I understand why.

Will wire with news from Fleurette as soon as it arrives, but I'll post this for now so you'll have it for your records.

With everlasting gratitude,

Constance A. Kopp

TELEGRAM FROM FLEURETTE TO CONSTANCE

September 6, 1918

SHE TOOK HER SWEET TIME BUT I AM FREE LETTER TO FOLLOW

MAUDE MINER TO CONSTANCE

September 7, 1918

Dear Miss Kopp,

It was with great relief that I received your wire informing me that Fleurette had been released, followed shortly by your letter, which told me all that I had suspected about Mrs. Winters and doings in Ohio.

I'm sorry to say that what happened to Fleurette is exceptional only in that she was so quickly set free. As you might imagine, any other girl in her circumstance would have been detained for whatever period of time the local committee deemed appropriate—and you know as I do that weeks can stretch into months, and months into years.

When I was first called to Washington to work with the War Department on a role for women, I had in mind exactly the sort of work your sister Norma is doing in France, or your service for the Bureau, or any of the more routine tasks, from stenography to switchboard, that women might capably perform.

But after the war commenced—just as you and I parted at the National Service School—it became apparent that the War Department had something else in mind entirely when they talked of women's affairs. Mr. Fosdick took charge of the Commission on Training Camp Activities, and asked me to lead the women's division. I did have hope that there would be something in the way of actual useful training for women in his plans.

That isn't at all what Mr. Fosdick had in mind. His concern was centered entirely on the behavior of girls living and working near the men's camps, and—more to the point—for the safety of the men themselves, who must be sent into war in fighting form, healthy of body and moral of spirit.

At first, I didn't object. You and I have both done this sort of work with girls. We know that it's no small task to keep them on the right path. It's perfectly true that girls are drawn to a man in uniform. At a dance not long ago in New York, half the men were National Guardsmen and the other half were new draftees, attending in their civilian clothes. Those not in uniform hardly danced all evening, while the Guardsmen had their pick of dancing partners. Such is the glamour of the uniform.

What we must do is to give these girls an occupation. I proposed a division for women and girls that would include the training of women workers, a war service league for women and girls who wished to be of use, educational programs, an industrial division to support women who work in the camps, and—yes—a protective bureau staffed by local matrons, with houses of detention and reformatories.

Before you blame me for the proliferation of these reformatories, remember that the Army camps are mostly located away from large cities. The small towns nearby have no facilities of any kind for girls. Anyone arrested would be thrown in the town jail, with (most likely) no woman on duty. We had to anticipate that and be ready with an alternative.

I'm sorry to say that it was only the protective work and detention facilities that attracted any interest—and money— at all. Fear-mongering took over, particularly among the old-timers who still remember the War Between the States, and the moral degeneracy and disease that the camps fostered in those days.

We also battle endlessly against salacious rumors. A story circulated recently that fifty girls became pregnant within the vicinity of a training camp. I investigated myself and found no truth to it, but the rumors persist.

The punitive aspect of this program—which has taken over, and is now all that's left—is directed entirely at the girls. No soldier receives punishment for his part in any illicit behavior. Isn't it strange that it's called a Protective Committee, when the entire emphasis is on the protection of the soldier? I've seen the interests of the girl subordinated entirely.

You asked on the telephone if I had any idea how many girls might've been detained since the war began. I should have the answer, but I don't. These local committees are hardly accountable to me. They've taken on a life of their own. I tell you with shame that the number has to be in the thousands, and more likely in the tens of thousands, if you believe (as I do, as I must do), that some are detained only briefly and released, along the lines of what happened to Fleurette.

President Wilson has just approved an outrageous sum to build more detention centers and reformatories. States are passing laws making it explicitly legal to detain a suspected party until he or she can be shown to be free of social diseases —but in practice, it is of course never the men who are detained. Instead every woman arrested for any transgression is now subject to medical examination and testing against her will. If you can believe it, our own Congress has put a million dollars toward a civilian quarantine and isolation fund.

This is more than you asked to know. In writing to you I've unburdened myself, at least for the moment. The truth is that I don't know how much longer I can put my name to an effort that I so wholly oppose, but if I leave, who will stand up for our girls?

Yours,
Maude Miner

FLEURETTE TO CONSTANCE

September 7, 1918

C—

Please take this letter directly over to Helen when you're through with it—I can't bear to write out this tale of woe twice.

I don't know what Mrs. Winters told you, but every word of it is untrue. I've never met a more mean-spirited, unreasonable woman. She looks at an unaccompanied girl and sees a prostitute—or, at best, a charity girl, who trades dinners and stockings for special favors. As if any of these soldiers have a nice dinner or a pretty trinket on offer!

Well, the girls in that detention center are not those kinds of girls, at least, not the ones I met. I spent two nights there, and had a chance to talk to everyone in my dormitory. I know you'll believe me when I tell you that these are ordinary girls, many of them working in their families' businesses—you know the little stalls that crop up around the camps, selling candies, cigarettes, and the like. Naturally the girls fall into the company of soldiers. There are thirty thousand men here—one can't help but meet a few of them!

And there are romances—the girls confessed that readily enough. It isn't easy to find a secluded place—you must imagine rows and rows of the most ordinary wooden barracks and tents, stretching all the way to the horizon, with nothing like a nook or a cranny in which to hide. Couples go out into the countryside, following the old roads at the edge of camp, but of course those places are well-known to the Mrs. Winterses of the world. Several of the girls here were rousted from some secluded love-nest behind a tree, as they scrambled to put themselves back together . . . well, you can picture the scene.

It hardly need be said that the man is never punished. The girl is forced into an auto and driven to a detention center, while the man is left to stroll back to camp, whistling a tune.

Call it immoral if you like, but is it illegal? And if it is illegal, when is the trial? What attorney defends the girl in court? A few of the girls were startled to even have the idea put before them like that. Everyone seems to accept that if a girl is caught, she'll go away. Of course, a few of them are pregnant, or found to be diseased—but why must they be made to suffer either condition in jail?

And it is like a jail. The food is worse than what your inmates ate in Hackensack, the blankets are thin, and there's nothing in the way of books or pictures or even a window to look out of. Everyone is sick and miserable: half the girls had a stomach ailment, or a cough, or something that looked awfully like the 'flu. A nurse comes but once a week. I picked up a sniffle myself, which is to be my souvenir of Camp Sherman. It's settling into my throat now, and quite liking the accommodations.

You'll naturally want to know what I did to get myself locked up, so I'll stop putting it off and confess: It's true that I was out after curfew, and that I was still in costume. The costume was only an ordinary dancing frock, and I had reason to be out late.

May Ward had another one of her nights that night—you know what I mean by that—and we were obliged to practically carry her out of the theater. She refuses to stay at camp. Usually there's a man to drive her back to her hotel after the show. But we couldn't find the man, and Mrs. Ward didn't recall his name. We waited around for an hour, and asked everyone who passed by, but it was beginning to look like we'd have to smuggle her into the Hostess House for the night.

Just as we were about to abandon hope, the fellow came strolling up, easy as could be, having found himself a card game to wile away the hours. He seemed to have no idea that he had an obligation to collect Mrs. Ward promptly following curtain call. It's entirely possible that she never told him. She's not known for managing practicalities.

Never mind—we were happy to see him at all, and poured May into his back seat with great relief. I was by then so wound up after being on the receiving end of Mrs. Ward's barbarism all evening (she is not a polite drunk these days) that I just wanted a few minutes to myself before retiring.

So I strolled—not far! Only a block or two, by city standards—and stopped to answer a question put to me by a soldier. We spoke in a friendly manner for just a minute. He'd been in the audience that night and asked the most ordinary questions—how do we find Camp Sherman, what other camps have we visited and do I prefer one over the other, where will we go next and when—that sort of talk was the sum of it. But along came Mrs. Winters with her walking-stick and her iron grip—and you know the rest.

The soldier, by the way, behaved honorably. He came to my defense, insisted that he'd stopped me, not the other way around, and that he was only offering to escort me back, as curfew had passed. (He hadn't in fact offered to escort me, but I appreciated the lie.) In spite of his efforts, Mrs. Winters hauled me off to her detention house.

Charlotte passed a frantic night with no idea of my whereabouts. I convinced Mrs. Winters to send word to her and to let her visit, so that she could take down a note to my family. Charlotte ran right over, and dispatched the telegram to you immediately.

I suppose you must've telephoned or wired, but Mrs. Winters didn't let on at first. She kept me another night, for good measure, and gave me reason to think she might transfer me to the state home (the implication being, I assume, that no older sister at the Bureau of Investigation could secure my release from a state home). I was left to worry and fret over this, and also to wonder what would become of me if the troupe moved on without me.

At the last possible second, Mrs. Winters told me that you'd intervened. She set me free under a barrage of stern warnings. I ran back to the Hostess House, to find that the troupe had in fact already left for Chicago. The lovely and loyal Charlotte stayed behind, though. Clutched in her hand were two train tickets, secured from Mrs. Ward only after the entire troupe threatened to quit if she abandoned me entirely. There's a remarkable spirit that develops when you travel with a group of chorus girls. I suppose it's not unlike a band of soldiers. I hope I never have to kill a German for one of them, but I would certainly try.

Charlotte had made all the arrangements, and we were spirited off to the train station. I was not sorry to put Camp Sherman behind me.

We've just arrived in Chicago, where we are at last housed in a decent hotel. It's my turn for a hot bath, which I very much hope will tame the throbbing in my head and the scratch in my throat.

Don't worry about me! I'm in the very best of company, and I'll be entirely well in a day or two. You can be sure that I will not set foot outdoors after sundown, nor speak to a member of the opposite sex, as long as I live, or rather, as long as Mrs. Winters lives.

We have three more weeks of bookings at the eastern camps, then a break at home. I'll send the date when I have it.

You know I'm just sorry sorry sorry for the trouble this might've caused and hope I didn't worry you overmuch.

Love and home soon,
F.

TELEGRAM FROM CONSTANCE TO FLEURETTE

September 10, 1918

STAY IN BED OR COME HOME AT ONCE IF YOU ARE
SERIOUSLY ILL YOU DID NOT EXPLAIN ABOUT
THE BIRD HELEN KNEW BUT WOULD NOT TELL ME

FLEURETTE TO HELEN

September 11, 1918

Dearest Helen,

Greetings from what I once would've called a shabby hotel
room, but that was before I spent weeks at a time living in
Army camps. This place is the Ritz, as far as the Eight Dresden
Dolls are concerned. We enjoy hot baths, tea brought up to
our rooms, and the most delicious clean white sheets, changed
daily if we demand it (and I do).

Did Constance show you my letter? I left out the worst
part, because it concerned Laura. You didn't tell Constance
about Laura, did you, you darling discreet girl? And I know
how she can trick one into telling the truth—I know it better
than anyone! She won't approve of my acquiring a parrot, so
why bother her with it?

Laura, poor dear, had a more dreadful ordeal than I did at

the detention center. At the time of my capture (I refuse to call it an arrest, for there was no police officer present), I had Laura on my shoulder. Our tiny room at the Hostess House is windowless and airless, and as I am obliged to keep her hidden from both Mrs. Ward and the ladies who run the house, I was afraid Laura was practically suffocating. She's a bird—she wants the wind and the sky and the sun. I took her out that night so that we could both have a breath of fresh air, and so that she could stretch her wings and have a look around at the world.

The soldier who stopped me was, of course, intrigued by the bird—more intrigued by her than he was by me, which you will understand when you meet Laura—and when Mrs. Winters grabbed me, I thought at first to give Laura to him, and to ask him to sneak her into the Hostess House. But it was after curfew already. He'd never be allowed inside.

I did beg Mrs. Winters, during our brief struggle, to allow me to return Laura to my room before I was taken away. (I expected, at that moment, to be locked up in a little office as Bernice had been. I didn't know that Camp Sherman was equipped with a detention house right on its grounds.)

Mrs. Winters refused. An inability to listen to reason is her chief personality trait. But when we arrived at the detention house, the problem became clear to her. She wasn't about to allow Laura to stay with me, but where was she to keep a bird?

Now, why do you suppose Mrs. Winters didn't simply open a window and set her free, the way George Simon's aunt threatened to do? Would you believe that it was a legal argument, not a matter of compassion, that won the day? The detention center has very strict rules about the storage of girls' property, and the return of said property to the girl upon release, or to her family if she is not to be released and is instead to rot in jail all her life. (That isn't quite how Mrs. Winters put it, but rotting away for life was most definitely implied.)

I argued that Laura was property, and that she was quite a rare bird of some value, and that she was, in fact, not my property but the property of a young private just shipped off to France. I said that she had no authority to simply open a window and toss out the valuable possession of a soldier.

I won on that admittedly bureaucratic point, but at great cost: if Mrs. Winters didn't hate me before, she hated me then. She agreed with a snort of resentment to turn Laura over to "my designated representative" at the earliest possible hour of the morning. I also insisted on being allowed to send a letter to my family, "so they don't go to the police and report me kidnapped," which is why I was allowed ten minutes to write a note to you and a telegram to Constance.

With that, Laura was put into a wooden crate in the storage room for the night. (Oh, that poor bird! How I suffered for her all those terrible dark hours!) In the morning, Charlotte came to fetch her, along with my hastily scribbled notes.

That took care of Laura, for the moment, anyway. But then, as the troupe was readying to depart Camp Sherman without me (and Mrs. Ward was threatening to leave me behind, with neither my wages nor a train ticket to anywhere), Laura's cage was left uncovered and she gave a whistle loud enough to attract Mrs. Ward's attention.

I wasn't there to see it, of course, but I'm told Mrs. Ward turned every shade of purple and demanded that the bird be left behind, along with all of my things. That's when the girls rallied and insisted that I be allowed to rejoin the troupe — and that Laura be permitted to stay with me—or they would all go home, and leave Mrs. Ward to finish her tour alone.

I'm told that she thought about that at some length, and very nearly took them up on their offer! Fortunately, we were booked in Chicago for three enormous charity concerts. She couldn't possibly carry those shows on her own. The almighty dollar won the day, and Mrs. Ward relented.

But I'm not allowed on stage as long as Laura remains with me. I am to sit in my room and sew. I'm still nursing the most miserable sore throat, so for the moment, that suits me and Laura just fine. We spend cozy afternoons together, me with my sewing machine and a pile of costumes in need of mending, and her perched atop her cage, watching me curiously and whistling at me from time to time. I can hardly croak out a tune right now, but I do try to whistle back.

We're held over in Chicago for another week as there was a cancellation at this theater and they hired us as the replacement act. The eastern camps are over-subscribed with entertainment anyway, so it hardly matters to them when we arrive. A bit more hotel living suits us all. May Ward even managed to smile at me once, but I think it was only because she'd forgotten, momentarily, what I'd done wrong.

Also, her husband, Freeman, is due to pay us a visit this week-end, which she finds cheering, as they seem to be reconciled for the moment.

I hope that you've had a word from your father and that the boys are behaving themselves.

Love to all of them, and to you—
Fleurette

CONSTANCE

Paterson, New Jersey

September 10, 1918

Dear Miss Kopp,

Your report on Mrs. Wilmington and her ceramic figurines raises intriguing questions, but it is of course the words she muttered in German that concern us the most.

My office has nothing on Mrs. Wilmington apart from the record of her immigration with her husband. We recorded her as a British citizen, not German, at the time. My counterpart in London reports the same: she claimed to be British-born on her certificate of marriage, which is the only other official document, apart from her British passport, that they can find in connection to her.

Proceed along this new line of inquiry and forget about her husband and the printing shop. Watch her house, learn her daily routine, find out where she goes, get to know her associates, etc. It's a shame she's seen you already. Have you any sort of disguise?

Or, if you'd rather, I have a whole raft of eager League men at the ready. I would even allow you to hold auditions and choose the one most suitable.

Yours very truly,

A. Bruce Bielaski

CONSTANCE TO BIELASKI

September 12, 1918

Dear Mr. Bielaski,

Disguise not necessary. I have a better idea.

Yours very truly,

Constance Kopp

CONSTANCE TO MISS BRADSHAW

September 12, 1918

Dear Miss Bradshaw,

The word from Washington is that you've made yourself useful at the War Department and they hope to keep you on. There's quite a bit of room for advancement if you wish for a career. From my recollection of our first meeting, I believe you do.

My assignment has grown more complex, and I could use your help. You wouldn't be returning to the print shop—I suspect you've lost interest in doing so anyway. Instead, I've a far more important role that requires discretion and a sharp eye. I can arrange for time away from your desk at the War Department if you're willing.

And if I'm wrong—if you'd rather finish your assignment and go back to the print shop—you'll have the opportunity within a few weeks. It's entirely up to you.

I don't want anyone working for me who isn't volunteering wholeheartedly, so think on it and please give your honest answer at your earliest convenience.

Yours very truly,

Constance Kopp

CONSTANCE TO NORMA

September 12, 1918

Dear Norma,

You asked once if every American child is required to write letters to France. In fact, it appears they are. Bessie has been busy at Frankie and Lorraine's school for the last month, preparing for an ice cream social meant to raise money for the Red Cross. A new project this year was to have the students write letters of friendship to French children, to be delivered by the relief organizations. I suspect they get quite a bit of assistance from their teachers, but the sentiments are stirring. Frankie's letter said:

"The war has brought us little hardship and as yet no real suffering, and for a time we could not realize how terribly it has altered the lives of the children of France. But now that our own fathers, brothers, and friends are fighting side by side with yours on the battlefields of France, it has become OUR war, and we are proud and glad it is!"

Lorraine's letter suggested that she had a much longer memory than would be expected of a girl of thirteen, but it was nonetheless quite well put and I thought you'd appreciate it:

"We have never forgotten and can never forget how your country helped us in the days of our first great struggle for that same liberty which we are fighting for now, and we only wish we could do much more than we are doing to show our gratitude. Please think of us as your friends."

They wanted so much to write letters to the children in your village, and were quite disappointed to learn that you're too far removed from the fighting to be served by the groups leading this effort. Bessie pulled them aside after and whispered in their ears a promise to let them write their own letters, at home, to the children of your village.

Here, then, are six letters, all nearly identical to the above, for you (or Aggie, I suspect it will be Aggie!) to distribute as you see fit. Your letters haven't mentioned any children in this village, but you must have some.

Frankie and Lorraine wanted Francis to help them translate the notes into French, but he continues to pretend he's never spoken anything but good American English in his life. It didn't matter—I sat with them after dinner on Sunday night and wrote each of their notes in French for them to copy. I think they did a fine job, don't you?

Francis, by the way, has a new project. When I arrived on Sunday, he'd come directly from his American Protective League meeting and settled into a corner with his notes, a pencil, and a Paterson directory. He didn't want to tell me what he was doing, but I coaxed it out of him eventually.

"We're starting a drive to collect pictures of occupied territories," he said.

"What sort of pictures?" I asked—a natural enough question! But he was so secretive about it.

"Does it matter what sort? Drawings, paintings, photographs." He turned back to his city directory, making little marks in the margins. I swear, Norma, he was holding his hand over the book, as if to shield me from seeing what he was doing.

"I understand what you mean by a picture," I said, trying to remain calm, but you know how Francis can get to me when he's like this, "but are you after any particular subject matter? And what do you intend to do with them?"

Oh, how he sighed and rattled his paper and tried to ignore me, as if it simply wasn't women's business! But if it was a matter of government secrecy, he could've taken it into another room. I suspect he wanted me to see it, if only so he could tell me it was highly important and none of my concern.

"Bridges," he said, at last. "Bridges, roads, buildings, towns, in any place occupied by the Germans in France, Belgium, or Luxembourg, or any part of Germany west of Hamburg. We're conducting this drive at the request of the War Department, in case you're about to accuse me of running off half-cocked on a phony mission."

"I wasn't going to accuse you of anything," I muttered. I was feeling awfully deflated by then. He hates it that I'm working for the government, while he puts in his time at a basket importer. The Army has no use for baskets, and no use for him —at least, that's how he sees it. I tend to forget that, and to forget that he needs a little shoring up from his family.

"It's a fine idea," I told him, "and sure to be of use. Are you going around to businesses, or schools, or how do you intend to collect the pictures?"

He muttered something about approaching newspaper offices, lecture bureaus, and art schools, but I could see he didn't really want to tell his sister anything more about it.

At least he's found something worth doing! I don't suppose we have any old pictures of European bridges back at the farm, do we?

There's so little I can tell you of my assignment, but I will say this: Mr. Bielaski seems to like having a lady agent so much that he wants another. I'm about to bring on my first recruit, and train her myself. I'd be perfectly happy to have a dozen under my command, if I could find them, but this is an awfully good start. The Bureau's reach is only going to grow after the war. We might investigate any sort of Federal crime, from liquor smuggling to gambling to kidnapping. I can't think of a single Bureau function that a female agent couldn't handle.

There's a change here, Norma, and you'll feel it when you come home. Women go to work in all the factories, and you see them in the streets, carrying their lunch pails like any working man. You see them in offices, bent over columns of figures, and even running elevators. I saw a woman operating a railroad crossing yesterday—really! No one seems to give it a second thought. The jobs must be done, and so they are.

Yours,

Constance

September 13, 1918

Dear Miss Kopp,

Thank you so much for your letter. It's been a thrill to have anything at all to do with the workings of the War Department, even though I spend my days filing correspondence in triplicate and maintaining a cumbersome index to the correspondence so that we might find it again someday if we ever need it. Although I read the papers and try to inform myself about the daily machinations of the war and our role in it, I simply never could've imagined the armies of secretaries (and we really could be an army) required to maintain any sort of order. The sheer volume of supplies and equipment being sent overseas is extraordinary—five hundred crates of egg powder one week, ten thousand boxes of matches the next, and requisitions for a thousand more canteens every time I turn around, each of them demanding a better design and slightly larger capacity, for our men cannot fight on the little pouch of rations we were giving them at the start of the war.

The girls I work with have been nothing short of astonishing themselves. So many of them are away from home for the first time as I am, missing their old friends and their old diversions, but they put in twelve hours a day at their desks quite willingly, eager to do anything at all that might help to ensure that their brothers and beaus return home in one piece.

They're offering an examination next week for women who'd like to work in the finger-print department. It might not sound terribly exciting, but there is an element of detective work to it. All the men give their finger-prints when they register for service. It's the task of the finger-print clerk to assign a classification number to each print according to its shape and whorls and ridges and so on.

Then, when the police pick up a deserter who refuses to give his name, they take a finger-print and send it in. The clerks classify it according to the same characteristics, and search the files for a match using only their numbering system. Would you believe they can find one in five minutes? They do hundreds of searches every day—not only for deserters, but also, I'm sorry to say, for dead bodies that can't be identified.

Well. I was thinking of taking the test myself, until I had your letter. The finger-print department can wait. I have been thinking often of you, and wondering how you managed to land the assignment you now have, and what it would take for a woman to advance up the ranks, so to speak, as you have done. I suppose you didn't start as a secretary. It's led me to wonder if perhaps I started in the wrong place. Now that I've had a taste for work at the War Department, I'm eager for more.

This is my way of saying "yes" to whatever you might ask of me. I apologize for taking six paragraphs to do it, but after long days of typing and tallying inventories, I find that my heart just spills out onto the page. I'll meet you at the time and place of your choosing.

Yours very truly,
Anne Bradshaw

CONSTANCE TO MRS. BAILEY

September 14, 1918

Dear Mrs. Bailey,

The Bureau will require Miss Bradshaw's assistance for what I hope will be an assignment of only a few days. Please excuse her until such time as you hear from me again.

Yours very truly,

Constance A. Kopp

CONSTANCE TO MISS BRADSHAW

September 14, 1918

Dear Miss Bradshaw,

I'll see you Tuesday at noon, in front of Robertson's on Lexington Avenue. All is arranged with Mrs. Bailey.

Yours very truly,

Constance A. Kopp

CONSTANCE TO BIELASKI

September 17, 1918

Dear Mr. Bielaski,

I'm pleased to report that Miss Bradshaw has the makings of a fine agent. I met with her today to give her the broad outline of her new assignment. I'll tell you exactly how the conversation went so that you might be assured that she's both sharp and eager.

I asked her to meet me in Manhattan, near her office. We met in front of Robertson's on Lexington. I was pleased to see that she arrived early and was looking in the window, as any passer-by would, while she waited for me.

"I was afraid you wouldn't come, and I'd be staring at bottles of iodine for an hour," she said when I arrived.

"It would've been a good test," I said, "because what you'll be doing for me involves quite a bit of waiting around and pretending not to look at what you're looking at."

"It sounds riveting," she said with good cheer, "although I wouldn't have thought anything could be more exciting than filing correspondence in triplicate." She took my arm and we walked up Lexington together as old friends, talking over the mission in low voices.

"You know that I was sent in to keep an eye on your boss and to watch for any sort of suspicious activity," I said.

"Yes, and I certainly hope you've found nothing amiss," she said. "I wouldn't like it if you discovered he was conspiring with the Germans and I never noticed it."

"Then you'll be relieved to know that there's absolutely nothing out of the ordinary at the print shop," I said. "It's the most mundane operation I've ever seen."

"Yes, he's the very picture of mundane," Miss Bradshaw said with a sigh.

"It's the wife who has come to my attention," I said.

She looked at me with interest. "The wife? I never met her, but she was always such a cold fish on the telephone."

"Has she any friends?" I asked. "Did Mr. Wilmington ever mention her having a group over for cards, or going out to meet anyone?"

"If she has a friend in the world, I never heard of it," Miss Bradshaw said.

"But you spoke to her on the telephone? What would you say about her accent, if you had to describe it?" I asked. (I was testing her powers of observation, and I was also interested to hear what she could recollect with a little prompting.)

Miss Bradshaw didn't hesitate. "It was a straightforward British accent, always proper and forthright, and very steady. Her voice never rose in greeting the way a woman's might, and she never spoke in a quieter, confiding tone, either. Of course, she had no reason to, when she was addressing her husband's secretary."

"And did she sound like a Londoner?"

"I wouldn't know enough about London accents to make a guess."

"That's fine," I said. "I don't want you guessing. When you don't know, admit it without any shame or apology. A spy should never invent or assume."

She gasped and squeezed my elbow. "Am I to be a spy?"

"Something like it, if you want the job. You're to continue collecting your paycheck from the War Department, but you'll report to me. I've reason to believe Mrs. Wilmington is not British at all, but German."

She glanced at me quickly, then looked very seriously ahead. "Mr. Wilmington never said a word about that. Surely he would know."

"Oh, he certainly would," I said. "She let a word of German slip when she thought I was out of earshot, but there'd be no hiding it from her husband. Her British accent isn't perfect. Any Londoner would mark her for a foreigner."

"But—what has she done? It's no crime to be born in Germany, is it?"

"Of course not," I said. "But there's quite a bit more than that."

I told her about the figurine with the suspicious rattle. She recalled several such packages arriving during the time she worked for Mr. Wilmington, but naturally she never opened the boxes and couldn't have known what was inside.

Miss Bradshaw was more than willing to join the operation. Her instructions are to disguise herself as much as possible, and to station herself near the Wilmington residence and observe. (I'm not taking on this role myself because, as you rightly point out, Mrs. Wilmington has seen me, and my height makes me too conspicuous. Miss Bradshaw can more easily disappear into the street-scape and only has to avoid Mr. Wilmington's gaze when he leaves for the shop in the morning and returns home at night.)

I've told her to make a careful note of any visitors, and to follow Mrs. Wilmington when she goes out. I hope, within a few days, to have a better idea of her activities.

I don't expect Miss Bradshaw to need my help, but if she does, she's been instructed to stop into a hotel lobby or a train station, where she may telephone Hudson Printing. As I usually answer the telephone, we have some hope that she might summon me on short notice. We also worked out a code in case I'm unable to answer and she has to leave a message with Sam Archer.

It's a better plan than putting a gang of overzealous League men on the corner, wouldn't you agree?

Yours very truly,
Constance A. Kopp

BIELASKI TO CONSTANCE

September 20, 1918

Dear Miss Kopp,

Run this one as you see fit. You have the makings of a good supervisor if you know when to put your agents on the more interesting jobs. You're right to see that as a spy your value is diminished as soon as you're recognized. We like our agents to be inconspicuous, and there's no avoiding the fact that you're known to both the Wilmingtons and will be noticed and remembered.

I look forward to your report, and to Miss Bradshaw's. Please extend to her the Bureau's congratulations on her first assignment.

Yours very truly,
A. Bruce Bielaski

P.S. I know the overzealous League men all too well. Last week eighteen of them busted into a card room and rounded up five young men, all of whom were too young for the draft. These raids make a mess of my desk. The League men like to file a report on their every move and submit it in triplicate. I often get four or five reports on the same raid, as each of them enjoys having their secretaries type a letter to "Mr. Bielaski at the Bureau."

MISS BRADSHAW TO BIELASKI

September 21, 1918

Dear Mr. Bielaski,

Miss Kopp passed on your words of encouragement, which mean a great deal to me. Thank you for placing your trust — and the trust of our government — into my hands. I hope I won't disappoint.

At Miss Kopp's request I'm writing the report this week. The first few days were unremarkable: From across the street and down a few doors, I observed the Wilmington residence and followed Mrs. Wilmington as she conducted the sort of ordinary business one would expect of any woman: a visit to the market, to the druggist, and so on.

This morning, however, was different.

She left the house promptly at 8:30, shortly after Mr. Wilmington departed for the print shop. She stopped first at a newsstand, bought a paper, and tucked it under her arm. From there she went on to the Hotel Manhattan on Market Street and sat in its lobby for about ten minutes, pretending to read the paper. I say that she pretended because she spent exactly a minute looking at each page — or, more precisely, she spent that amount of time with her head turned in the general direction of each page. I don't think she read a word. She spent as much time on the front page as she did the ladies' page and the sports page. She never once turned the page to finish a story. No one reads a paper like that.

At the end of ten minutes—precisely ten minutes, by the standing clock in the lobby—she folded the paper, dropped it on the table next to her, and walked off.

I didn't like to let her go, but I suspected by then that I was following the paper, not the woman.

I was seated across the lobby, behind a wallpapered column, where I had a clear view of the chair she'd vacated and the paper she left behind.

Almost immediately a man arrived with his own paper— the Bergen County *Record* this time, while she'd left behind a copy of the *New York Times*—and he sat for another five minutes, reading first his own newspaper and then Mrs. Wilmington's.

I'll give you as close a description as I can of the man: he was perhaps only five feet and six inches, and stout, with thick black hair that fell over his forehead and a mustache just as dark. He had the round red cheeks of a drinking man and smoked a cigarette while he sat there. He wore a red waistcoat under a gray worsted suit and black shoes shined to perfection. I saw no rings, pins, or even a watch, although I couldn't see his watch-pocket from my vantage point. His eyes were brown or black, rather rounded, under heavy eyebrows, his lips fuller than average, his nose wide and flat. When he walked, his gait was unremarkable.

At the conclusion of precisely five minutes he stood, with Mrs. Wilmington's copy of the *Times* still in his hand. He tucked it under his arm and strolled out of the lobby, appearing to be in no particular hurry and looking neither to the right nor the left. He seemed in every way to be a man at his leisure. His copy of the *Record* remained in the chair he'd just left.

I wasn't sure at that moment which newspaper to follow. It was entirely a guess that I ought to stay with Mrs. Wilmington's *Times*. I saw immediately that I'd made the right decision, for the man walked straight to the train station and repeated his performance: he took a bench on the platform, pretended to read the *Times* again, then walked off, leaving the paper behind. His departure coincided precisely with the announcement that the 9:02 to New York was arriving.

By then, as you can imagine, I was looking breathlessly around, wondering who would snatch the paper up. It was a crowded platform and anyone might've taken it. Another man sat down almost immediately (the two must've seen one another, although I didn't observe it), picked up the paper, glanced at it, tucked it under his arm, and boarded the train.

As I had no ticket, I couldn't follow. I can only assume that this performance has been repeated many times before and will be again.

Let me tell you about the second man: he was perhaps five feet and eight inches, with fine blond hair parted on the right side and slicked down, a wide forehead, thin nose and lips, and wire-rimmed spectacles. He wore a brown and burgundy checkered overcoat, an ordinary brown suit, and had on his left hand a plain gold wedding band. He was a most ordinary-looking man, but I'd recognize him if I saw him again.

I returned to the hotel and found the *Record* still sitting in the chair. There was nothing tucked inside and no evidence of markings or other codes made within the pages of the paper.

Miss Kopp feels quite certain that Mrs. Wilmington was, in fact, using the newspaper ruse to send a message to someone. If it happens again, I'm to slip a coin to a newsboy and send him running over to Hudson Printing, where he'll barge in and try to sell an extra to Sam Archer. That will be Miss Kopp's signal to meet me at the train station. Next time, we plan to follow both men.

Yours very truly,
Anne Bradshaw

BIELASKI TO CONSTANCE

September 23, 1918

Dear Miss Kopp,

My thanks to Miss Bradshaw for a thorough report. It looks like you're on to something. Now that we have three subjects to watch—Mrs. Wilmington, the first man, and the second man—I want you working with a team. I'll put another agent at your disposal with the idea that Miss Bradshaw will continue to follow Mrs. Wilmington, and you and the other fellow can track the two men.

I've no choice but to send you a League man, but he'd be under your command and you can dismiss him if he isn't up to standards.

As usual, we're looking for names, addresses, known associates, and so on. As soon as you can supply me with the men's home addresses, we'll intercept mail.

Yours very truly,

A. Bruce Bielaski

CONSTANCE TO BIELASKI

September 25, 1918

Dear Mr. Bielaski,

By some stroke of luck, I happened to be working the counter yesterday while Sam Archer made a delivery. Another package arrived for Mrs. Wilmington — not from England this time, but from a hosiery shop in New York.

As no one saw me receive the package, I tucked it into my bag and took it home last night.

The package was (disappointingly, at first) filled with stockings, not contraband. But there was something unusual about them. They were of a slightly darker shade than the stockings most commonly on offer around Paterson, but there was also something to the texture that struck me as odd — something that might only be noticed by a woman who wears a pair of stockings all day.

I dipped the toe into a basin of water and — you guessed it — the water ran brown.

I recognized a secret ink as soon as I saw it. I called Miss Bradshaw over at once and told her to keep an eye on Mrs. Wilmington's clothing when she follows her, and to try to spot any other small article of clothing that might be impregnated with ink — scarves, socks, handkerchiefs, and the like. She was thrilled to be let in on this bit of spy-work and said it sounded like the sort of thing one might find in Berlin, but never here in Paterson. I explained that we'd seen quite a bit of it before our country went into the war, as the Germans started with lemon juice and worked their way up to more sophisticated methods.

But what type of ink is it? The British are miles ahead of us on working out the type of ink and the chemicals required to make it reappear. I hoped this was one the Bureau had seen before.

Sure enough, I took the stocking to our man on Lexington and was relieved to find that he recognized the ink at once and was able to supply me with a small quantity of the reagent. Miss Bradshaw and I have had a fine time writing "secret messages" in the ink, watching it disappear into the paper as it dried, and then seeing it reappear when the reagent was applied. But enough fun and games—our task now is to take hold of one of these newspapers she's passing along, and to scour it for a hidden message.

I did go into New York to make inquiries at the hosiery shop whose label appeared on the package, but they claimed to know nothing about it and don't appear to be in the mail-order business. The address is enclosed nonetheless if you'd like to investigate.

Yours very truly,
Constance Kopp

P.S. In reply to your offer of help, Miss Bradshaw and
     I will manage on our own. As soon as we decide we
     can't function without a League man, we'll send

for one—but don't hold your breath. Did you hear about the League's latest raid in Hackensack? They interrupted a play during the second act— brought the whole thing to a halt—and dragged out twenty-five men they suspected of avoiding the draft. Most were too old or too young. A few simply weren't carrying their papers. All were hauled to the police station, leaving the ladies without escorts home.

The play was entirely disrupted, of course, and the players felt they couldn't go on. The theater was forced to refund tickets to anyone who demanded it.

Surely the League could've handled it quietly, during intermission or after the performance. I strongly suspect they enjoy barging in, waving their badges around, and hollering to the ushers to bring up the lights. My brother swears he wasn't a part of it, but I have a hunch he was and doesn't like to admit it.

My younger sister, Fleurette, has witnessed all too closely the overzealous matrons at the Army camps, locking up girls on the flimsiest of charges. These all-volunteer efforts have a way of veering off-course. I'm sure I don't have to tell you that, but for now—no, thank you, we'll do without the League men.

BIELASKI TO CONSTANCE

Dear Miss Kopp,

We looked into the hosiery shop and found nothing amiss. The stockings might've been purchased there, but we don't believe the shop had anything to do with impregnating them with ink and shipping them to Paterson. The shop girls have no recollection of suspicious purchases, customers with German accents, etc.

I can send in the police to search the Wilmingtons' place as soon as you're ready. I expect you'll find messages written in secret ink in the newspaper, but look for a message done in pinpricks as well. Did I tell you about the new fellow we hired here in Washington to work in our cryptography department? We handed him the corpse of a German messenger pigeon, which we'd saved because the quills and feathers were riddled with holes and we suspected some sort of code. It didn't look like anything he'd seen before, but he decided to collect some feathers around town and try puncturing them with his own code, just to see how it might work. He put the feathers he'd gathered in a drawer with the German bird, and a few days later all the feathers had holes in them. Turned out the dead bird had mites.

Yours very truly,
A. Bruce Bielaski

CONSTANCE TO BIELASKI

September 29, 1918

Dear Mr. Bielaski,

Pigeon mites? You really could use Norma in the code room.
Yours very truly,
Constance Kopp

NORMA

Langres, France

September 7, 1918

Dear Constance,

Your sister has done something extraordinary. She'll never wear a medal for it, but she deserves one. I can't tell you what happened, but you must demand the whole story when you see her *après la guerre*. All I can say is that she helped to secure a victory for our troops, and she has proven at last what she can do. Her commanders recognize it. She's having an easier time now, and working harder than ever. You'll be so terribly proud of her when you find out why.

But that's as much as I'm allowed to divulge. Norma says I ought to stop going on about a story I'm not allowed to tell, and instead to say something about what's happened at the hospital. You know all about crimes and investigations. I'm sorry to say that we have one of those on our hands now—and it concerns me.

Fortunately, I can tell about it, as there are no military secrets to conceal. It's just a terrible misunderstanding that I don't know how to set right.

As you know, I'm a nurse at the American hospital here, where I have charge of all the medical supplies. It's my responsibility to catalog every pill and vial when it arrives, to make sure it's all stored properly, and to mark down everything that's dispensed to the wards. Once a month, I reconcile my inventory and hand a report to my supervisor, Mrs. Clayton.

The system works quite well and was, in fact, designed by your sister, who took one look at the French method that we were on the verge of adopting, and announced that it was "as if a committee of poets and painters had been convened to design a record-keeping system." We American nurses found that quite funny, but it didn't seem to translate very well to the French. Regardless, Norma invented a much better system, which managed to reconcile American hospital practices with Army protocol and the Red Cross management style, and we are thoroughly satisfied with it.

Imagine my horror, then, when Mrs. Clayton told me this morning that supplies were going missing and I was the one to blame! There isn't so much as a drop of iodine that can walk out of my supply closet without my knowing it, and I told her so.

"I give you my report every month," I said. "It reconciles perfectly."

"This goes beyond your report," she said. "You'll have an easier time if you confess now."

"But I have nothing to confess! And I've no use for anything in the supply room. If I were ill, I'd need only go to one of the doctors and he'd fix me up. That's how it is for all the nurses."

"I never said you were stealing it for yourself," Mrs. Clayton said. She was so vague about it! I think she hoped that if she said very little, I would stutter and stammer and confess my guilt. But I was more confused than ever.

"We have three hospitals in this village," I said, "a French one, a British one, and ours. We're practically awash in pills, powders, and ointments! What's the point of stealing them?"

"That's for you to tell me," she said, maddeningly.

Can you imagine how frustrated I was to be accused of a crime—a pointless crime at that, truly—and to be given no specific charges against which I might defend myself?

Regardless, Mrs. Clayton refused to say a word in answer to my questions. In the end I was sent home—in tears. I wasn't courageous about it at all. I ran up to our little room in the attic, burrowed under the blankets, and simply dissolved. Constance, I've never been accused of any wrongdoing in my life! You can't imagine how ashamed I felt. To be charged with stealing the very medicines that we so desperately need for our soldiers—who would do a thing like that? It's a horrible thought. I feel—well—*stained* by the mere accusation. Haven't I done everything in my power to earn Mrs. Clayton's trust?

Norma came home after a long day at the fort and found me sniffling and feeling sorry for myself. She didn't say a word, but turned right around on her heel and went down the street to the Patisserie Confiserie.

The shop was closed at that time of night and, as always,

sugar and butter are so dear that only the officers living at the Cheval Blanc can afford a cake, but somehow Norma roused Madame Bertrand from her apartment upstairs and talked her out of a slice of the most astonishing frangipane cake, with brandied cherries sunk to the bottom. The cherries must come from an ever-dwindling supply of Madame Bertrand's preserves, inherited from her brother, the former proprietor of Patisserie Confiserie who, as you know, died last year, poor man, and how she comes by the almonds these days is anyone's guess.

Regardless, a bit of cake, along with Norma's wise counsel, helped enormously. I intend to go back to Mrs. Clayton in the morning to demand that she furnish proof. Norma has said that she will come with me. She says that she does not entertain baseless accusations at her post, and neither must I. Do you see what a great deal of good your sister does for me?

Tendrement —
Aggie

NORMA TO CONSTANCE (ENCLOSED)

September 8, 1918

Dear Constance,

I thought I would wait to mail Aggie's letter in the hopes that we'd clear the matter up first thing this morning and I could tell you to forget all about it. Quite the opposite has happened, and Aggie finds herself in a real mess.

I went with her to the hospital at the beginning of her shift.

She thought it better to make an appointment with Mrs. Clayton, but there's a war on and I haven't the time for appointments. I went straight to the woman's office, stood in the doorway, and said, "You and I must sit down and put to rest this business with Agnes Bell. She's never stolen anything in her life."

Would you believe that Mrs. Clayton refused to hear it? She said, "Any testimony coming from Nurse Bell's bosom friend can have no bearing anyway, being obviously biased."

"Bosom friend, what nonsense!" I told her. "As if any of us are given a choice in bunk-mate. We're put into rooms in the order in which we arrive."

She started to wave me off, but before she could, I informed her that I'm biased only in favor of defeating the Kaiser and returning home, and that if I saw any evidence of theft or wrongdoing, I would hand Aggie over to the authorities immediately. Aggie, standing right behind me, nodded vigorously at this.

With that, the two of us stepped into her office, uninvited, and took our seats. Mrs. Clayton didn't like that at all. This woman is a battleship, accustomed to giving orders and hearing no guff about it. You know the type—a rather tall, stout, stern-looking woman in her forties, with the kind of broad shoulders and thick arms that come from lifting invalids for twenty years. These nurses know their business when it comes to keeping their patients alive, but that does not make them any sort of criminal investigator.

We made our case, but nothing we said made a difference. After much arguing back and forth, and poring over supply records that might exonerate Aggie, Mrs. Clayton has refused to back down. In fact, she intends to dismiss Aggie from the hospital and send her home in disgrace. Already she's put someone else in charge of supplies and demoted Aggie to orderly duty.

Aggie is twisted in knots over it, as you can imagine. There's no one but me to defend her or to say a word on her behalf. She's too ashamed to tell the other nurses—although they will work it out for themselves, soon enough, when she shows up to work in an orderly's uniform. But for the moment I'm the only one who knows, which means that I'm also the only one who can speak up for her.

Nothing more is going to happen to her immediately. It's no simple matter to send a trained nurse back to America—reports must be written, approvals granted, travel passes secured—and that gives us some time.

As Mrs. Clayton is clearly incapable of conducting the simplest of investigations, Aggie and I will pursue other means of establishing her innocence.

As ever,
Norma

P.S. Tell Fleurette to keep sending her jars of this and that to Aggie—she needs it.

AGGIE TO CONSTANCE

September 14, 1918

Dear Constance,

It's awful of me to pour all my bad news into a letter like this, but you've heard the beginning of it and you might as well hear the rest. I've been absolutely miserable this week. Another girl

is running my supply closet now, while I'm reduced to changing sheets and carrying lunch trays. At first I didn't want to tell
anyone what had happened, but there was no getting around
it. The nurses all demanded to know why I was out of uniform
and working as an orderly, and I had to confess. The trouble
is that I tend to burst into tears every time I try to tell about
it, and I'm afraid that only makes me look guilty. My friends at
the hospital rush to reassure me, of course, but there's something else in their reaction—a bit of suspicion, a note of worry.
If there's a thief among us, it's either me or it's—well, one of
them, isn't that right?

I don't accuse them, but an accusation hangs in the air.
There's a distance now, between me and the others. We were
in this together before, and that's what made it possible to
carry on, even on the most difficult days. But now I feel like an
outsider or, worse, a traitor. I know I've done nothing wrong,
but can I blame the others for having their doubts? Wouldn't I
have done the same?

Norma has been telling me all about your days of policing
and detective work, perhaps hoping that it will shore me up
now that I'm in the middle of my own investigation. I'd never
have the nerve to chase down a criminal and put him under
arrest, but she says you did it all the time! I can only imagine
how surprised the criminals were to find a female cop dragging
them off to jail. However, I'm not sure I'm made of such sturdy
stuff. I'm simply collapsing under the weight of this. Isn't it
strange—I could bear the war, I could bear the men with their
legs half-rotted away, their faces burned beyond recognition—
but to be falsely accused? It's too much for me.

Norma, on the other hand, has strength for both of us. She

must have something of the lady detective in her just like you do, for she's already set out a course of action for me. First, she told me that I must determine the nature of the crime, and not to trust Mrs. Clayton's account of it.

"Always know for yourself what sort of problem you're dealing with," she told me. "What exactly has been stolen, and when, and where, and how much?"

This has not been so easy to work out, as Mrs. Clayton refuses to say. I'm left with no choice but to go through patient records and compare what I've issued to the nurses against what's been dispensed to patients (all on my own time, of course). Would you believe it—I did find some discrepancies. Typhoid vaccines in particular are disappearing in large quantities, which is to say that I dispense them as requested, but a rather sizable share of them are never given to patients. I believe we have a similar problem with antiseptics, but it is of course more difficult to judge exactly how much of an antiseptic might be used on a given patient. Other medicines are missing in much smaller quantities that might not be the result of theft but of simple errors or carelessness.

But who would want vaccines and antiseptics? Anyone who hasn't had a vaccine will get jabbed whether they like it or not. And if someone were wounded, they'd simply come to us for treatment.

No one has a key to the supply closet but me and Mrs. Clayton. I give out supplies three times daily, more often in emergencies. For the rest of my shift, I perform my routine nursing duties and the closet remains locked.

As puzzling as it is, that's the situation. When I explained it to Norma, here's what she said:

"Now begin looking for guilty parties. Watch everyone and trust no one."

I had to explain that it's simply not in my nature to distrust everyone around me. How could anyone go through life like that?

What do you suppose Norma said? "You don't have to distrust everyone—only the one stealing the supplies. Whoever's done this doesn't deserve your trust."

Honestly, I don't know who would steal medicine from sick patients—especially from Americans, come all this way to give their lives for a free Europe.

But what else can I do? Mrs. Clayton is no help. She's certain that I'm to blame and can't wait to send me home. I continue to insist on my innocence and demand proof if I'm to be punished. We are, for the moment, at a standstill.

Norma says I can only be cleared of wrongdoing if I apprehend the guilty party myself. "We must take matters into our own hands, you and I," she tells me.

And so we shall. What choice do I have?

Tendrement—

Aggie

NORMA TO CONSTANCE (ENCLOSED)

September 14, 1918

Dear Constance,

As Aggie has told you, we're conducting quite the investigation here. I have insisted that Aggie make a list of any and all suspects, and cross them off only when we can definitively say that they couldn't possibly have stolen the supplies.

Aggie took my advice rather too literally and made a list of everyone who might have the opportunity to pocket a bottle of pills, which turns out to be almost everyone who works in the hospital. I told her that a list like that only tells us who has the *opportunity* to steal. What we need to know is who has *reason* to steal. What would be their purpose in snatching medicines from a cart?

This question yielded another list. Aggie is to be commended for her list-making abilities—it speaks to the sort of orderly mind one wants in charge of the supply cabinets. Here is what she put down:

REASONS TO STEAL FROM A HOSPITAL

To treat oneself, if one is ailing. (Although if anyone were personally in need of gallons of antiseptic, we would all know it on account of their gaping wound.)

To treat a friend or relation. (But why steal hundreds of vaccines, when one will do?)

To treat an entire village or encampment of refugees. (But if there were so many in need, why not tell the Red Cross about it? It's what they're here for.)

You can see, from this short list, that Aggie doesn't know how to get inside the criminal mind. It hadn't occurred to her that anyone would steal the supplies for money.

"You mean they'd sell them?" she asked. "But—to whom?"

I told her that there was a way to sell everything in a war:

sugar, liquor, tires, and bullets. She didn't believe me, particularly about the bullets, so I took her over to Monsieur Paquet's dry goods store and showed her the scale where he weighs out nails by the pound. A pound of nails makes for a parcel no larger than my fist, and costs only a franc or two. But I've seen Monsieur Paquet weigh a parcel of the very same size, and the same weight, but charge ten times as much for it. He's not even subtle about it: I saw a man walk in and ask for *"un petit quelque chose pour les Boches,"* as if I couldn't understand a word he was saying. What other secretive, small, heavy object would he want "for the Germans"?

To confirm my suspicions, I followed him home—the village is only a mile or so in length, so it's never far to anyone's house—and stood on the street outside, listening to the unmistakable sounds of a man taking apart and cleaning a rifle.

In case you're wondering, I didn't report it. The Germans will surely never make it this far, but if they did, I fully expect them to be defeated by an army of elderly Frenchmen with creaky rifles and pockets full of ammunition.

I told Aggie that I've seen no signs of a trade in medical supplies around town, but that we must both watch for it and notice small irregularities of the sort I spotted at the hardware store. Why the hospital administrators haven't already taken up this line of inquiry is beyond my comprehension.

What I do know is that Aggie is not going home. If they dare to put her on a train, I'll stand across the tracks myself to stop it.

As ever,
Norma

NORMA TO CONSTANCE

September 16, 1918

Dear Constance,

If we lose the war, it will be due to the auditors. Did you know we had such a species as an Army-decorated American auditor in our midst? What they're doing skulking around France is anyone's guess. This is no time for inventories and penny-pinching. We have a war to win, and what we need to accomplish that properly is everything, and then more of everything, and then still more of everything. When America comes to help, she brings her all. There should be no squabbling over it.

But an auditor, we have learned, is the direct cause of Aggie's misery, and I won't stand for it.

After a week or two spent dithering over these unfounded accusations, and having no idea how to go about finding the crook—if there is one—Aggie was summoned back to Mrs. Clayton's office to discuss the plans for her removal and arrangements for sending her home. Aggie was heartbroken and utterly defeated by the prospect. She wanted to go alone to the hour of her humiliation, but you can be sure I wasn't about to allow that.

Mrs. Clayton leapt to her feet at the sight of me and hollered for me to get out—she fancies herself quite the authority figure, as you will see—on the grounds that Aggie shouldn't bring "a chum" to work under any circumstance, and particularly to a meeting such as the one that was about to commence.

I told her—and this took her by surprise—that we had further questions about the crimes themselves, and required answers so that we might more quickly locate the real thief.

It was entirely apparent that Mrs. Clayton believed with every fiber in her considerable being that the criminal was seated before us in the person of Aggie Bell. By suggesting otherwise, I believe I left her speechless for a moment.

After some arguing back and forth I was allowed to stay. Mrs. Clayton was, as threatened, preparing papers to send Aggie home. She thrust them across the desk at the poor girl. This sent Aggie nearly into hysterics. It was not a fit of anger, but of weeping and pleading. Mrs. Clayton was entirely unmoved and seemed to want only to tell Aggie of her decision and send her away.

Aggie started to push herself out of her chair, sniffling, but I pulled her back.

"You obviously have it within your power to send Aggie anywhere you like," I said. "You've decided that she's the guilty party. You've refused to say anything about the evidence against her, in the hopes that she'll break down and confess. But she hasn't, and she won't. Now that you're sending her away, you might as well tell her how this came about."

That's when Aggie and I learned, for the first time, about the auditor's report.

The auditor came and went in July. He scampered around the hospital with his ledger-book and a fistful of pencils, putting bits of adhesive plaster on every shelf as he counted, and not bothering to remove them when he finished, which is to say that for such a meticulous man, he left a mess behind. Aggie recalled his visit but thought nothing of it, as it was a routine matter for someone to come by and inspect her records from time to time.

His findings, we've now learned, arrived on Mrs. Clayton's desk just last week, after having spent most of the summer passing from one officer to another. It's a good thing that the war isn't being fought by stenographers and men behind desks, because we'd lose—only in triplicate, and ten years behind schedule.

The auditor found the hospital in good order. The number of beds, linens, chairs, surgical tables, and scalpels were as expected. All manner of equipment could be accounted for and tracked with a high degree of accuracy in the hospital's inventory. The kitchen was likewise running efficiently, with its pots, spoons, serving trays, plates, and so forth carefully accounted for. The quantity of food ordered was, by his calculations, in keeping with the number of patients fed each month. (If you're getting bored reading this brief summation, imagine what it was like to sit through Mrs. Clayton's recitation, line by line. You asked for longer letters—"pages and pages," you said—so here they are.)

The only discrepancy, he reported, was found in Aggie's supply closet. The quantity of medicines ordered for the hospital, and dispensed according to Aggie's own meticulous records, was in excess of those typically required for a hospital of this size. In particular, vaccines and antiseptics were given out at a rate much higher than that seen in other hospitals of the same size. (This, you will recall, is exactly what Aggie found when she undertook a far more painstaking examination of the records, having not been told that the auditor had already reached the same conclusion.)

The auditor finished his report by saying that he could only assume that the supplies were being stolen, and stolen regularly. His recommendation was that the nurse responsible for the supplies be removed from her duties.

When Mrs. Clayton reached the end of the report, she looked up with an air of inevitability. "There, you see? I've told you more than I should, but now you have the whole of it. The auditor has made his decision. I'm to bring the matter to a close and report that I've done it."

Aggie was, naturally, stunned to learn all of this. Why hadn't she been given an explanation before, and a chance to respond?

I could tell that Mrs. Clayton wouldn't tolerate an argument from one of her staff, but I don't work for her. There's only one way to handle a woman who doesn't like her authority questioned, and that's to further prop up her authority.

"The auditor seems to think that he runs the hospital, and can hire and fire at will," I said.

"Nonsense!" said Mrs. Clayton, just as I'd hoped she would. "This is my hospital, and I decide."

Aggie started to plead for mercy, but I stopped her. She always wants to tug at the heart-strings, but it was obvious to me that Mrs. Clayton doesn't run the hospital with her heart, nor should she.

"The auditor plainly knows nothing about how a hospital is run," I said. "He fails to understand that you don't have one person in charge of supplies, but dozens. Once dispensed, the medicines go out on trays and carts all over the hospital. He seems to think that patients are wheeled directly over to Aggie to be given their pills and injections. He's either lazy, dim-witted, or inexperienced."

"All three, I'd say," pronounced Mrs. Clayton—coming around to my point of view.

"He hasn't thought it through, and there's no one to tell him so," I said. "He hands out these reports and expects them to be obeyed, but what real authority has he, except to write another report?"

Mrs. Clayton considered that, but then said, "I haven't the time to prowl around day and night, looking for a thief. I'm expected to write my response and show that I've taken care of it."

"Then put the truth in your report," Aggie said, quite firm and stalwart, which is the only way to behave at a moment like this. A nurse needs to have some pluck, and I believe Aggie has found hers. "Tell him that you've found no wrongdoing on my part, and that the situation is under investigation."

"You've had plenty of time to investigate," Mrs. Clayton said.

"I've had no time at all!" Aggie protested. "Give me two weeks and let me see what I can do. Surely you don't mean to take the word of an auditor over one of your own nurses!"

Mrs. Clayton sniffed—she doesn't like to be told what to do—and said, "But when no thief is found—"

I'd had enough by then. I pulled Aggie out of her chair. "There's nothing so difficult about catching a thief. Criminals aren't as clever as we make them out to be. Aggie and I will take care of the crook, and you take care of your reports."

It's never a good idea to wait for an answer at a moment like that, so I didn't. We've won Aggie a reprieve for the moment. Now to catch our thief.

As ever,

Norma

FLEURETTE

Chicago, Illinois

FLEURETTE TO HELEN

September 26, 1918

Oh, Helen, you just won't believe it —

There I was, all alone in my room, repairing frayed red piping on the hems of skirts because there is no red piping of this sort to be had any more — it's out of date and anyway there's a war on — but Mrs. Ward insists on it, so what was I to do but get out some red thread and bring the poor things back to life.

My throat was just a little better. I was starting to put it to work again, very gently, with the hope that Mrs. Ward would forgive me and put me back on the stage. As I stitched, I sang a little line, and Laura whistled it back at me. Once or twice she opened her beak, and I swear she was trying to sound out the words! Truly, she's the most remarkable parrot you've ever met.

Just then, a knock came at the door. It was Freeman Bernstein, passing by in the hall on the way to his wife's suite.

"I thought I recognized that voice, but who's this?" he said, grinning at Laura. "Let me hear a tune."

I pulled myself together, made apologies for my voice, and lifted Laura from her perch. She settled quite easily onto my arm, and the two of us sang a bit of "Over There," the first song she ever whistled for me.

And would you believe it—Laura danced up and down my arm, across my shoulders, and along the other arm as we sang! She's never done anything like it before. She bobbed her head in time to the music, and flapped her wings a bit, and even once—I didn't imagine it, truly!—kicked a leg up, like a chorus girl would!

Well, that just set Mr. Bernstein spinning like a top. "I love a bird act! What else can she do? If you can work up twenty minutes of material, I'll have the two of you on stages all over the country!"

I thought it sweet of him to say, but what do I know about a bird act?

"You know Mrs. Ward is entirely opposed to birds," I said. "She doesn't allow me on stage at all right now. She wouldn't stand for me and a parrot."

"Oh, I won't book you with May. You can go out on your own with an act like this! Say, can the bird do any other tricks?"

"I try not to overtire her," I said. "She's been moved around too much as it is."

"Moved around? She's a bird! They fly through the air! I've seen them do it. Travel is their business."

"I suppose so," I said, but I wasn't so sure about that. He went on, absolutely undaunted.

"You'll need to work up some fresh music. These boys are going to come home from France, and they will have seen the

Paris style of theater. They will have heard a different sort of tune. They will have seen girls do things on stage that they just don't do back home. An act like May's—that's not what they're looking for any more. They'll want someone younger, someone more exotic. You and this bird—they'll go for something like that. I don't suppose you could make yourself a dress out of feathers, could you?"

I didn't answer, but I was already imagining a quite stylish shift made of gold feathers, to better set off Laura's raiment of green.

While I was thinking that over, Mr. Bernstein snapped his fingers and said, "I've got just the thing. Do you suppose she could be trained to remove some item of clothing with her beak?"

Well, Helen, I thought I was too old to blush, but I turned red all over! Very quickly he said, "Nothing too risqué! A scarf, perhaps?"

I know full well that if Laura could pull a pin out of Charlotte's hair, she could be taught to remove a scarf, but where exactly would this scarf be placed, and what would be revealed?

"You do know that I speak French," I offered, mostly to take his mind off the scarf.

"My stars! I forgot. Sing me something."

I gave him a few little lines, in the most beguiling voice I could summon:

Je ne veux pas guérir
Je ne veux pas guérir
Car j'adore ma jolie infirmière

Laura had never heard the song before, but she cooed along. Mr. Bernstein was practically in tears.

"You're wasting your time in this hotel room," he said. "Go home and rest your voice, and work up a little act. Write to me the very minute you're ready. Within two weeks I'll have you booked all over the country. Just imagine: Mademoiselle Fleurette and Her Fine Feathered Friend."

By now I was warming to the idea. "But I'd always pictured myself with a stage name," I said.

"When you're already called Fleurette? Is there a prettier name on Broadway?"

I had to admit that there wasn't.

"Listen to me, girlie. May's act is going to stink like old fish *après la guerre*. She doesn't know it, and I'll be damned if I'm going to be the one to tell her, but that's the truth. If you want to make a life on the stage, you need to be working up an act for the 1920s, not singing the same old numbers from the 1910s. A girl on the stage always has to look ahead, to the next big thing. Can you do that?"

Oh, Helen, what could I say? I told him yes—yes, yes, yes! It seems outrageous, the idea of Laura and me as permanent traveling companions, appearing on the stage every night, but I'd be a fool not to try. And you know I'd never be cruel to Laura. If she showed any sign of distress, I'd take her home right away and forget all about it.

Of course, George Simon could return for her at any time, but if he saw the two of us together, he'd want me to keep her, wouldn't he? Just for a year or two?

Anyway, I'm tired of these Army camps, and of singing the same old songs every night, and the dry sandwiches and weak tea at the Hostess House, and May Ward thinking only of herself and growing ever more difficult. Why *isn't* she looking to the 1920s? And why shouldn't I?

Don't answer that. I'm coming home. I'll see you in the flesh soon enough. Between Constance and Bessie, I'll be nursed and fussed over, and so will Laura. When I have my voice back in fine form, I'll be ready for my next act.

With all my love—and kisses to be delivered in person—
Fleurette

TELEGRAM FROM FLEURETTE TO CONSTANCE

September 27, 1918

ARRIVING IN PATERSON TOMORROW 3 O'CLOCK
NOT SICK MERELY SICK OF MRS. WARD

KITCHEN TABLE NOTE
FROM CONSTANCE TO FLEURETTE

September 28, 1918

F—

What a surprise to have you home! If you're seeing this note, Mrs. Spinella let you in as I requested. I hope she's left a cot for you. I'll be home by six.

Might you be persuaded to stay in town for a few days? I have an assignment of a highly sensitive nature that requires both your acting and your seamstressing skills.

You have a letter here from Norma, and Bessie left a plate of sandwiches.

C.

KITCHEN TABLE NOTE
FROM FLEURETTE TO CONSTANCE

September 28, 1918

C—

You phrase it as a question but I don't suppose you're going to allow me to refuse. I'm not sleeping on that miserable cot, though—not with this nasty old cough. Find me a bed or I'll move over to Francis and Bessie's.

I'm running over to see Helen. I'll be back at eight. The parrot's name is Laura.

F.

NORMA TO FLEURETTE

September 10, 1918

Dear Fleurette,

Soldiers over here like to complain that they aren't allowed to make a single decision for themselves, but now I see why they're not. What man in his right mind hands off a parrot to a chorus girl, who is traveling from one stuffy old room to another and boarding trains at all hours of the day and night?

A pigeon is one thing and a parrot entirely another, but

if I remember my Bishop's guide correctly, parrots are hardy birds and will teach you as much about how to care for them as any book might. For instance, if a bird is uncomfortable or distressed, it will pluck its feathers or grow costive, which is to say that it will refuse to speak. If you feed it something disagreeable, you will know at once from its droppings. Pay attention in this manner and the bird will show you what to do.

If you ever took any notice of my pigeon loft, I hope you learned the importance of keeping a bird's enclosure scrupulously clean. Newspapers must be changed daily, and the entire cage taken out once a week and scrubbed with ordinary soap and water, then left to dry in the sunlight. Take care with its perch and feeding-dishes, too: You wouldn't want to drink from a dirty cup, and neither does your bird.

A parrot will take all manner of seed, but hemp and sunflower are best. Offer them sparingly, though. Think of them as treats that will spoil the health if eaten too often. Corn and bananas are fine food, and berries when you have them. Give a plain diet of boiled rice if the bird shows signs of illness.

Let the bird stand in the sun when possible, or even in a brightly lit window, but take care to make sure that it is not forced to sunbathe all day. Think of its life in the jungle: it might sit on an uppermost branch and preen its feathers, but then retreat underneath a canopy of leaves in the heat of the afternoon.

Of course, you must put the bird in the largest cage you can possibly find. For that you might try Miller's Hardware in Hackensack. If they don't have something for you, they will build it. A pretty brass cage in the shape of a palace is charming for a canary, but a parrot wants to stretch its considerable wings, and you must give it space to do so. Likewise give it a good perch outside of its cage and allow it liberty when you can.

As for training a bird, the way to go about it is to discover what the bird naturally likes to do and to reward it for doing so. Seeds make a fine reward, but give only one seed at a time, not a handful. Never punish a bird for failing to learn: it simply won't understand and will come to fear you.

As long as you keep it away from other birds (and you must), you won't have to worry about mites or worms. If you run into any other difficulties of an urgent nature, go through my books and you'll find Bishop's and a few others. The library likewise has a collection of aviculture books and periodicals, which will serve you well.

As ever,
Norma

FLEURETTE TO NORMA

September 29, 1918

Dear Norma,

Thank you for your advice on bird-keeping. You'll be happy to know that she's no longer being made to sleep in dreary old dormitories and hotel rooms. I've returned to Paterson to rest my voice and rehearse a new act. Constance intends to put me to work. I'll be doing something in service to my country, although she won't let me say what it is.

I have only just now caught up on your letters and enjoyed hearing about the baker mailing her cakes off to Belgium. I was heartbroken to read about the soldier with the picture of his mother concealed behind a button. I do hope Aggie has settled her troubles at the hospital by now—the letters take forever to arrive, and sometimes we get bunches of them at once, so it's entirely possible you've already written and told us how you took care of it.

I enclose a feather from my fine new friend, Laura. Have you ever seen such a dazzling color?

Yours,

Fleurette

CONSTANCE TO NORMA

September 29, 1918

Dear Norma,

It is now apparent that you knew about this bird of Fleurette's all along and never thought to mention it to me. Now that she has your instructions on its care and feeding, I suppose it will live forever—but surely not with us! The parrot was given to her by a soldier and will be returned to that soldier as soon as the war ends. I'm telling you this so you won't encourage her in her attachment to the bird. As it is, she carries it everywhere, wears it on her shoulder out on the street, and has of course taken it over to Francis and Bessie's so that the children can fall in love with it, too.

Fortunately I have the basement room at Mrs. Spinella's. No one can hear the bird when it whistles (and Fleurette is teaching it to whistle, and sing, and talk, and dance—it's like a little feathered version of Fleurette herself), and Mrs. Spinella has agreed, for an extra fee, to allow it, as long as no one complains.

You bear some responsibility in this, you know. Fleurette told me that the young man—George Simon is his name—only gave the parrot to her when he heard that she had a sister who kept pigeons.

Fleurette will earn her keep and the parrot's, as my assignment has grown more complicated and I need her help.

Our thoughts are with Aggie. Do send us a line when you can.

Yours,
Constance

FLEURETTE TO GEORGE SIMON

September 30, 1918

Dear George,

Laura and I (you see, I kept her name, I promised I would!) just returned home to New Jersey, and your postcard arrived the same day. Yes, you may write to me at this address any time you like, and I will always write back!

Laura has been an absolute love. She's whistling more every day, and she tries to sing sometimes, too—and I do mean real singing, with words, or what sounds she can make to resemble words. She's proving to be quite dexterous as well—she loves to take hold of any sparkling object and try to hide it away.

I'd even say that she has a sense of humor, if it's possible for a bird. Do you suppose it is? Can a bird tell a joke? Because I believe Laura is a great wit, and is only working out the means to express it.

It wasn't at all difficult to find food to her liking during our travels—she did just fine on a diet of bread, corn, apples, and bananas (which pretty closely describes my diet, too), but now that she's home, she's feasting on all manner of seeds as well.

Constance (my eldest sister) was a bit surprised to learn, when she offered to share her living quarters with me, that a bird would be part of the bargain. I'm happy to say that she's come around quickly. I catch her sneaking treats to Laura, and teaching her to say "Constance," which is a difficult word for a bird. So far all that Laura can manage is a sound like "Aw," but Constance finds that amusing and keeps at it.

I did have a letter from Norma waiting for me when I arrived, filled with good bird-keeping advice. I can assure you that Laura is in capable hands.

I hope you're well and safe. If there's anything at all we can send you, please write at once.

With all best wishes—

Fleurette and Laura (who does not say "George" but will try something like "Or")

FLEURETTE TO FREEMAN BERNSTEIN

September 30, 1918

Dear Mr. Bernstein,

I didn't see you before I left Chicago, so I wanted to write and tell you that I've taken your advice. After Chicago I went straight home to New Jersey. I parted with Mrs. Ward on the best terms possible under the circumstances. My voice still sounds like sandpaper but it will recover on a steady diet of my sister-in-law Bessie's chicken soup.

Laura (that's the parrot's name) seems to learn something new every day, whether I teach it to her or not. She's picked up the whistle of the tea-kettle and likes to fool me by starting that whistle as soon as I put the kettle on. I never know any more when the water's actually ready.

But don't worry—our act will be far cleverer than that! I expect to have something marvelous to show you within a few short weeks.

You may write to me at this address. I remain—

Yours very truly, with everlasting gratitude,

Fleurette

FREEMAN BERNSTEIN TO FLEURETTE

October 2, 1918

My dear Miss Kopp—

You're a clever girl to take Freeman Bernstein's advice. I've already been up and down Broadway, telling them all about your act, but I'm not going to let New York have you first. We'll put you on a regional tour, and let you fill a house in Newark, then Allentown, and then Lancaster. Theaters you've seen before— May's sung in all of them, and you were there with her.

Once we've collected some good notices, it'll be on to Boston and Philadelphia, maybe over to Chicago—and only then will we let Broadway have a look at you! This is the way to turn you into a sensation.

Don't worry, they'll all be begging for a booking. I'll see to that.

The first order of business is for you to have a picture made with that bird. Get yourself up in three or four costumes, and go down to Schwab's Studio in Fort Lee. Tell him Freeman sent you, and to charge my account.

The girls are starting to bob their hair, or to tuck it under and pretend they have. Would you consider anything of the sort?

Think about it before you go for the pictures.

Yours devotedly,

Freeman Bernstein

P.S. Have you told those sisters of yours about our business arrangement? One of them put a gun on me last year. I wouldn't like her to get into the habit of it.

FLEURETTE TO FREEMAN BERNSTEIN

October 4, 1918

Dear Mr. Bernstein,

Norma is the sister you ought to fear, but she's in France, so you have until the end of the war to reform your character and win her over.

When I first told Constance I was going to tour the Army camps with Mrs. Ward, she knew there was no point in trying to talk me out of it. She even went so far as to say that I am a grown woman, capable of conducting myself honorably when in the employment of Ward & Bernstein, and that in spite of your reputation, she knew perfectly well that I've never come to harm or disgrace due to my association with you, and so on and so on.

However, she isn't entirely aware of our new arrangement, or perhaps I should put it to you plainly and say that she hasn't an idea about it. She's assigned to a rather difficult job right now and wants my help with it. I thought it best to stay quiet and do what I could to assist her. Once the job is concluded and I've helped her to make a success of it, I'll tell her all about Mademoiselle Fleurette and her new act.

Laura and I sing together every day. She's quite an accompanist when she whistles. She does tend to rush, so I keep the tempo and give her cues. All of my costumes will require a pouch for seed, because she only sings for treats. Like every girl who works for you, she expects her wages.

About my hairstyle—shall I keep you guessing? Just wait until you see those pictures!

Yours very truly,

Fleurette

CONSTANCE

Paterson, New Jersey

CONSTANCE TO BIELASKI

October 4, 1918

Dear Mr. Bielaski,

I've found a way to get inside the Wilmington household. As you might recall, I've observed that Mrs. Wilmington can't sew, and she cares little for clothes. Even the curtains and upholstery are shabby and neglected.

With so much in disarray, an able seamstress could find a week or two's worth of work for herself at the Wilmington residence. To that end, I've sent in my younger sister, Fleurette, who grew up as I did speaking French and German. As she is only twenty and stands a good head shorter than I do, we may be assured that the Wilmingtons will not suspect that she's related to me.

"What am I to call myself?" was her first question. For once, her flair for the dramatic proves useful, as she does require a name other than the German-sounding Kopp. She settled on Gloria Blossom, which sounded obviously phony to me but I couldn't persuade her otherwise.

She insisted on a disguise and I likewise didn't object: a spy likes to put her own operation together, so to speak. She'd had a red rinse in her hair for the stage, but she darkened it considerably and cut it a few inches (she's sneaking closer to a bob, I suspect). She put together the wardrobe of a working woman of modest means, which in her case is quite a disguise. We are, of course, of modest means ourselves, but you would never know it from looking at Fleurette's collection of silk, crepe, beaded slippers, and furs. To be noticed is always her objective, and to make herself plain is a remarkable trick.

It was up to me to get her hired on. Fortunately, Mr. Wilmington's coat is nearly in tatters. It hangs all day on a coat-rack just outside his office. I had no difficulty at all in ripping a few seams in his pockets when he wasn't looking.

He cursed loudly the first time a handful of coins dropped right out of his pocket and onto the floor. I looked up calmly from my typing and said, "I know a very good seamstress."

"We require a dozen seamstresses," he said. "Everything's falling apart. I don't know what Mrs. Wilmington does all day."

I, of course, am likewise curious as to what Mrs. Wilmington does all day.

"If you'll allow me," I said, "I'll send a note to Mrs. Wilmington making an introduction to the girl I know. Her rates are quite reasonable. She'll have the entire household stitched back together in no time."

This was easily accomplished. By yesterday afternoon, Fleurette had secured employment in the Wilmington household. She noticed right away that most of Mrs. Wilmington's dresses fit her poorly and has scheduled a number of fittings to make alterations to almost everything she owns. It helped considerably that Fleurette let it be known that she could put her hands on fabrics not generally available in war-time—bits of silk, velvet, and so forth, to dress up a collar or a cuff. This might not sound like much to you, but Mrs. Wilmington's face lit up at the sight of even a few scraps of hard-to-find fabric in Fleurette's mending-basket.

I've encouraged her to expand her role as seamstress-spy in any way that might keep her in the house longer. She's offered her services for other domestic tasks as well, such as polishing furniture and dusting picture-frames.

You may expect quick progress now that we have my sister on the inside.

Yours very truly,
Constance A. Kopp

P.S. By the way, Fleurette reports that the ceramic figurine sits alone on a curio shelf, untouched.

BIELASKI TO CONSTANCE

October 6, 1918

Dear Miss Kopp,

I never expected to have an all-girl spy network on my hands, but I have no doubt you'll make a success of it. I'm sending under separate cover two identification badges like yours, one for Miss Bradshaw, and one for your sister. If they get into any trouble and have to send for the police, they are to present them just as you do and expect prompt co-operation. The police should let you use their call-boxes as well. If they give you any guff about it, send them to me.

Yours very truly,

A. Bruce Bielaski

MISS BRADSHAW TO CONSTANCE

October 8, 1918

Dear Miss Kopp,

Pursuant to our conversation tonight, I submit this report to document a most eventful day.

As you know, I've tried twice to follow the messenger and have twice been foiled. I've been able to track Mrs. Wilmington's newspaper as it travels from the newsstand to the hotel in Mrs. Wilmington's possession, from the hotel to the train station in the hands of the first messenger (it's always the same man), and again as it is picked up at the station by the second messenger and taken on board the train.

The trouble is that the second messenger is in the habit of evading detection. He changes rail-cars frequently, steps off at any convenient stop, switches from the express to the local and back again, and manages to thoroughly lose me when he does. No one will let a lady step from car to car unassisted, so I attract too much attention when I try to follow him. I've lost him twice so far and was near despair—but today I had a stroke of luck.

As is his custom, Mr. Wilmington departed for the office precisely at eight. At 8:30 Mrs. Wilmington walked out and went directly to the news-stand on the corner to purchase the *New York Times*.

With the *Times* in hand, she walked once again directly to the Hotel Manhattan. She sat in the same place near the window, in a high-backed green chair next to a potted palm.

I took my usual spot behind a column, across the lobby. I had a book with me and pretended to read. Mrs. Wilmington sat for precisely ten minutes, reading the newspaper but not reading it, as previously described. She seemed merely to pass her eyes across each page, for a minute at a time, giving equal interest (or a lack of interest, as I've yet to see Mrs. Wilmington interested in anything) to each page, even a page filled almost entirely with advertisements.

After ten minutes passed, she stood, dropped the paper, and left.

This time, however, no one came to pick it up.

I waited a full fifteen minutes. Men and women walked in and out of the hotel. The paper sat, untouched, ignored by porters and waiters who circulated through the lobby.

At that moment I had a decision to make. I had no specific instructions from you regarding what I was to do if the newspaper was simply abandoned. Had the messenger failed to appear? Surely Mrs. Wilmington wouldn't have simply left it if she hadn't seen him. Had someone interfered with him, and prevented him from coming into the hotel?

I suppose we'll never know. I didn't see the man approach, nor did I see or hear any kind of scuffle on the street. My best guess is that he was spotted by someone who knew him and was forced to abandon the mission.

But there I was, staring at the discarded newspaper across the lobby. A porter started walking around, picking up stray papers and abandoned cups. He began at the other end of the room, which gave me only a moment to act.

I dashed over to the green chair, picked up the paper, and started to read. Tucked in between the pages I found a grocery list, written in Mrs. Wilmington's hand.

I withdrew from my pocketbook a handkerchief and held the grocery list gingerly, as you instructed, to avoid leaving finger-prints or damaging any already put down. I don't believe anyone saw me doing this—the green chair is high-backed and deep, so that it's easy to avoid being seen.

There was nothing remarkable about the note. If it holds any useful information, it must be in secret ink or code.

After spending only about three minutes in the chair, I tucked the note into my handbag (discreetly, behind a curtain of privacy afforded by the newspaper), folded the paper, and walked out.

Both the note and the paper are now in your possession. Per your instructions, I'll stay at my post and continue as before.

Yours very truly,
Anne Bradshaw

MRS. WILMINGTON'S GROCERY LIST

Oat flakes
Butter

Laundry soap
Cabbage
Evaporated milk
Mincemeat

CONSTANCE TO BIELASKI

October 8, 1918

Dear Mr. Bielaski,

Enclosed please find Miss Bradshaw's report. The note she intercepted appeared at first to be a grocery list, unremarkable, and in Mrs. Wilmington's hand, as confirmed by Fleurette, who was able to smuggle out other notes written by her.

We brushed on a coating of the reagent. It is quite miraculous to watch the writing emerge in its ghostly fashion. Quite apart from the spectacle of it, we did uncover what appears to be code written across the list. I've enclosed a complete transcript—as you can see, the format is as follows: three numbers, separated by a period.

25.8.3
163.20.4
439.40.8

. . . and so on. I only wish my sister Norma were here, as she's never met a code she couldn't decipher. Absent any help from Norma, I entrust it to you and await your reply.

Yours very truly,
Constance A. Kopp

BIELASKI TO CONSTANCE

October 10, 1918

Dear Miss Kopp,

The code looks like book cipher. Is there a book to which Mrs. Wilmington is particularly attached? The code works as follows: If the line reads 2.5.6, the first digit represents the page number, the second digit represents the line of text on that page (counting down from the top), and the third digit represents the position of the word in the line, starting from the left.

Thus, 2.5.6 instructs the recipient of the code to turn to the second page, count down five lines, and read the sixth word on that page.

It only works if both sender and recipient possess identical editions of the same book. It's generally not a slim book of prose or a volume on a narrow subject, but some doorstop of a book covering a wide range of topics and therefore containing, somewhere within its pages, every possible word a messenger might have cause to use. Dictionaries, encyclopedias, and Bibles are likely suspects.

Yours very truly,
A. Bruce Bielaski

TELEGRAM FROM BIELASKI TO CONSTANCE

October 11, 1918

ON SECOND THOUGHT DO NOT PUT SISTER IN DAN-
GER OVER HUNT FOR TREASURED BOOK WE HAVE
CAUSE TO ARREST PULL HER OUT AND I WILL SEND
IN MY MEN

TELEGRAM FROM CONSTANCE
TO BIELASKI

October 11, 1918

NOT YET

CONSTANCE TO BIELASKI

October 12, 1918

Dear Mr. Bielaski,

Beg pardon for the abrupt telegram, but we can wrap up this
operation ourselves and bring in the rest of the ring if you'll
only let us. You know you wouldn't have pulled three men out
—you would've let them finish their work and you would've rewarded them for doing so. We deserve the same.

Fleurette has made herself quite useful at the Wilmingtons' and now has reason to be there almost every day.
Whenever Mrs. Wilmington leaves the house on some small
errand, Fleurette starts going through drawers, files, and

even paging through books in the library in search of hidden notes.

It comes as no surprise, then, that Fleurette knew immediately what the book in question might be. She'd found it on the floor in Mrs. Wilmington's bedroom only last week. Supposing it had been knocked off the night stand, she picked it up, dusted it off, and was about to replace it when Mrs. Wilmington walked in.

You would've thought Fleurette was fingering her jewelry box! Mrs. Wilmington snatched the book away, furious, and told Fleurette to never again touch her things.

But it's Fleurette's job to touch her things, of course: she's there to repair clothing, put upholstery and curtains in order, and so forth. She managed to settle her employer down and to assure her that she was only tidying as she went about her work.

The book in question is *Dr. Chase's Recipes or Information for Everybody, Enlarged and Improved Edition,* published in 1902 by Thompson & Thomas of Chicago, in red binding. I haven't any idea how she and the person with whom she is in communication happened to come into possession of two copies of this particular volume, but it is a good choice for a book cipher, as it is filled with information on everything from gunsmithing to beekeeping to cooking for the convalescent, and offers a detailed index of some ten pages, listing entries from Ale, Homebrewed to Worm Lozenges.

As you said, a book cipher is no good unless the book contains the words you wish to use. I can't imagine a single word that wouldn't be found in this dense volume.

As soon as Mrs. Wilmington discovered Fleurette with the

book, she hid it away, but all women hide things in the same places. Fleurette needed only an hour alone in the apartment to retrieve it. The book was too large for a flour canister, leaving the mending-basket as the next most likely place, but Mrs. Wilmington has no mending-basket (if she could mend, Fleurette wouldn't be there). The lingerie drawer might've been another likely spot, but Fleurette was in and out of her bureau every day, as Mrs. Wilmington well knew.

Fleurette's next idea was to search for a drawer with a false front in her writing desk—and she quickly found one. The false front was cut out of paste-board and fitted with nothing but a few tiny furniture nails to hold it in place. My mother had one just like it. If you ever meet a woman who hasn't carved out some tiny hiding place in a desk or drawer, be very suspicious. It doesn't mean she has no secrets: it means her secrets are too large or dangerous to be hidden in her bedroom or sitting-room. Look for a gun under the floor boards in that case, or a body buried in the garden.

The code Mrs. Wilmington tucked into her newspaper translates as:

Will proceed on the first quiet night

There's more. We found a bit of scrap paper tucked inside *Dr. Chase's*, written in another hand. In faint pencil was another series of book codes, which we have transcribed to read:

Rubber gloves
If glass breaks bury underground

1 inserted into nostril or feed or water
2 into muscle with syringe

I can only hope that the intended recipient of the syringe is not Mr. Wilmington, and that Mrs. Wilmington will have to leave the house to carry out her plan, whatever it is.

We're working three eight-hour shifts now. Fleurette takes the day shift inside the apartment, Miss Bradshaw spends the early evening watching from across the street, and I have the night watch from midnight to eight in the morning.

When Mrs. Wilmington proceeds with her plan, we will follow and apprehend if necessary.

Yours very truly,
Constance A. Kopp

P.S. I'm not at all worried about being spotted. Fleurette has proven herself to be a master of disguises. With a complete change of wardrobe, theatrical face-paint, and gray powder in the hair for me and a pair of glasses for Miss Bradshaw, we are practically unrecognizable even to each other.

BIELASKI TO CONSTANCE

October 14, 1918

Dear Miss Kopp,

Would I have allowed three men to stay on the job and wrap it up themselves? I admit that I would, if one of them were a trained agent with some background in law enforcement— and you are. I concede defeat. Please proceed.

No reason to work overnight duty and then try to stay awake all day at Hudson Printing. Give your notice and let Mr. Wilmington shift for himself. He can find another secretary. You, Miss Kopp, and Miss Bradshaw ought to finish what you started.

Yours very truly,
A. Bruce Bielaski

CONSTANCE TO MR. WILMINGTON

October 16, 1918

Dear Mr. Wilmington,

It is with regret that I submit my resignation from Hudson Printing Company, effective immediately, owing to a pressing family matter. I thank you for the opportunity and wish you and Mr. Archer all the best in your future endeavors.

With best regards,
Winifred Sedgewick

MISS BRADSHAW TO MR. WILMINGTON

October 19, 1918

Dear Mr. Wilmington,

I'm in receipt of your kind letter, forwarded from my boarding-house in Paterson, and your offer of return fare so that I might resume my position at Hudson Printing Company. I'm sorry to say that my mother's health has only deteriorated, and she requires constant care. I'm sure you'll find many an eager applicant for the position of secretary. With much gratitude for your kindness and forbearance, I remain—

Yours very truly,

Anne Bradshaw

CONSTANCE TO NORMA

October 19, 1918

Dear Norma,

Fleurette has made herself comfortable in my little basement apartment. She refused the cot and demanded a proper bed, which Mrs. Spinella declined to furnish. She (Fleurette, that is) still suffers from a cough she picked up last month, so I want her to be comfortable.

To that end, Francis and I went out to Wyckoff on Saturday, had a look around the house (which is fine but dusty—there's not a leak or a broken window-pane anywhere), and hauled out the little day-bed from Mother's old room for Fleurette. I took a few extra blankets as well, and a lamp for her bedside, and a couple of your bird books, which she demanded because she spends hours training that parrot to whistle and sing. She wants to know how to keep her feathers lustrous, and what sort of toys might best amuse her while we're away at work. I told her I didn't think that you ever gave a toy to your pigeons, but I'll let you answer that.

You should know that Fleurette has proven herself to be an able investigator. She's made a discovery that changes the course of our work. Mr. Bielaski wanted to rush right in with the police, but I told him I'd rather take just a little longer to watch and learn. If the woman we're following is up to anything at all, I suspect she can lead us to the next link in the chain, and the one after that. Someone is giving her orders — or she's giving someone else orders. We're going to stay on the job until we find out.

Yours,
Constance

CONSTANCE TO AGGIE (ENCLOSED)

October 20, 1918

Dear Aggie,

Just before I posted my letter to Norma, a batch of letters arrived telling us more about the alarming accusations against you. I only wish I'd had them earlier and could've dashed off some advice.

I hope your troubles are solved by now. But please know that if the unthinkable were to happen, you would not be returning friendless to the United States. Bessie, Fleurette, and I would be here to meet you, and to help you get on your feet again.

If everything isn't resolved yet, let me just say this: Norma is absolutely right that we must all look out for ourselves and not depend upon anyone else to come along and rescue us. If you can point to the culprit, you've solved your own case, and what could be better than that?

My sister, as you might've learned, is indefatigable once she's set herself upon a particular course. If she's decided that a thief is afoot and that catching him is the only way to clear your good name, then she won't stop until it's done. This sort of brute force is, after all, exactly how she managed to get herself and her pigeons to France. She was relentless about it. (I should know! I lived through years of militaristic pigeon campaigns, mounted from my sitting-room, begun practically the day the Archduke was assassinated.)

Please remember that only in novels do investigations run smoothly, with a new clue turning up in each chapter until the whole is finally revealed. In fact, the usual progress of an investigation is something more like this:

Day One: Nothing out of the ordinary.
Day Two: Nothing out of the ordinary.
Day Three: An idea! The idea is pursued, but leads nowhere.
Day Four: A witness is interviewed, but they know nothing.
Day Five: Nothing.

And on it goes, until one day, you find the answer. And the reason you find it is that you've been looking.

I promise you that discouragement, boredom, and the questioning of one's own sanity are the workaday characteristics of any investigation. You might feel, as I often do, that you have nothing to offer—no insight, no clever ideas about where to go and who to ask, and no special genius for ferreting out the odd and obscure detail that will lead to the truth. But you do have something to offer, and that is your perseverance. It's the one quality that you and you alone can bring to this matter.

No one else is looking for the thief. But you're looking—every day. Perseverance alone counts for a great deal. In fact, it's everything.

Yours,
Constance

NORMA

Langres, France

NORMA TO CONSTANCE

September 12, 1918

Dear Constance,

Aggie's case has been quite firmly stuck—until yesterday. Believe it or not, a clue has been delivered to us by the town drunk.

Our village is in possession of exactly three town drunks. As unlikely as it may seem, they've provided our first and only hint in the matter of Aggie and the missing supplies.

Our billet is situated just off the town square. The village's main avenue begins there and runs right down to the old gate leading out of town. Along this avenue are the sorts of shops you'd expect: druggist, butcher, tailor, baker, tobacconist, and so on.

This square is where the drunks spend their days, so they won't miss anything. Every afternoon, except on the coldest winter days (when they huddle in a church basement), these three station themselves under an enormous acacia tree, directly between a statue of historical significance (that I shall not name because ours is the only village with such a statue), and the office of the village newspaper. The editor sits in the window, overlooking the square, so that he, too, won't miss anything. Town drunks and newspaper editors have a number of habits in common, including loitering, drinking, dishevelment, and keen powers of observation.

I'm surprised they (the drunks, not the newspaper men) sit out every day in sight of all the American soldiers, who have no tolerance for inebriants. Idle, unemployed men back home would either be conscripted into the Army or locked up. Here they are not only tolerated but viewed by the French as a necessary part of village life, like the mortar that holds the cobblestones together.

The eldest of the three drunks, Julien (you will learn in a minute how it is that I came to know his name), is a gaunt and grizzled old man with enormous red ears and a nose that grows continuously, more in length than width, like that of Pinocchio. He wears a battered straw hat, even in winter, and offers a toothless grin and salutation to everyone who passes by.

I've never stopped to speak to him as I've no reason to do so, but he seems to be quite a story-teller. He speaks incessantly to his companion, a young man of about twenty-five who by all rights should be hunkered down in a trench along the Argonne, except that he's so jumpy and prone to hallucinations that no soldier would tolerate him in close quarters. He'd be sent out as a misdirection, to draw German fire, and he'd be dead in a minute. Although he has no redeeming qualities and contributes nothing to village life, he has nonetheless been spared this fate.

The third is a person of indeterminate sex—even long-time villagers can't be sure—who wears chin-length stringy hair, speaks in a high but not feminine voice, and mostly addresses ghosts, spirits, and other apparitions. He—or she—goes around wrapped in shapeless blankets and robes, has nothing to say to the other two, but is prone to screaming and thrashing about if addressed directly.

The three are always seen together, the first talking incessantly to the second, and the third saying nothing at all except for the occasional round of incoherent shouting.

There—you have the picture. Yesterday, Aggie was walking along the main avenue and stopped to linger at the window to the bakery with which you are now familiar. With your most recent package lost and a few other food shortages of the type that occur often but not always simultaneously as they are now, we've all grown tired of potato soup, dark bread, and, for a Sunday treat, what they call *gâteau de guerre*, which does nothing to earn the name *gâteau* as it is made only of grated potatoes, eggs, and a pinch of sugar.

The bakery has very little on offer either, but Aggie tortures herself by going to look anyway. I tell her that it's best never to think of home, or treats, or small luxuries, or good meals, but she does it anyway and makes herself miserable as a result.

At just that moment—while she was looking in the bakery window—Julien approached with a little bundle of something in a nasty old handkerchief. He held it out to Aggie as if presenting a gift.

She naturally withdrew. She's polite to a fault, thinks she owes the world a smile, and doesn't know how to be stern as you and I do, so merely said *merci* and inched away.

But the man did not take this as a refusal—how could he, when she didn't refuse?—and persisted, holding out his hand and unwrapping the handkerchief to reveal its contents. One wouldn't want to guess at what sort of horror he was preparing to unveil, but Aggie looked anyway.

Inside the handkerchief were three aspirin bottles, all full and unopened. They were labeled with Aggie's own inventory numbers.

What on earth gave him the idea to offer them to Aggie? She was in her uniform, of course, but so were a dozen others walking up and down the street. She'd never been on speaking terms with him and assures me that they'd not so much as exchanged a word of greeting. Why would he choose that moment to approach her?

She believes it to be divine intervention. I call it suspicious behavior on the part of an untrustworthy individual.

She tried, in her broken French, to extract from him some explanation of where he found the bottles. She couldn't understand a word he said, but she took the bottles nonetheless and presented them to me that night as her first official bit of evidence.

I went out the next day and interrogated him myself, which was how I came to know his name. I could, of course, understand his French, but what he said was mostly nonsense. After much stern questioning, he claimed first to have picked the bottles up in the street moments before handing them to Aggie, thinking she'd dropped them. Then he said that he found them on a rubbish-heap near the engineering school. Finally he told me that he unearthed them while digging an improvised latrine for himself.

The third explanation made me very much want to sanitize the bottles, but we are trying to preserve evidence. If you happen to have a packet of finger-print powder at hand, send it along, but the bottles are so dirty and appear to have been handled so much that I don't think a print could be found. Even a perfect print would only be of use if we could match it against the culprit's own hand, and we as yet have no way of doing that.

Nonetheless, Mrs. Clayton accepts the vials as evidence that we're making headway. She has, for the moment, withdrawn her threats to send Aggie away, though she doesn't want to admit it. Regardless, Aggie remains on orderly duty as we endeavor to clear her good name.

Julien is, at this moment, our only suspect. He might not be a suspect at all but merely a witness. It is nonetheless our duty to keep a much closer eye on him. I consider it wholly unpleasant to trail around town after an unsavory character, but that is, of course, the very definition of detective work.

Of my own work I will say only that things have picked up lately.

As ever,
Norma

AGGIE TO CONSTANCE

September 20, 1918

Dear Constance,

I promised I'd write if we had any news in the case of the missing medical supplies (it sounds like one of those Sunday serials, doesn't it?)—and we do!

You have (I hope) a letter from Norma about a villager, Julien, who approached me on the street and handed me three bottles of aspirin, which appeared to have been taken from our hospital. Although we still don't know how they came to be in Julien's possession, finding those three stolen bottles did buy me a little time. Mrs. Clayton understands that something is amiss, and is allowing me the opportunity to work it out.

Now we have another clue. Here's what happened: Just last night, Norma and I were gathered in our room along with Betty, the Signal Corps operator who was instrumental in— well, this terribly heroic act that your sister insists mustn't be discussed through the mails. Suffice it to say that we've become fast friends and were gathered to celebrate Betty's birthday.

For the occasion, she'd managed to put her hands on a dusty bottle of *piquette* so raisiny that we suspect it was spoiled, but we drank it anyway. Norma jumped up at the last minute, declaring that we needed something sweet to go with our farmhouse wine. She went around the corner to the Patisserie Confiserie. Our little village has been awfully low on sugar and butter lately, but Madame Bertrand had delivered a tray of the most beautiful little tarts to an officers' dinner party just a few days ago, so we believe she's put her hands on some ingredients.

Norma found the bakery closed but not locked. She could see through the window that Madame Bertrand was not upstairs in her apartment but only just in the back, baking. Norma walked right in. When Madame Bertrand didn't come out from the kitchen to greet her, she simply went behind the counter.

In this way she startled Madame Bertrand, who jumped when she heard Norma behind her and dropped the cake pan she was in the middle of greasing. Norma picked it up and looked it over—your sister is nothing if not observant—and asked her what sort of cake goes in a pan like that. It was round, with a mold in the center (like an upside-down coffee can, if you can picture that) so that the middle of the cake would be hollow.

Norma was suspicious from the beginning, but she only asked very calmly what sort of filling went in the center. Madame Bertrand was so flustered that she couldn't summon an answer and instead told Norma that the bakery was closed and there would be no slices on offer tonight.

Norma kept hold of the pan, turning it over and examining it from all sides. She told me that it looked to have been made by hand and hammered together, not made in a factory. It was, in other words, irregular.

"Cream? Jam?" Norma suggested, trying to help Madame Bertrand give a plausible answer.

"Yes," Madame Bertrand said hastily. "Just so. Strawberry jam and cream filling."

Norma handed the cake pan back. "What's the name of that cake?" she asked next. Every sort of pastry and bread loaf has a name in France.

Madame Bertrand rolled her eyes and muttered, "Angels in heaven."

"*Anges du paradis,*" Norma repeated. "That's a strange name for a cake. I'll order one someday."

"Go on, now" was all Madame Bertrand had to say to that. "I closed hours ago."

"But there's half a *clafoutis* on the rack," Norma said. Without waiting for Madame Bertrand to argue, Norma cut a slice for each of us and left a few coins in payment. I never would've had the nerve, but Norma has a way of walking into a place as if she owns it. No one stops her, not even a formidable baker.

That cake pan with the hollow center made Norma suspicious. While we ate our *clafoutis* (if you've never had one, it's a custard with fruit baked inside. Madame Bertrand had to substitute rice flour for wheat, but at least the eggs were fresh), Norma laid out the whole story as she saw it: Madame Bertrand with her bread carts rolling back and forth to the hospital each day, the trips to the post office to ship cakes to a sister in Belgium that no one had heard about before, and poor old Julien, right in front of the bakery, producing three stolen bottles of aspirin that might well have fallen off the bread cart or out of a pocket.

Could it be? Is Madame Bertrand snatching up supplies to send to her sister in Belgium?

You can't imagine how intrigued we became, all at once, about the sister in Belgium! Fortunately, we knew exactly who to ask—Madame Angevine, the proprietress of the hotel, who had known Madame Bertrand's brother for decades, and bought desserts from him. She was herself responsible for reviving him once or twice when he went into one of his diabetic spells.

The three of us traipsed downstairs at once—unable to wait even until morning—and found Madame Angevine in her little parlor, bent over her ledger-books. She doesn't like an interruption, but we went with an offering: a bit of *clafoutis*, and the last dollop of that rose-scented hand cream Fleurette sent.

It was a terrible sacrifice but it had to be done, as Madame Angevine is a business-woman. If you want something from her, you'd better not come empty-handed.

And she did have something for us! As she tells it, Monsieur Bertrand arrived in the village as a young man in about 1884, took a job in the bakery, and assumed ownership of it when the previous owner became too frail to run it any longer. For nearly thirty years, Monsieur Bertrand was at the very center of village life, baking wedding and birthday cakes, pouring chocolate eggs at Easter, and creating *Galette des Rois* for every Epiphany dinner in town. He knew absolutely everyone, which is not difficult in a village of only a few thousand inhabitants. He and his helper, Fernand Luverne, were always quick with a joke and had a treat on offer for every child who came in with his mother. In addition to Fernand, he kept company with a good crowd of men about his age: other shop proprietors, landlords, and so forth. They would gather in a café in the evening for a drink, a smoke, and a game of *crapette*.

What Madame Angevine did not recall was any mention of Monsieur Bertrand's family. It's not that he refused to speak of them, only that he was such a part of village life that it never occurred to anyone that he might belong to someone else. She suggested that we talk to Fernand, or to some of the other men he used to meet in the evenings. Perhaps they would've heard about a letter from a sister in Belgium or Toulouse, or any mention at all of his relations. She named a few people we might ask, and I wrote them down.

Norma, of course, was the only one who could think of a question, and it was an important one.

"If he never mentioned his family," she said, "how did anyone know to write to Madame Bertrand in Toulouse after he
died?"

Madame Angevine looked puzzled at that. "You're right.
Someone must've known. The constable, perhaps, or the coroner."

As you can see, we have our lines of inquiry!

Norma says that I should have the pleasure of catching
Madame Bertrand myself. If she's stealing, it's a matter of following her into the hospital kitchen during her bread delivery,
and following her out again, without being detected. Betty is
of course thrilled to be involved and will keep an eye out herself. Neither one of us can be away from our stations for long,
but we will do what we can, and I'll solicit the help of a few
other nurses as well. (Carefully chosen nurses, Norma warns.
Your sister doesn't like the idea of too many investigators trip-
ping over each other in the pursuit of a likely suspect.)

To have a plan—to have any idea at all of what I might do
next—is a tremendous relief. I might not have conveyed, in
my previous letters, the depths of my fear and worry over these
accusations. I try to keep my spirits up and to sound cheerful
when I write to you. To be honest, we all put on a smile when
we write home. A letter filled with worry and gloom does nothing for our families, who can only worry and feel gloomy in
return. And my troubles are nothing if you put them alongside the widows, the orphans, the soldiers blinded, the villages
bombed to ruins. My only difficulty is a false accusation from
an auditor. If I'm sent home over it—well, the war will go on,
with or without me. But the fact is that I'm terribly ashamed to

have been accused of a crime and to wake up every day knowing that my name has not been cleared. I feel sullied by it.

It's an awful burden to carry around. But tonight, that burden is a little lighter, and I owe it to your sister. She is such a
gift to me. I thank you again for loaning her to me for the duration of the war, which I pray will be short.

More as I know it—

Tendrement—

Aggie

P.S. You asked about library books. We do receive a
   shipment, from time to time, of books and magazines for our patients. Newspapers are also welcomed enthusiastically—you can't imagine how
   much a man from Chicago, for instance, cher-
   ishes a copy of the *Tribune*.

   The books come through a central depot and
   are parceled out according to need, so Bessie's library should just keep doing what it's doing and
   we will get our share. She's right about the books
   being burned—we must take a quarantine very seriously. As you can imagine, those in a locked, isolated ward are most in need of some way to pass
   the time and take their minds off their suffering.

   But that's not the only reason we burn them.
   I need hardly say that in a hospital, with so many
   wounded and ailing men, the books suffer all kinds
   of damage that render them unsuitable for further
   circulation. I can't put it any more delicately than

that, but I'm sure you can picture it. The point is
—yes, we can always use more books, and the librarians are doing their part heroically.

September 23, 1918

Dear Constance,

I can hardly believe it happened, but I did, in fact, catch Madame Bertrand in the act. Honestly, I thought my heart would
stop. I don't know how you survived it, chasing criminals
around. Truly, I could hardly breathe and found myself, at a
crucial moment, dizzy and seeing spots.

She wasn't all that difficult to catch, once I knew to watch
her! She delivers her bread promptly at seven in the morning,
so for the last few days I arrived early, lingered about, watched,
and waited.

The kitchen is situated at the back of the building, down
a half-flight of stairs. It's wholly inadequate for our purposes,
as this place was built as a school for children, not a hospital filled with nurses, doctors, orderlies, and patients, all of
varied appetites and all dining according to their particular
schedules. The kitchen staff is mostly French, as we are short
on American personnel and the villagers turn out to be most
skilled at procuring extra potatoes and making every leaf and
stem count. They use everything: the woody, pockmarked cabbage stalk, the reptilian feet of chickens, the greens atop a car-
rot. Did you know you could eat those? We do.

Into this cauldron of French cooks—old women, mostly,

and a few boys too young to go to war but old enough to carry coal and heavy iron pots—Madame Bertrand wheels her bread cart every morning. I soon noticed that she summons one particular kitchen boy to help her wrangle it down the stairs. The bread, wrapped in linens and packed in baskets, is unloaded and replaced with a load of empty baskets and used linens. The same boy helps her push the cart back up the stairs, and she wheels it home.

As you can see, she doesn't even come into the hospital. She barely steps foot into the kitchen. The kitchen ladies don't want her there anyway—they don't forgive her for withholding sweets from them, and never did get over the way she dismissed Fernand Luverne when she took over the bakery. In fact, they hardly speak to her. (No one, not even your sister, can hold a grudge the way the French do.)

I might've been at a loss to explain how Madame Bertrand could possibly be stealing supplies, when she so plainly comes and goes without ever seeing so much as a roll of gauze. But your sister has turned me into a suspicious person, I'm afraid, and I knew at once who to suspect—young Gilbert, the cook's helper who carries the cart in and out.

The supplies had to be hidden in that jumble of dirty linens and baskets. I just knew it. But how was I to intercept them?

Should I follow Gilbert and apprehend him in the act of thievery?

Should I find some pretense to rummage through the dirty linens just before Madame Bertrand arrives?

Or should I simply waylay her in the street on her way back to the cake shop and insist on inspecting her cart?

At that moment, I did nothing. I waited until that evening and consulted your sister.

She told me in no uncertain terms what I was to do, which was: none of the above.

"Do not allow yourself to be distracted by the kitchen boy," she told me. "He's a petty thief, trying to put a little money in his pocket. That's not the real crime."

"Isn't it?" I asked, still failing to grasp Norma's idea. The theft, after all, is what cost me my job. I find I often don't understand what Norma's driving at (did you ever have that problem with her?), but in this case she explained it clearly enough.

"The real crime is the smuggling of the supplies out of France," she said. "That's why we want to catch her. Keep an eye on things at the hospital, and if you can, make sure that the scheme works as you suspect it does. But don't interfere. We must intercept her on the way to the post office."

Well! This gave the mission a new dimension. It had not occurred to me to think of the sending of the supplies as the greater crime, as I was still imagining Madame Bertrand shipping medicine to her ailing sister or to an entire ailing village.

Norma, however, had discovered something else.

Actually, it isn't what she discovered, but what she hasn't discovered. Norma is the only one among us who speaks French well enough to go around and interrogate the villagers about Madame Bertrand's deceased brother. She hasn't spoken to everyone yet—as I said, her duties keep her away from dawn to well after dark—but so far, no one she's interviewed recalls him mentioning a sister in Belgium or Toulouse, or, for that matter, any relations at all. They had the general impression that his break with his family had been an unhappy one, but none of them even recalled how they knew that much. Monsieur Bertrand was such a light-hearted man, so companionable, and so pleased with his friends and his livelihood, that it simply never occurred to any of them to bring up old unpleasantness and demand to know more about it. Even his old friend and helper, Fernand, knew nothing of his family.

They all admitted to being surprised when Madame Bertrand turned up, but she was so disagreeable that her presence only confirmed, in a general way, what they'd assumed all along about his family—that he'd split from them years ago, for good reason.

None of them recall who summoned her after his death. Norma has several more people to interview. Meanwhile, we are to treat the sister in Belgium as fictitious, and to proceed with the understanding that property of the United States Army and the American Red Cross is being shipped out of France for an unknown and possibly nefarious purpose.

Having settled that, I went back to work. It was not, I'm sorry to say, at all difficult to catch young Gilbert in the act. The only difficult part was in restraining myself from stopping him and turning him in.

I would guess Gilbert to be about twelve or thirteen—young enough to be treated as a child or a younger brother by the nurses, but old enough to put in a day's work. He carries trays upstairs and sometimes delivers them to the wards when the orderlies are short-handed. He comes again to take the trays away, and of course he does any sort of errand requested by the cooks. In this way he is in and among us constantly. It is a testament to how swift, quiet, and unassuming he is that I had never before noticed him.

This is obviously a very good quality in a thief.

I followed him when I could, and so did Betty (we have decided not to tell the other nurses about Gilbert for fear they'll bungle our operation—listen to me! I sound like Norma), but as you know we have our duties and cannot trail along behind him all day.

Nonetheless, after a few days of spying, I did catch him pocketing a jar of antiseptic from a nurse's cart. He thought he was alone in a corridor, but I had ducked into a closet only seconds before, as he came around the corner with his load of used trays and dishes. He was quite some distance away, but there was no mistaking it: he saw the cart, sidled up to it, and reached out quick as you please to snatch a jar and tuck it under his shirt. Had I been walking by him on some errand of my own, with my mind on my business, I might not have noticed at all, he was so swift and light about it.

I've yet to see him hide a parcel among Madame Bertrand's linens and baskets, but Norma tells me to be patient. We're so very close.

If I had more news I'd give it, but as you can imagine, I'm consumed with this case every waking hour (and every sleeping hour, for I dream about it most nights). How did you ever turn your attention to anything else when you were in pursuit of a criminal? I find I don't want to eat or sleep or say a word to anyone. I just want to catch my crook.

Tendrement—
Aggie

NORMA TO CONSTANCE

September 26, 1918

Dear Constance,

Madame Bertrand has been apprehended. I'm sorry that Aggie didn't get to do the honors herself, but the opportunity was there and I had to act.

The difficulty has been in catching Madame Bertrand on her way to the post office with packages addressed to the so-called sister in Belgium. The obvious solution is one I'm sure you've thought of, which is to involve the postal master in our scheme, but we simply couldn't trust him not to gossip.

Even worse, he might have gone to the town constable, unable to resist the excitement of bringing the police in on this bit of intrigue. I'm quite sure Madame Bertrand would've spied the police before they spied her. This is a practiced criminal we're up against.

So we had to wait until she happened to go out of her shop with her packages. The trouble was that she never went at the same time of day. The post office closes at four, and Aggie and I rarely return from our duties until after seven.

I just happened to have reason to be in town yesterday— some nonsense about the mayor issuing a proclamation thanking our unit for its service. (You can be sure I told him to forget all about it. We want not a word of gratitude until the war is won, and even then, we don't deserve it, for we've done nothing for France that she wouldn't do for us.) Nonetheless, I was ordered to collect the medal and told not to return without it, so I had no choice.

I made it my business to pass through the town square both coming and going from the mayor's office, and was rewarded with the sight of Madame Bertrand stepping out of her shop, locking it behind her, and teetering over to the post office with her arms full of packages.

I didn't hesitate but ran right into her, knocking her down and scattering her boxes. I managed to put a hand right through one of the packages and to roll on top of another, which is to say that I came away covered in cake. Madame Bertrand went down on one hip and might've sprained something. Those cobblestones are unforgiving.

This prevented her from jumping up and pushing me away. While she floundered on the ground, groaning and sputtering, I bustled about and did my best impression of a careless and apologetic American. I made it look like I was trying to gather up the packages and put them back together, but of course what I was doing was reaching right inside those cakes and retrieving the stolen bottles and vials.

A crowd had gathered by then, including any number of young soldiers eager to help a pair of ladies in distress. A constable approached, too, and this time I had a use for him.

Madame Bertrand was by now sitting up and accepting the attention of a village girl. It took her a minute to look around at all the faces staring down at her and to see plainly that it was I who had run her down. Her eyes traveled down to my hands, which were outstretched to show her the crumb-covered bottles.

"These rolled right out of the package," I told her. "Are they yours? They look just like American medicine bottles." I wiped one clean and saw Aggie's inventory numbers. "How on earth did you come by them?"

I said all this in English first, as if I'd forgotten that Madame Bertrand spoke only French, but in truth I was doing it to catch the attention of the American soldiers. Then, as if remembering my mistake, I repeated it all in French, for the benefit not only of Madame Bertrand but the town constable as well.

Then I added (stating the obvious, but people can be slow), "They seem to have been buried inside your cakes. Who on earth wants a cake filled with pills and potions?"

"Pills and potions" sounds silly and lacks specificity, I know, but I was trying to pretend that I didn't already know exactly what was in every bottle.

Madame Bertrand was too flustered to say a word and (wisely, from her point of view) let her eyes flutter and her chin wobble, and then she fell back in a fine imitation of a fainting spell.

A soldier was now rummaging through the other packages. Between the two of us we fished out twenty bottles in all, mostly vaccines and antiseptics, plus the odd bottle of whatever young Gilbert had managed to snatch—aspirins, a packet of sleeping powder. This explains why Aggie found almost everything missing in small quantities: when he couldn't find what Madame Bertrand had requested, he simply took what he could get.

There was nothing left for me to do but to have a quiet word with the highest-ranking American within earshot, who happened to be a captain in the engineering school. I first told him (and a British officer, for good measure, as the British have been here so much longer and take a proprietary interest in any sort of wrongdoing) that the American hospital was under investigation over missing supplies very much like these. Then I said the same, in French, to the constable. The three of them started haggling over questions of jurisdiction, with me acting as interpreter as they were speaking at cross-purposes and in languages unintelligible to each other.

None seemed to wonder where the supplies were going, so I slipped that question into my translations, to make it appear that they each had thought of it themselves. Suddenly the ruined packages were of a great deal more interest, the mailing labels scrutinized, and the postmaster summoned.

I didn't want to give them too much more to grapple with —really, the three were having such trouble putting the puzzle together, having originally thought they were coming to rescue two ladies in distress and finding it difficult to turn their minds around to a criminal investigation—but I did manage to drop in a question about the apparent recipient of the supplies.

"Madame Bertrand mentioned a sister in Belgium," I told the constable, as Madame Bertrand slept on (a doctor had by this time been sent for, and I knew I could count on him to put an end to the play-acting with either smelling salts or a painful injection of anything at all), "but no one seems to recall Monsieur Bertrand mentioning even the sister we have before us, much less a second one in Belgium."

There. It is now a matter for the police.

As ever,
Norma

AGGIE TO CONSTANCE

September 28, 1918

Dear Constance,

This will be brief, as my days at the hospital are much longer now, but for good reason: I've returned at last to my original post! I'm sorry to say that the supply room was in terrible disarray without me. I've put it back in good order, but it will take me a while to sort out the disastrous record-keeping my replacement left behind.

The next installment in our little adventure, Norma insists, is mine to tell about, but first I must say that I can hardly believe that Norma tackled Madame Bertrand single-handedly. I will regret for the rest of my days that I wasn't there to see it. Norma is quite literally the talk of the town: everyone speaks of *la petite Américaine culottée* and wonders how the Germans must be faring against our boys, if this is what our girls are capable of. When I say that I share a room with her, I am looked upon as a celebrity myself.

Of course her act of daring took place directly in front of the newspaper editor's window, which is positioned quite deliberately so he won't miss a thing. And in fact he didn't. Try to imagine a rotund little man in a battered felt hat and a pipe perpetually between his teeth, rushing out with his shoes barely slipped on (he's known to pace about barefoot when composing his prose), the laces flapping and the pages of his note-book blowing about in the wind. The newspaper possesses but one camera, and the photographer was out at the train station at that moment to make portraits of some visiting

French officers, so I'm afraid the incident is left to our imagination and the colorful prose of the newspaper editor.

I insisted that Norma translate the story for me, and I've copied out her translation for you, enclosed. I'm sure you'd have no trouble reading the French version, but I pasted my only copy into my diary before I thought of sending it to you. Norma tells me that you've been in the papers hundreds of times, and all over the country to boot. This is but one notice in a village paper, but I know you'll enjoy it, and it will tell you something of Madame Bertrand's fate, too.

As for what happened next at the hospital, I will admit this: I don't have it in me to do any sort of policing. Norma insisted that I point my finger at the boy who aided Madame Bertrand with her thievery, but I just didn't have the heart to do it. I can only imagine that Gilbert is desperately poor, and eager to please, and surely has no way of understanding the import of what he's done. To him, it probably seems like the Americans came to town with endless riches, and that a little bottle of this or that couldn't possibly be missed.

Oh, Constance, I wish you could see him: more child than man, with dark hair in little ringlets around his face, and a soft, shy smile. He's no criminal, I'm sure of it.

But Norma convinced me that something had to be done about him. We don't know how much longer this war will last, she argued, or what other schools or offices or hospitals might be established here. Is he to be allowed to steal from all of them? Who will catch him next time, and what might the punishment be?

If I turn him in, she said, I can make a plea for mercy. There might be no one to make such a plea next time.

It was only this possibility—that he might someday do far greater harm to others, and come to far greater harm himself —that convinced me to do what I did. I had to act quickly, as word of Norma's run-in with Madame Bertrand was circulating around the village, and he would soon find out that his co-conspirator had been caught.

Here, then, is what happened: Norma, after her tussle with Madame Bertrand, picked herself up, dusted herself off, and went straight to Fernand Luverne to tell him that the American hospital would be in need of a bread delivery in the morning, as Madame Bertrand had been arrested. Fernand was delighted to hear it. Having worked in the bakery for so many years, he knew exactly how to step in and get the hospital's order ready. Although Madame Bertrand had changed the locks when she took over the bakery, the village locksmith was a friend of Monsiéur Bertrand's and of Fernand's, and didn't hesitate to open the bakery for him.

The very next morning, after sitting up most of the night talking it over with Norma, I arrived early to intercept the bread delivery. I asked Mrs. Clayton to come with me, as our thief was about to be unmasked. I had no way of knowing what Gilbert knew about the events of the previous day, but this was my only chance, so I took it.

Mrs. Clayton and I were lingering nearby when Fernand arrived with the bread delivery, to be met by a panic-stricken young Gilbert who had only just begun, a few moments earlier, to hear conflicting rumors about what had befallen Madame Bertrand. He was standing with his pile of dirty linens, empty baskets, and pilfered bottles, turning this way and that, not sure what to do.

Fernand walked in and made ready to accept the little bundle. Gilbert started to back away, mumbling excuses. I knew then that we had him. (I must stop at this point and tell you that in the seconds just before his capture, a remarkable feeling of calm came over me, and I felt somehow able to see all sides of the situation at once and my role in it, as if I were a bird gliding overhead. You must know that sensation.)

I nodded at Mrs. Clayton—we'd been lurking in a corner, pretending to sort through a bin of potatoes, which no nurse would ever have reason to do but somehow we didn't attract notice—and the two of us moved in on him at once. The poor creature was so terrified that he just crumbled. The armload of contraband fell to the floor.

There was a great deal of yelling and scuffling after that, but I wasn't a part of it. I just clutched those stolen supplies to my chest and took the first tranquil breath I'd enjoyed in weeks. At last, this matter could be put entirely to rest.

Nothing's been put to rest for Madame Bertrand, however, as you'll see from the attached.

I wasn't as brief as I meant to be. There's such a great deal to tell!

Tendrement—
Aggie

(ENCLOSED)

SCUFFLE IN THE PLAZA LEADS TO ARREST

SEPTEMBER 26 — It appeared to be an ordinary trip to the post office for Madame Bertrand, who last year assumed ownership of Patisserie Confiserie following the death of her brother, Monsieur Bertrand.

She crossed the plaza carrying an armful of packages and was unsteady on her feet as a result. An American woman stationed here with the United States Army dashed across and collided with Madame Bertrand, sending both the baker and her packages to the ground.

It was soon discovered that the packages contained medical supplies stolen from the American hospital, secreted within the hollow centers of cakes whose ingredients must have been themselves smuggled or stolen, for no one in the village has been able to purchase such confections in months.

The American, who refused to give her name but was identified by others as Mademoiselle Norma Kopp, held aloft the vials and confronted Madame Bertrand. Soon American and French officers gathered about, and were joined by Constable DeCamps.

"I know these to be stolen," declared Mademoiselle Kopp. "A nurse at the hospital has been wrongfully accused, but here is the culprit."

Madame Bertrand, having fainted, gave no reply.

A doctor from the American hospital was summoned and revived the baker. She insisted on being escorted home, but Constable DeCamps would not have it. The postmaster, who was also by now on hand, told those gathered that Madame Bertrand had regularly been in the habit of sending packages to the same address in Belgium.

"There exists the possibility," Postmaster Simond said, "that Madame Bertrand has engaged for some time in the practice of smuggling stolen medicines out of the hospital, and using the French post to do it, while simultaneously depriving the people of this village of such confections and baked goods as might otherwise have been available to them, and were available, prior to the death of her brother."

Following his pronouncement, there ensued a disagreement between the constable, the American officers, and the doctor over who ought to take custody of Madame Bertrand. The constable won, having agreed (after some urging by the doctor) to bring in a nurse to sit with her all night.

She was taken immediately to jail, requiring the assistance of two American soldiers to walk upright, and remains there still.

The American officers have sent telegrams to their counterparts in Belgium to investigate the identity of the sister who received the packages. The French officers, preferring to conduct their own investigation, have done the same.

What is known at this time is that Monsieur Bertrand never mentioned a sister in Belgium. For that matter, he never mentioned a sister in Toulouse, where Madame Bertrand is said to have lived before she was summoned here following her brother's death.

It is also not known, at this time, who wrote to Madame Bertrand to tell her that her brother had died. Every man interviewed thus far could name an-other man who must've been the one to notify her, but in actual matter of fact, none of them did.

Miss Kopp was to receive commendation from the hospital for her heroism in unmasking the scheme, but she has refused it, claiming that she merely stum-bled over a cobblestone and doesn't merit an award for that.

CONSTANCE TO NORMA

September 28, 1918

Dear Norma,

We haven't had a letter from you in ages, but it's the same for everyone here. As the fighting grows worse, the mail slows down. Our men seem to be taking the upper hand—is it pos-sible? Dare I to hope that we'll prevail in the Argonne?

We're desperate for news from either of you, and particu-larly eager to hear that Aggie has been cleared of wrongdoing. As long as there are no urgent telegrams from either of you, we'll hope for the best.

The enclosed is from Fleurette, who wanted to put to-gether a package of whatever pretty and perfumed items she could come by. I hope Aggie can make good use of them. I can only imagine what a day in her hospital must be like now, with wounded men coming in droves. We just read about a train loaded with injured soldiers that had to be off-loaded during a rainstorm, the men in their stretchers simply dropped into the mud, face-up to the rain, because of a switching problem and a need to change trains. I shudder to think what condition they must be in when they arrive.

I don't know how a bit of hand cream makes up for any of that, but we're happy to send what we can. I hope this goes through — I hear they're limiting packages to the soldiers, and I don't know if the same restrictions apply to you. You'll see that Bessie baked another trench cake, this one with apple preserves. Do you remember last year, when we picked them at the farm? You can tell Aggie all about our gnarled old apple tree, and the apples that are too tart to eat and must practically be drowned in sugar and cinnamon. We've told the girls at the dairy that they can have this year's crop, if they can figure out what to do with them. I suspect they'll get fed to the pigs.

Did you hear that they've opened the draft to men aged forty-one to forty-five? You can be sure that Francis ran down to the draft board the minute it opened. He was not the only one: it was a little heart-breaking, really, to see so many eager men, most of them fathers and husbands, practically climbing all over themselves to get to France.

We don't think there's any possibility that Francis will be sent — you know he wheezes when he climbs a flight of stairs now, and I doubt he's run a mile in twenty years — so Bessie only smiled and encouraged him. She saw it as a harmless fantasy and baked a particularly good Saturday pie to celebrate his enrollment. She makes the crust out of broken crackers, fills it with scraps of this and that, covers the whole in beaten eggs (from our own hens, who continue to thrive in her backyard) and any cheese she can put her hands on.

It's a far cry from our old Sunday dinners—do you remember the breasts of duck? The roasted goose?—but we devour it. It's hard to imagine that we'll ever go back to eating the way we used to before the war. Everything's so plain and simple now.

    Yours,
    Constance

NORMA TO CONSTANCE

September 30, 1918

Dear Constance,

I've strictly forbidden Aggie from writing another word about her situation, as it is no longer a matter of petty theft, and might well be pertinent to war-time activity. I'd be surprised if the censors have allowed any of it to go through, but I cannot risk another word falling into German hands. Suffice it to say that Aggie has been reinstated in her position and the matter resolved to everyone's satisfaction.

Now we go back to work. You must see the same news from the front that we do. Our men are advancing, but the effort is punishing and the casualties high. It isn't unusual for Aggie to work all day and all night, then take four hours to sleep, only to return for another shift.

The wounded who reach Aggie's hospital are the ones considered gravely injured but likely to survive. (The men who are certain to die are left at the hopeless wards near the front, as there is no use in transporting them this far.) Aggie's patients are generally expected to pull through, but at a cost: an alarming number of them are coming back not just blind, but missing most of their faces. We now have a rope strung up around the hospital and down the main street so that they might hold on to it and walk a bit when they are able. We've grown accustomed to the sight of strong, young men with heads wrapped entirely in bandages. Some of them are learning to be masseurs for the mutilated men.

My work is a picnic in comparison. I'm at the fort from dawn to dusk, hovering over the incubators. We can't hatch pigeons fast enough these days. It has only just now occurred to my commanders that it's a waste of the Army's resources for me to walk three miles each way to work. I won't be run around in an auto, but I've been given a trap and a good horse, which I keep at the stables behind the hospital.

As ever,
Norma

AGGIE TO CONSTANCE AND FLEURETTE (UNSENT)

October 4, 1918

Dear Constance and Fleurette,

Norma has once again refused to let me write to you and tell of all she's done, because it concerns a military matter. I'm putting it down on paper anyway, but at her insistence I won't mail it. I've made her promise to put this letter in your hands herself when she returns home. I only wish I could be there to see your faces when you find out!

Constance, Fleurette, Bessie, Francis: Your sister has caught a spy! A real spy, a dangerous criminal, a woman sought by the French authorities for two years.

It took a bit of time and a great deal of detective work on the part of the local constables and the various British, French, and American officers who got involved, but here's what we have learned: Madame Bertrand—which is not her real name, but only one of many names by which she was known—has been carrying out her treasonous scheme by turning up in one town after another where some Allied military unit established its home, be it British, American, Canadian, Australian, and so forth. She would look for an opportunity to insinuate herself, and would then take advantage of the foreigners' naivete to secure some kind of position, even though she was a newcomer with no sort of reputation or references. She has variously posed as a nurse, a seamstress, a baker (as you know), and she even once dressed as a man and pretended to be a chaplain. She would then proceed to steal what she could for the enemy: valuable information, medical supplies, ammunition, and even fuel.

The authorities have been looking for her for two years, but she always managed to slip away and turn up in the next town under a new name, with a new disguise. This is the first time she's appeared more or less as herself, not bothering with a wig, glasses, or any other contrivance that might hide her identity. Perhaps she thought that her last, best disguise was to simply wear none at all, and to stay on here until the end of the war.

It was a stroke of luck on her part that Monsieur Bertrand had only just passed away and his shop was there for the taking. It's a testament to her skill in deception that she was so readily accepted as his sister.

None of the local authorities had any idea that a lady spy was on the loose and that they ought to watch out for her. This is not a slight against the police in this village: you must understand that even here, so safely removed from the front, war can be awfully chaotic. We're practically swimming in paperwork, much of it outdated, damaged, or simply unintelligible. It's easy for official alerts of any kind to go unnoticed.

You must be wondering where, exactly, those pills and vials were going, and for what purpose. I'm afraid we aren't being told much, but this is quite a small village and rumors do travel. The most credible idea is that she's been shipping supplies to a handler in Ypres, it being the only city in Belgium not occupied by the Germans, and that from there they'd be handed over to Fritz quite easily.

Imagine: our medicines were being stolen to keep German troops alive, just as our soldiers are being deployed to kill them! Of course, I wouldn't deny an aspirin or a clean bandage to some poor German boy who wants nothing more than to see the fighting end and to return home, just as we do. Nonetheless, it's the worst sort of betrayal, and everyone in the village is outraged.

Norma is seen as a mastermind around town for uncovering the scheme. She can hardly walk down the street, for all the outstretched hands waiting to shake hers, and the endless expressions of gratitude. Everyone wants to hear her tell the story, although they know every word of it by heart.

Now you know the truth. When you see her again, I hope that you'll greet her as the returning war heroine that she has become. None of us will return home just as we were before we left. This will be truer for Norma, I believe, than for the rest of us.

Tendrement—
Aggie

AGGIE TO CONSTANCE AND FLEURETTE
(UNSENT)

October 12, 1918

Dear Constance and Fleurette,

I've had to resort once more to writing a letter I cannot send, having received only a grunt from Norma in response to my entreaties to pass these pages on to her family upon her return.

Nonetheless—the entire village can talk of little else!

Here is what transpired.

Norma was never satisfied that we'd heard the end of Madame Bertrand's case. After she was arrested and sent away (to some French dungeon or another, we haven't been told), Norma kept puzzling over one question: How is it that Madame Bertrand came to arrive in our village just as Monsieur Bertrand died, and how did she know enough about him to convince the villagers that she was his sister? A spy has ways of finding things out, but—what were her ways?

Norma said very little to me about this. She ruminated over it—your sister is quite a ruminator—and from time to time I caught her muttering to herself and scribbling something down in a little note-book. She would disappear in the evenings, offering no explanation, and come home hours later, with her brow furrowed, her lips pursed, and an even more exasperated air about her than before.

Unbeknownst even to me, her closest confidante, Norma was conducting her own investigation.

She was going around to the hotels and looking—sometimes with the proprietor's permission, and sometimes without it—for Madame Bertrand's signature in the guest registration book. Her idea was that Madame Bertrand must've stayed in a hotel for at least a few nights before taking possession of Monsieur Bertrand's apartment, and perhaps someone else at that hotel might've remembered something.

It took Norma all week, given the reluctance of hotel desk clerks to open their registers, but eventually she examined every page of every register, starting the day Monsieur Bertrand died, and continuing for three weeks thereafter, well past the date Madame Bertrand took over the bakery.

Not a single register in town had her signature in its pages.

Norma inquired of every widow with a spare room for rent, or anyone at all who might be known to take in boarders. Everyone, of course, knows Madame Bertrand, and no one recalls renting a room to her.

Did Norma give up? You know your sister! Of course she didn't.

After stewing over it for several nights (remember, I had no idea any of this was going on), she went back to the hotels and looked again at their registers. This time, she looked at the weeks prior to Monsieur Bertrand's death. And this time she found Madame Bertrand—under an assumed name and disguised as a man.

She recognized the signature only because she recalled the handwriting on those packages bound for Belgium. Can you imagine, remembering a thing like that?

While you're holding your breath—because surely by now you've guessed at the truth—let me quickly tell you that the constable had saved the ruined packages from that fateful day when Norma and Madame Bertrand collided on the square. However, they'd been sent off as evidence when Madame Bertrand herself was taken away. Norma therefore had no way to prove, with absolute certainty, that the writing matched.

Fortunately, there were all manner of receipt-books, ledgers, recipes, and so forth in the bakery, which was once again being operated by Monsieur Bertrand's old friend, Fernand. Norma was able to persuade him to show the receipt-books to the town constable, so that the signature in the hotel register might be compared against Madame Bertrand's own handwriting.

And only after she had done that—only after she was entirely certain herself, and the constable was likewise satisfied—did she tell what she knew, and explain what it meant.

If Madame Bertrand arrived before Monsieur Bertrand died, then it was almost certainly she who killed him.

I don't know how Norma managed to convince the constable and the coroner—well, I do know, it's because she's absolutely indomitable in three languages, only one of which was necessary in this case—but she put the evidence before them and insisted that they take another look at the circumstances surrounding Monsieur Bertrand's death.

The coroner in this village serves also as a justice of the peace, druggist, and a few other small official roles whose exact meanings are obscure to me. He hasn't had a great many suspicious deaths on his hands over the years, and his records are, as Norma puts it, insufficient. Nonetheless he did agree to open his files and even permitted Norma to look over his shoulder.

The coroner's notes, of course, gave no suggestion of foul play. The baker was found dead in his shop at eight o'clock on a Tuesday evening, after he failed to meet his friends for their usual game of *crapette*. Fernand and another man went over to the shop and found it locked and dark within. Fernand saw, through the window, that Monsieur Bertrand had collapsed on the floor behind the counter. After some frantic fumbling for a key, he rushed inside but was unable to revive him.

The coroner arrived ten minutes later and declared that the baker had been dead only a few hours. There were no marks on him nor any sign of a break-in or any kind of struggle. His difficulty with diabetes being well-known, the corner made the entirely reasonable conclusion that he'd slipped into a diabetic coma from which he did not recover.

There was only one line in his report that might mean anything at all. The coroner had noted that it was possible that an attempt had been made to bring him around with frangipane. Norma asked what led him to make that remark. The coroner could not at first remember, but then said that he'd noticed the sweet smell of almonds and assumed Monsieur Bertrand had taken a bite of some small delicacy, in an effort to save himself.

It was immediately apparent to both Norma and the coroner what he'd missed—although it was not so apparent to me, when Norma told me about it later.

That almond scent could've been cyanide.

The thing to do would've been to examine the body more closely. There was, perhaps, a test they could've run at the chemist's.

Or, at the very least, someone that night could've looked in the bakery case to see if anything made with almonds had been on offer.

But nothing of the kind was done. There had been no reason at all to suspect a murder. And in case you're wondering, Monsieur Bertrand has been buried for over a year and there is no talk of exhuming him.

You can only imagine the lecture Norma gave those two Frenchmen. Always suspect! she said. *Toujours!* They've never had such a scolding, I'm certain of it.

The plan—hatched between Norma, the coroner, and the constable, in secrecy—was to notify those parties now engaged in trying Madame Bertrand for treason that she was under a further cloud of suspicion. It seems entirely likely that the treason charges will punish her for life, if not put her to death. None of us are sure if a murder charge makes any difference at all at this point. But the evidence has been put forward, and we hope that justice will be done.

I said that they hatched this plan in secrecy. Norma, the constable, and the coroner all thought it best to never reveal what they knew, so as not to agitate the villagers or cause further heartache to Fernand and Monsieur Bertrand's many other friends. Besides, they can't be certain, and perhaps they never will be.

There might've been some idea, on the part of the coroner and the constable, that they would like their own reputations protected as well. After all, the murder had happened on their watch, and had only been uncovered through the efforts of an American girl. *Quel embarras!*

Nonetheless, there are no secrets in a village this size. Within a day or two, everyone knew. Even in the midst of this war, with so many unjust and cruel deaths, they're taking this one especially hard. There's quite a bit more outrage over the possibility that Madame Bertrand murdered their beloved baker than there was over the very real, demonstrated fact that she'd been smuggling supplies to the enemy. What does it matter to the people of this town if a few Germans get vaccinated? But to think that Monsieur Bertrand might still be here today, beaming from behind his counter, dusted in flour, the name of every customer on his lips and a kind word for all —in these terrible times, that is too much to bear. They are in mourning all over again.

And quite honestly—I am not exaggerating—they put your sister just below General Pershing on their list of favorite Americans. You wouldn't believe the dinner invitations we've had! Norma tries to decline them, but if I have anything to say about it, we go. In the last few nights, we've feasted at a dozen tables. For the first time I think I might return home stouter than when I left. Who can say that, after a year of war rations?

Norma has just returned and is horrified to see how many pages I've written. Must close—

Tendrement—

Aggie

CONSTANCE TO NORMA AND AGGIE

October 20, 1918

Dear Norma and Aggie,

I had four letters from you all at once yesterday. What a time we had at Francis's house, reading through each thrilling installment of the cake shop mystery! Fleurette saw the theatrical possibilities at once and jumped to her feet, brandishing the first letter of the bunch, and reading it aloud in the most dramatic fashion. The children were all too eager to play the parts of the town drunks. Bessie tried to put a stop to that, it being an entirely unsuitable sort of play-acting for children, but they were so charming and quick-witted about it that we all succumbed. Frankie Jr. teetered around dizzily, offering aspirin bottles to Fleurette, and Lorraine played the other one—the talkative one—bickering in the corner with a houseplant. The plant was meant to represent the one who didn't speak at all except for the occasional "incoherent shouting." (The shouting was, fortunately, left out of the performance.)

In the next act, Bessie took the part of Mrs. Clayton, and I was conscripted to play Madame Bertrand. No cakes were knocked to the ground in our reenactment, however. A stack of pillows had to do.

Well done, both of you! It's an absolute triumph of investigative work, what you've accomplished. Justice has been served, and a mystery solved. The fact that you provided us with an evening's entertainment is merely—I'm sorry, but Bessie insisted that I put this in—the icing on the cake.

Encore, encore!

Constance

CONSTANCE

Paterson, New Jersey

CONSTANCE TO BIELASKI

October 22, 1918

Dear Mr. Bielaski,

You've heard from the police already, but their report is incomplete.

Early Monday morning, at 4:10 a.m., Mrs. Wilmington left her apartment and I followed. She wore a heavy cloak over her coat, which is not her custom.

She walked briskly and intentionally to the stables next to the train station. As you might expect, the stables are hardly in use any more, but a few horses remain. The stable was dark and unguarded.

Mrs. Wilmington stood across the street for some time, watching the entrance, which consists of three wide barn doors with nothing but a half-gate across each.

All was quiet. One could dimly see the horses in their stalls, perhaps five in all.

After standing for some five or six minutes, she walked around to the back of the stable, and I followed. As there was no moon, it was easy enough to stay in the shadows. There was a rusted rail-car nearby, where I could linger undetected.

The rear of the stables faces onto the train tracks. It's not unusual for horses in the back stalls to push their heads out of a row of rough-cut windows and observe the rail-cars going by. When they heard her coming, a few of them staggered to their feet and looked around for her, perhaps expecting a treat from a stable boy.

There Mrs. Wilmington stopped. She patted the nose of one horse and walked on. At the next, she held out a gloved hand and allowed the horse to sniff it.

She then proceeded to the third—a heavy chestnut draft horse, from what I could observe—and reached under her cloak. I had to inch a bit closer to see, but there was no mistaking the object she withdrew.

It was the ceramic figurine.

I couldn't believe she would risk smashing it and attracting attention, but there was no one around. The freight trains run at all hours of the night, and there's always a whistle or a rumble of a train on the tracks. Mrs. Wilmington did just as I would have done and waited for the next train to approach. With the noise of the engine as cover, she dropped the figurine and smashed it, gently, against a rock. It fell easily apart, disgorging its stuffing of sawdust.

She already wore rubber gloves—she must've left the house wearing them. She bent over carefully and picked two glass vials from among the sawdust and broken bits of ceramic.

I'd seen enough. I couldn't wait any longer. Once the vials were open, I had no idea what poison might be released.

There was no way to sneak up on her. Speed and surprise were my only advantages. I ran as swiftly and silently as I could and grabbed her from behind. She gasped in surprise but kept hold of the vials.

"Drop them," I said, and was rewarded with an elbow to my gut.

I squeezed her a little tighter and moved one arm up around her neck. "Federal agent. I'm arresting you."

She stomped on my foot—a smart trick, ordinarily, but her boots were no match for mine—and I kicked her in the back of the knee and threw her down. She did what any good saboteur would do and tossed the vials as far as she could. In the struggle she had little choice as to her aim. It was my good luck that both sailed right into the barn and I heard no sound of breaking glass.

I kept a knee in her back and put her in handcuffs. She groaned and complained, in German, about her shoulder. I spoke directly back to her in her mother tongue.

"Um was für ein Gift handelt es sich?" I asked. ("What's the poison?")

She only sputtered. I'd given her a face full of dirt and she couldn't wipe it off. I twisted her arm as hard as I dared, but she only gritted her teeth.

"Never mind, we'll test them ourselves," I said. I had with me a box of matches. I expected to find a lantern within the stable and I did. It hadn't been lit in some time and the oil was nearly gone. Mrs. Wilmington didn't make it easy for me —she struggled and kicked and fought to get away, until I was obliged to push her to the ground and put her face-down on the stable floor. It's an undignified position, but one she could've avoided had she been more co-operative. I then settled myself on top of Mrs. Wilmington's recumbent figure and went to work on the lantern.

Once I had a little light, it didn't take long to find the vials. Both had landed softly on a bed of straw, and neither had been trampled by a horse. (The horses, by the way, observed all of this in stoic silence. A New Jersey carriage horse is not surprised by anything, not even an attempt on its life.)

I didn't like to carry the vials and had no secure case in which to transport them. With great trepidation I wrapped them in Mrs. Wilmington's rubber gloves and put them in my pocket, then pulled Mrs. Wilmington to her feet. I worried all the way back to her apartment that she would throw me off my feet and smash the vials, but covering her in manure and moldy straw seemed to subdue and humiliate her sufficiently. She gave me little trouble as I marched her home.

Miss Bradshaw was rooming not far from the train station, so along the way I stopped to rouse her. (Fortunately, her room faces the street. A few pebbles tossed up to the window woke her.) She dressed quickly and came along. It wasn't until we rounded the corner and the Wilmingtons' residence came into view that Mrs. Wilmington put up a fight again, digging her heels in so that I was forced to drag her. She began to shout, obviously hoping to wake the neighbors.

"Get your hands off me!" she yelled, followed by "Where are you taking me?"—intending, perhaps, to give the impression that I was carrying her off, not bringing her home.

When we gave no answer, she tried again. "My husband will have you arrested!"

That was enough to cause the lights to come on in a few windows. We were in front of her apartment building by now. I rummaged around in her pockets for a key.

"Mrs. Wilmington, I'm an agent of the Bureau of Investigation," I said, as quietly and calmly as I could under the circumstances. "You're under arrest. Shouting will do you no good."

Apparently I failed to convince her, because she screamed, "Thief! Help! Thief! Police!"

I will never understand a criminal who screams for the police, but as you know, they sometimes do. By now the neighbors were awake, and I knew the police had been summoned.

Officer Sweeney's report begins here. It's accurate insofar as he claims that I refused to relinquish Mrs. Wilmington. She was in my custody and I wasn't about to hand her over until he understood the situation, which he did not. Miss Bradshaw had by then produced our badges, but he refused to look at them and was treating us like three disorderly ladies in a late-night brawl.

It is not true, however, that I assaulted Officer Sweeney. I merely prevented him from placing Miss Bradshaw under arrest. He might have stumbled backwards into a brick wall in the process, but I hardly put a hand on him.

We had by then located Mrs. Wilmington's key. I persuaded Officer Sweeney to accompany us upstairs, where Mr. Wilmington waited. The possibility that another man might sort out this mess seemed to appeal to him. The four of us went upstairs fairly calmly.

As you know by now—and of course, I did not know, or I would've pulled Fleurette out of the house—Mr. Wilmington had been lying abed for two days with aches, fever, and a cough. Fleurette suspected influenza but didn't think to mention to me that she'd been looking after him, as Mrs. Wilmington paid him little attention.

He was hardly able to speak or to understand questions put to him. I was of course worried that Mrs. Wilmington had poisoned him before she went to the barn. I sent Miss Bradshaw into the hall to call for an ambulance.

Officer Sweeney had by then examined our badges in the light and begun to wonder if we were telling the truth. When Miss Bradshaw returned, he went out to telephone the station. That's the call that eventually made its way to you. I apologize for disturbing your sleep, although I don't suppose you get much rest these days. Under your orders I kept possession of the vials until your agent was dispatched to retrieve them.

By then, two more officers had arrived, followed shortly by an ambulance for Mr. Wilmington. Mrs. Wilmington was detained in the hallway by another officer. Miss Bradshaw and I insisted on accompanying the police on a thorough search of the apartment. That took some convincing. Officer Sweeney, still nursing a grudge and a bruised elbow from our tussle in the street, insisted that his men were more than capable of searching for evidence.

"That's fine," I said. "I suppose you've already put your hands on the book, then."

"This place is full of books," he said. "I'm not hauling off a library."

"She's a spy," I told him. "She wrote her codes in book cipher. Do you know the book?"

He wouldn't admit it, but he did not.

"And certain of her undergarments are soaked in secret ink. Have you been through her lingerie?"

"I most certainly have not," he said, with some pride. Apparently even lady criminals deserve their privacy in Paterson.

With that, Miss Bradshaw and I simply pushed our way past him and proceeded to search the house, gathering up *Dr. Chase's Recipes*, along with a dictionary, an atlas, a guide to the trees of New England, and a few other titles that seemed unusual, in case she used more than one book for her messages. We also collected notes and papers of all kinds, many of which were in Mr. Wilmington's hand, but I would not put it above Mrs. Wilmington to use her husband's correspondence as cover for her own secret messages.

We looked inside every kitchen canister and shook any object, however small, that might conceal a vial within it. As we were looking for anything that might contain messages written in secret ink, I seized three old cookbooks with notes jotted down between the recipes—some in English, and some in German. I can only assume that they come from both Mr. Wilmington's family and his wife's. If I wanted to put a note in a place where it would not be disturbed, I'd choose an old family cookbook.

At the conclusion of our search, we accompanied the officers to the police station to see for ourselves that Mrs. Wilmington was to be locked in a cell. (She was by then loudly protesting her innocence and claiming that I'd planted the vials myself, although she was unable to explain what she was doing at the stable.)

Once assured that she was in custody, Miss Bradshaw

and I went to the print shop to make one last search for good measure. We found nothing out of the ordinary. It was by then six in the morning, so I stopped in at home to tell Fleurette that she wouldn't have to report to work at the Wilmingtons'.

I found her feverish and shivering under the covers. It was then that I learned that she'd been nursing Mr. Wilmington.

Both are in the hospital now. I write to you from an uncomfortable wooden chair in the hall that is to be my home until she's released. Both she and Mr. Wilmington are under quarantine, as the vials were found to contain anthrax and glanders, and we don't know if they were exposed. As you know from your call to Dr. Hatch, there isn't a great deal to be done for either disease, short of excising pustules if they appear (and they haven't).

Mrs. Wilmington, of course, is the very picture of health —isn't that always the case with these German spies?—and she swears that no poison of any kind was ever unbottled in the house. (Then again, she swears that she's innocent, so why would I believe a word she says?) She sits in a jail cell in Paterson, isolated from the other inmates, although by the time this report reaches you, she will have been transferred to your custody.

I have more questions than I have ink and paper with which to ask them, but the nurse just walked by with some soup on a tray for Fleurette. I'll go in and try to coax her to take some.

Awaiting your orders.

Yours very truly,

Constance A. Kopp

BIELASKI TO CONSTANCE

October 24, 1918

Dear Miss Kopp,

"Awaiting your orders," she says, while her sister clings to life. Your orders are to stay at Fleurette's bedside until she's ready to walk out under her own power.

Our men in New York have sifted through all the evidence taken from the Wilmingtons' apartment. We found no trace of anthrax or glanders save inside the vials themselves, which raises the hope that Mr. Wilmington and Fleurette are not poisoned but merely ill.

You were right to take her old family cookbook. It yielded a roster of her collaborators in New York. She'd written a list of numbers faintly, in pencil, deep in the gutter of a single page near the back of the book. This time the code corresponded to letters on the page, not words. (For instance, 2.3.4.5 would refer to the second page, third line, fourth word, fifth letter.) Because you'd also snatched up the red-bound edition of *Dr. Chase's*, we were able to read the code and make arrests.

Of the four men named, two matched the descriptions Miss Bradshaw had given of the messengers spotted at the train station and the hotel. The other two had been picked up during that raid at the St. Regis restaurant that started it all. The police had released them, but we found them again easily enough, as the St. Regis had already re-opened its disreputable house in the basement. None of them possessed vials of anthrax or glanders. Unlike Mrs. Wilmington, they are apparently intelligent enough to keep it out of their homes.

Someone's making it in a laboratory, but we don't know who, and they won't say.

We gather that the men were engaged in a plot to destroy livestock, both the horses we send over to France and those still needed here at home on farms. We believe they further hoped to cripple our meat and dairy supply by going after cows, goats, sheep, and the like. If they were successful, they planned to spread disease to humans, particularly around Army camps.

It appears they were experimenting on carriage horses and intended to move out to dairies and farms around the camps next. We've found three stables in New York that have had unexplained deaths among their horses. It continues to astonish me that no one reports those incidents, in spite of notice after notice in the paper, hand-bills posted around stables, and even posters in the street, entreating everyone to report suspicious doings.

As for the men we arrested, we hope to persuade one of them to come over to our side and lead us to whoever gives the orders. So far they resist persuasion. It is nonetheless a victory to have them in our custody. It wouldn't have happened if you hadn't noticed the wife, worked out the book cipher, seized the cookbook, and so on.

Now we await Fleurette's recovery, and Mr. Wilmington's. As I understand it, he's too weak to answer questions. Get in as soon as the doctors will allow and find out what he knows.

Yours very truly,

A. Bruce Bielaski

CONSTANCE TO BIELASKI

October 26, 1918

Dear Mr. Bielaski,

You will have heard from the doctors directly by now, but Fleurette is believed to have been spared the worst. They suspect not anthrax or glanders but quite a severe streptococcal infection turning to scarlet fever in Fleurette's case, and pneumonia in Mr. Wilmington's case.

Fleurette suffers from the worst ulcerated throat I've ever seen. When the doctors tried to lance an ulcer and swab away the pus for a laboratory sample, she kicked and fought as they pried open her mouth. She would've screamed if she could make any sound at all—but right now she can't. She finally surrendered, and sobbed the whole while. It was horrible to watch.

Because she can't speak, I've tried to persuade her to write notes to me—but she won't. She merely nods in agreement or shakes her head in refusal when I ask a question. Beyond that she hasn't a word to say.

She still suffers from a fever, chills, and aches. Her appetite is gone entirely and it's impossible to get anything down that throat. She subsists on a sip now and again of thin broth. Our brother's wife, Bessie, has never met an invalid she couldn't tempt—but even Bessie's puddings, compotes, and stews go untouched.

The doctors tell me that until the fever breaks, the throat won't start to heal.

Of Mr. Wilmington I can say no more than you already know: he was in a far worse state than Fleurette when we found him, and he remains so. If he happens to rally and it appears we can get any kind of statement from him, I'll run right over, even if he's only capable of nods and hand signals. The poor man is allowed no visitors owing to the criminal investigation. I do look in on him from time to time, but he doesn't know I'm there.

As for whether he suspected anything of Mrs. Wilmington —it's entirely possible that he never had any idea. The two of them seemed to lead very separate lives, in a way that is not particularly unusual among married couples. He had his business to run six days a week, and she had charge of the apartment and their domestic affairs. From the little time I spent inside their home, I could see that his study was the center of his life: there was a tray-stand for his supper, a day-bed, and a rack for magazines. I could easily imagine him retreating to that room every evening and saying hardly a word to his wife, nor she to him. It might never have occurred to him to wonder where she went or what she did with her time.

It's maddening to sit in the hospital and wait, but you're right—I can't take another assignment until I see Fleurette on her feet and bound for home.

Yours very truly,
Constance A. Kopp

CONSTANCE TO NORMA

October 28, 1918

Dear Norma,

When you left, you made me promise that I wouldn't spare you any news, no matter how worrisome. I confess that for the last week, I have kept something from you—but it's all right now.

Just as we were wrapping up what turned out to be a rather dramatic case, Fleurette became seriously ill. For a few terrible days, I feared she'd been poisoned. The doctors are now certain that she wasn't. It appears that both she and the man of the house (the house in which our investigation had been taking place) were stricken with a violent streptococcal infection. In the man's case, it turned into pneumonia. In Fleurette, it turned to scarlet fever.

When she came home from her tour a month ago, she was nursing a sore throat. She might've been more ill than she let on, making her susceptible to any infection that came along. Regardless, you are to be assured that she's getting better. She remains in the hospital but is to be released in a few days if she continues to recover.

I'm afraid the infection ravaged her throat. She hasn't spoken a word in days. The doctors assure me that she'll be able to talk again. They encourage her to stay quiet for now and let it heal. She has no interest in corresponding by note but will nod yes or no when I put a question to her directly.

Whether she will be able to sing again is anyone's guess.

Please know that she's under the very best of care. She will most likely convalesce with Bessie and Francis, where she can be made much more comfortable.

In case you're wondering, I am looking after the bird. It has learned to say "Fleurette," or something quite close to it, and by saying her name seems to ask about her every day.

My assignment is nearly concluded. The man of the house is too ill to give his testimony and, in fact, the doctors aren't sure he'll survive. The case can draw to a close with or without him, but I'm waiting every day at the hospital to interview him if he happens to rally. I'll take another assignment as soon as Fleurette is well.

The news from the Somme is devastating, but surely this is the very end of the fighting.

Yours,
Constance

BIELASKI TO CONSTANCE

October 30, 1918

Dear Miss Kopp,

We had a British agent go personally to inform Mr. Wilmington's family in London of his death. The agent was instructed to say nothing of Mrs. Wilmington's activities. The family was told only that he died of pneumonia in the hospital, that American authorities have discovered that his widow is German-born, and that the United States government must confirm certain details of her story before deciding whether she will be allowed to remain here.

Every relation gives the same account: Mr. Wilmington knew that his wife was German and that she moved to London at the age of fourteen. They recall that she was eager to leave when the war began. In fact, the move to America was undertaken mostly at her insistence. At the time, everyone assumed that she wanted to remain above suspicion and sever all ties with the Kaiser. Now we know the truth. She intended to work against us, to impede our progress in joining in the war, and to weaken our position once we did. I don't believe Mr. Wilmington suspected any of that.

I'm in receipt of your report on the questioning of Sam Archer, the other men at the print shop, and Mr. Wilmington's associates. Their statements can't entirely clear his good name, but they will certainly go into the record.

I visited Mrs. Wilmington in jail and told her myself of her husband's death. She did cry a little and make a fuss, but that could be play-acting. She insisted once again that he had no hand in her treachery nor any idea that she was working for the Germans. It seems that he was her ticket to America and her cover story. That's some kind of marriage.

Another assignment is yours when you're ready for it. I have a simple enough case for Miss Bradshaw, but I want her reporting to you. She's back on a secretary's desk at the War Department until your sister is home and you can turn your attention back to Bureau business.

Talk of an armistice sounds serious this time. Our work continues regardless. Write when you're ready.

Yours very truly,

A. Bruce Bielaski

NOVEMBER 11, 1918

Armistice Day

CONSTANCE TO NORMA

November 13, 1918

Dear Norma,

I've imagined a hundred versions of this letter and written it over and over in my mind. But now that it comes time to put words to paper, I can't think what to say except that we wait, eagerly and impatiently, to greet your ship and to see you set foot on American soil again.

The news here is so garbled, as you can imagine—three extras a day and everyone clamoring over each other to spread rumors and speculation—but as I understand it, our soldiers will be needed for some time to keep the peace and make sure the Germans withdraw according to schedule. As long as there are soldiers in Europe, there will be nurses and canteen workers—but what about messenger pigeon operators? Might they send you—and your birds—home soon?

I can't promise that we'll have the farm habitable in time for Christmas, but Francis and I are going over tomorrow to see what needs to be done. I'm keeping my room at the boarding-house until we have everything settled. I might need to keep it regardless—I don't know how I'd get back and forth to any sort of job from the countryside. How did I ever manage it before? It seems a hundred years ago.

There are parades and parties and every kind of celebration here. Fleurette is out of the hospital and recuperating, but we're doing everything in our power to keep her indoors. Her doctors are starting to see cases of Spanish influenza at the hospital, and they advise me to keep her off the streets to avoid any chance of infection.

Tell us your plans, and Aggie's, when you have them. We feel that she's one of ours now, and we would welcome her here!

Yours,
Constance

NORMA TO CONSTANCE

November 25, 1918

Dear Constance,

The war has concluded but you'd never know it here. The hospitals remain full, the engineering schools are still holding classes (the Army intends to finish some of its bigger rail and communications projects before we leave), and our pigeon outpost is being gradually turned over to the French—only very gradually, as they've lost interest in all matters military-related and want only to rest and eat and tell their stories.

French life is resuming its old pace, in other words, while our Army wonders what to do with itself.

I'm to travel to Paris next week to make a final report on our pigeon school and the possibility for its continued operation in peace-time. I suppose they might decide to send me home from there. I'll cable as soon as I know.

As ever,
Norma

AGGIE TO NORMA

November 27, 1918

Dear Norma,

That was some trick you pulled, leaving for Paris without telling me. I know you don't like a long farewell, and there will be too many of them around here when we finally wind things down, but you're not finished with me!

I'm writing with an urgent message for you: If they offer to send you home, don't go! I want you to stay in Europe with me.

I've taken a two-year post in Belgium with the Red Cross. You'd be surprised at how many of us are going. It seems that most of the nurses here have become accustomed to the frenzied war-time life, and can't bear the idea of returning home to sit in their mothers' parlors.

I can't imagine going home either, even though—or perhaps because—there's no one waiting for me there. What am I to do, work a shift at some county hospital and return home to a furnished room at night? What kind of life is that?

If this war has shown me one thing, it's that the world is far bigger and grander, and more filled with tragedy and chaos and love, than I ever knew it was. There's more adventure to be had, out here, than I could ever hope for back in the same well-trod paths I took at home. There's more of a need, too. America can survive on its own. Europe is battered beyond recognition. The war doesn't truly end until these nations are back on their feet.

Don't you feel as I do, Norma? Admit it: Wouldn't you rather have another year here than anything else in the world? Of course we wished desperately for the fighting to end, but now that it has, who wants to go back to the way things were before? I don't, and I suspect you don't, either.

Here's what I'm working up to tell you: They are desperate for interpreters! I have a position absolutely promised to you if you'll take it. The committee was just here yesterday, holding interviews, and when I told them that I knew an American woman who understood our way of doing things, and spoke both French and German perfectly, they could hardly believe it.

I know it has nothing to do with pigeons, and might bore you at times, but, Norma, I simply can't imagine going without you.

Think of the countries we could visit, and the places and people we would see! There's useful work ahead for us, and who knows, perhaps another cake shop to investigate.

I hate to lure you away from your sisters, but when will you have another chance? Come with me, and if it doesn't suit you, go home any time.

I leave for Paris in a week. Wait there for me, won't you?

Au plaisir de te revoir—

Aggie

NORMA TO AGGIE

November 30, 1918

Dear Aggie,

You oughtn't to go running off to Belgium without any idea of what you're getting into. The reports here in Paris are that it's a mess and will be for some time. The German occupation will be slow to unwind, the numbers of refugees are overwhelming, and nobody knows what they'll find at the prison camps.

It isn't a nice quiet village with a wall around it. We think we've been in the war, but we've been living in the countryside. We never saw the bombing that Paris did, and we never suffered through the rationing they did. Country folk have a way of getting by, but this city saw real deprivation. Everyone here is skin and bones. You've seen suffering and misery at the hospital, of course, but Belgium will be another story entirely.

You're right that I'm expected at home. Everyone is—including you. It isn't true that no one is waiting for you. We would be waiting for you—the Kopps—all of us.

Nonetheless, if you're set on going to Belgium, I can't possibly allow you to go alone. Your French is terrible and you don't have a word of German. I'll speak to the Red Cross committee if you insist on following through with this scheme, and we can hear for ourselves what they have in mind for us.

Yesterday a man on the street said that the war is not over until everyone can go home. If that's true, the war will not end in Belgium for many months to come, perhaps years. I suppose you think that you'd be shirking your duty to go home now.

Of course, my sisters expect me back. They can't manage the farmhouse without me—neither of them know a thing about running a household—but they could shift for themselves a while longer while you and I go and have a look at Belgium.

I'm waiting for you in Paris.

As ever,

Norma

FLEURETTE TO FREEMAN BERNSTEIN

December 1, 1918

Dear Mr. Bernstein,

It's been ages since I've written. I'm sorry to say that I'm not yet ready to take Laura on tour, and that all my plans—for songs, for costumes, for bird tricks and whistles—all of it had to be put aside while I assisted Constance in a case of some importance. In the process, I fell ill again, or perhaps I never properly recovered from the bug I picked up at Camp Sherman—but the miserable truth is that I was in the hospital for some time, and then sent to my brother's home for strict bed rest and close watching by female relations.

I'm only just now up and about again, and starting to rehearse with Laura. My voice isn't entirely recovered, but the doctors say to rest it for another month before I try again.

Please don't forget about me! Until I'm well, I remain—

Yours very truly,

Fleurette

BIELASKI TO CONSTANCE

December 4, 1918

Dear Miss Kopp,

You'll see this in the papers soon, but I'll tell you now: I'm having to answer to my superiors over the League men and how they conducted their slacker raids. (Don't remind me of all the times you warned me.) I'll be testifying in front of Congress (and in front of a gang of reporters up to the rafters) for most of December. After that, I'm done. It's been suggested that I "pursue business opportunities." That's exactly what I intend to do.

That doesn't mean that you're done, too. My deputy, a Mr. William E. Allen from Fort Worth, Texas, will step in as acting chief of the Bureau in January. I've told him that you're to stay on after the war, and that you'll bring a few ladies along with you. We can't call it a division or a department, but in an unofficial capacity that's exactly what it will be. Since I'm the one who started our training school for agents, I'm still (for a few more weeks) the one who decides what goes on at that school. You're to train the lady agents and shepherd them along.

Allen's a good man. Come down to Washington and meet him now, while I'm still around to introduce you. And don't waste any pity on me. I've been director since 1912, which is too long. It's about time another fellow had a crack at it.

There will be a ticket for you at the station. You're to leave on the 9 a.m. on Monday. Wire to let me know to expect you.

Yours very truly,

A. Bruce Bielaski

TELEGRAM FROM CONSTANCE TO BIELASKI

December 6, 1918

I WILL BE ON THE TRAIN

CONSTANCE TO NORMA

December 9, 1918

Dear Norma,

I have news that can't wait until you return, or perhaps I simply can't wait another minute to tell someone. I'm at the train station in Washington now, having just spoken to Mr. Bielaski. In the space of one hour, I've made new plans for my life.

I won't make you skip ahead to the end of this letter to find out what I've decided. Here it is: I'm moving to Washington. I'm due there in January, which means that I might've already packed up and gone by the time you return.

I will, of course, meet your ship, wherever and whenever it arrives. I would invite you to join me in Washington—I can find an apartment for two—but I can't imagine you ever leaving New Jersey. I expect you'll want to stay on at the farm, or remain with the Signal Corps at Fort Monmouth. (Most likely the latter, although you haven't told us yet. Or perhaps you have. The mail delays are worse now than they were in wartime.)

Fleurette is desperate to get away from us both and will no doubt return to the stage as soon as she's entirely well. I could try to stop her, but on what grounds? She's a grown woman. She can do as she pleases. She'll always have a bed in Washington if she wants one, and a place at Bessie and Francis's table, and perhaps a place with you, wherever you land. But she's not going back to the farm any more than I am.

From such a great distance, it must be impossible to imagine the mood here. You're living in a ruined place among ruined people. Everywhere you turn, you see devastation.

But here it is the opposite. Everywhere I turn, I see a spirit of progress and forward momentum. We mourn our losses, and grieve over the wounded and shattered men returning home—of course we do—but with the war ended, there's a spark here that I can hardly describe. It's a sense that nothing can be the same again, and that what's coming next is—well, a new era. Something bright and almost unimaginably different from the old days, before the war.

You're not coming home to the country you left, that's what I'm telling you. Even our old home, and the way we once lived —all of that has been turned upside down. But please don't worry about where you'll fit or what you'll do—you can take all the time you like to rest, recover, and find your way again. I just thought it better to tell you now, rather than let you harbor one dream of home only to find something quite different waiting for you.

Now I'll tell you the entire story. Mr. Bielaski summoned me down to Washington to meet his replacement, as he plans to resign and go into business next year. You've never met Mr. Bielaski, so you must take my word for it that he is a more generous and good-humored man than the pictures in the papers might lead you to believe. In those pictures he's always the hard-bitten cop, with the brim of his hat down and a stern look in his eyes. And he certainly is a cop through and through —he has lived and breathed the Bureau's mission every day and night of this war. I don't imagine he's had more than four hours of sleep in a night for years.

They tell me that newspapers are getting through to France every day now, so you might've read about his testimony to Congress. If there's one thing you can learn about him from those articles, it's this: he had his hands on every case that ran through his department. There wasn't a move made by any one of us that he didn't follow. He's been testifying without notes, for hours each day, on every subject from propagandists infiltrating the newspapers to breweries harboring German sympathizers. He hasn't yet had cause to mention any of my cases, but he's nonetheless explaining, in meticulous detail, the work of countless agents (both volunteer League men and his own agents) on hundreds of cases over several years. It's extraordinary, what he's accomplished, and I for one am sorry to see his career in public service come to an end.

But I was summoned to Washington to meet the man who is to succeed him, and who will be my boss in the new year.

Mr. Allen is quite different from Mr. Bielaski in both temperament and appearance. Where Mr. Bielaski has the bearing and stature of a policeman on patrol, Mr. Allen reminds one of a scholar. He's tall and lean, with dark hair, round spectacles, and the measured drawl of a Texan. There's something of a young Lincoln about him, if that helps to fix a picture in your mind.

He practiced law with some distinction in Fort Worth, and had served most recently as an assistant federal district attorney before Mr. Bielaski made him a deputy at the Bureau. There's no end to the legal entanglements and financial crimes that the Bureau must investigate, and I take it that he spent most of his time on those matters. The more rough-and-tumble aspects of our work are, to put it mildly, unfamiliar to him.

When I was introduced to him, in the office that Mr. Bielaski will soon hand over to him, he stood cordially and said, "I've been learning all the Bureau's secrets this week, including the name of its only lady agent. Please accept my thanks for your service to the country, Miss Kopp."

To be greeted in such a courtly and . . . well, *approving* manner put me directly at ease. "It's been the greatest honor of my life," I told him. "I hope I might continue to serve in any way the Bureau sees fit."

"They want change," Mr. Bielaski said, pointing his thumb in the direction of what I suppose must've been the White House, or Congress, although there was nothing outside his window but bare tree branches, "and change is what they'll get. Mr. Allen is, at present, only the acting chief, although I hope we'll persuade him to stay on—"

Here Mr. Allen grinned widely but said, "I've a wife and four girls to consider, but we are thinking on it."

"That's just what we want you to do," Mr. Bielaski said. "Take Mrs. Allen to the theater, and show her a nice house on a quiet street. Why, when she sees the cherry blossoms this spring—"

"She's entirely immune to cherry blossoms," Mr. Allen said. "We have flowers on the trees in Texas, you know."

"Not like ours," Mr. Bielaski said. "But as I was saying, the Bureau's going to change. We're the only civilized nation of any size that hasn't been touched by this war. That means that our factories will equip the world, and our farms will feed the world. The risk of sabotage and the threat from the Bolsheviks haven't gone away just because the Germans stopped shooting. Mr. Allen's going to put the agency on a more professional footing, and see that our agents—including you, Miss Kopp—have all the resources they need to do the job."

At that moment all eyes turned to me. I realized that my turn had come. It was up to me to say what, exactly, I required. What my *department* required.

Fortunately, I'd had a long train ride to put it all together in my mind. I simply squared my shoulders and began.

"It seems to me that a separate training program for women would allow them to more quickly find their way and learn what, exactly, they might best contribute to the Bureau. Such a program would serve them not only as agents, but also as police officers, deputy sheriffs, or any other such work to which they are suited. In fact, we might open the course to women considering any position in law enforcement, and take the top candidates for our own. The others can finish our training and go on to find work in any police department."

Mr. Bielaski nodded at this and said to Mr. Allen, "I didn't know, until Miss Kopp told me, that most of these lady cops you hear about are given no training whatsoever, because the police chiefs don't know what to do with them. If the Bureau puts the course together, we'll have an influence over police departments all over the country."

Mr. Allen nodded. "That's fine, if Congress will give us the money. What would you see these ladies doing—let's say, if you had a class of thirty?"

Thirty! I'd hoped to recruit five! But I went on as if it was nothing. "Training in the law, of course," I said quickly, knowing Mr. Allen would want to see plenty of book-learning, "and training in Bureau procedures. I would also teach combat moves and holds, how to make arrests and use firearms."

Would you believe it, Mr. Allen didn't even blink at that! Perhaps all the women in Texas carry guns, I don't know. I continued on. "Surveillance methods, naturally, and interviewing techniques, along with some understanding of codes, secret inks, and means of concealment. I've spoken both French and German from childhood, so I would offer at least a taste of a foreign language course to see who had an aptitude for it."

Mr. Allen and Mr. Bielaski were both leaning back in their chairs by now, smiling. "That's everything the men learn, and a bit more," Mr. Bielaski said to Mr. Allen. "I guarantee you that Miss Kopp's agents will come out of the course better trained and qualified than some of the fellows. These boys think they know everything, so they don't listen in class. I've kicked out quite a few because they couldn't bother to do the work."

"You won't have that problem with my students," I said, and I meant it. Oh, Norma, you know how hard they'll work. You know how eager they'll be to have a chance.

There's so much more to tell you, but the train's coming. Must close for now. I'll post this from Paterson and write again soon.

Tell us your plans as soon as you have them. I know there's a great deal to be sorted out over there even though the fighting has ceased, but we're all impatient to have you home.

Love,

Constance

FLEURETTE TO HELEN

December 9, 1918

Dearest Helen,

I hope this letter catches up with you in New York. I can understand entirely why you and the boys would want to be there to greet your father's ship, and to wait nearby while the Army does whatever it must do to discharge him. I've heard of soldiers being quarantined for weeks when they return. I hope they'll let your father go without all that fuss.

I have some news that can't wait until you get home. I've just been bursting to tell you! Yesterday I had the most astonishing letter from Freeman Bernstein. I'd written him to say that I was terribly behind in putting an act together, and had only just returned to rehearsals after a miserable illness.

Would you believe it, he wrote back promptly and told me that nothing puts a girl back on her feet faster than a contract!

A real contract, Helen—and I haven't even finished my act! He offered me three hundred dollars per week, and bookings in five cities to start. He promised to work out a schedule as soon as I say I'm ready to go. I have only to sign at the bottom and send it back when I'm well.

Just the thought of it was enough to make me want to leap up and get to work this instant! Do you know that my first thought was that I couldn't wait to tell Laura? What do you suppose she'll make of a signed contract with a Broadway manager? I suppose she'll take a bite out of it if she can. Oh, I'd like to take a bite out of it, too, but instead I kissed it, and now I sleep with it under my pillow.

Everyone's talked for so long of *après la guerre,* and now here we are, and it's more than I could've imagined. All I ever wanted was to sing and dance, and to live my life as I pleased, and get off that rotten old farm and see something of the world. It felt like I was always too young, and under the watch of too many sisters, and without the funds or the wherewithal to put myself together and to—well, to launch myself, like a steamer leaving port.

But that's just how I feel now! Mr. Bernstein once asked me to imagine the 1920s, and at first I thought he said to imagine *my twenties,* but it's the same thing, isn't it? It's a bright and brilliant future, when the boys come home and the world is at peace and we can do as we wish and make our own fortunes.

Only I haven't told my sisters yet—so don't breathe a word about it! The truth is that I feel a bit sorry for both of them. What will they do, after the war? Constance is off in Washington now, learning her fate. I don't imagine the Bureau will have need of a lady spy any more, with the Germans defeated. I suppose she can find work at a jail somewhere, but doesn't that just sound like—well, like *jail?*

And what will become of Norma? I don't know how we'll break the news to her that messenger pigeons are going into retirement. Did you know that there are ten million telephones in this country? Truly, we mustn't tell her that she's coming home to a nation of telephones, automobiles, and electrical lighting, or she might just stay in France forever.

Is it too much to hope that when your father comes home, you'll be free, and we can make a duet and travel together? It's been too long since we've been on the stage, dear Helen, and as much as I love all the girls in May Ward's chorus, you're better than the lot of them. Mr. Bernstein is right—Broadway is going to want fresh young faces, and that's you and me.

I might sound delirious. I suppose I am. Let's go be delirious together. It's our turn!

With love and affection,
Fleurette

Historical Notes

AS WITH MY most recent Kopp Sisters novel, *Kopp Sisters on the March*, I've had to veer even further into fiction for this novel because I don't know exactly what the Kopp sisters were up to during World War I. For the next book in the series, which begins after the war, I'll be able to pick up their true story again. (And it's remarkable, what happens next. Stay tuned!)

Meanwhile, for this novel I've placed the real-life Kopp sisters into real-life situations—but their participation in these events is fictional.

Here's what I do know about the Kopps' lives during World War I: Constance's obituary stated that "during the world war she performed a considerable amount of secret intelligence work for the federal government." Another obituary said that she worked for the Sherman Service, which was a company that business owners could hire to snoop on their employees, with the aim of ferreting out acts of sabotage or union organizing. Opposing unions would've been seen (by some people, at least) as a patriotic endeavor at that time. The factories had to keep running if we were to win the war, and the fear was that worker protests would only get in the way.

I took those hints about Constance's wartime work and did all I could with them. Of Norma's and Fleurette's activities I know nothing at all. They completely dropped out of sight during World War I.

I sent Norma to Langres, France, where the Army Signal Corps did, in fact, have a messenger pigeon school at the Fort de la Bonnelle. I visited twice to see the site of the old school for myself and to interview local historians. Those were tough research trips, folks. I took the most beautiful walk of my life through the countryside to trace Norma's route from town to the fort, and stopped to interview the French-speaking goats along the way. I sat in sidewalk cafés and wrote sketches of the people walking by. Many of the physical descriptions of villagers come from those afternoons. When three "town drunks" sat right in front of me and proceeded to make mayhem on the village square, I thought, "Fine. I'm putting all three of you in my book," and I did.

With the help of local guide Maud Cauchois, I toured the abandoned fort, and visited the astonishing Petit Musée du Doughboy, a collection of artifacts from the Americans' participation in the war in that region of France. Its owner, Franck Besch, has an infectious passion for this moment in history. From his collection came the story of the button on Forrest Pike's coat and the soldiers' engravings on the mess kits. I can't thank Ms. Cauchois and Mr. Besch enough for their generosity and patience with my limited (okay, nonexistent) French. I couldn't have told this story without them.

The version of Langres in wartime that I present in this novel is based on letters and diaries kept by American soldiers stationed there, plus a collection of photographs and correspondence pertaining to the pigeon school held at the National Archives. It is very much the viewpoint of one highly opinionated American — Norma. I'm sure Norma's perspective is very different from that of the villagers who lived through those devastating years.

The pigeon service did not, to my knowledge, deploy any women overseas. There were Signal Corps women operating the switchboard in the nearby town of Chaumont. For more about them, I highly recommend Elizabeth Cobbs's excellent book *The Hello Girls*. Also, the Signal Corps did not, as far as I know, ever consider discontinuing its messenger pigeon program, although all the problems with the program I described were real problems faced by military pigeon programs at the time. Norma's opinions about her superiors, as well as her contempt for the "British method" and the "French method," stem entirely from Norma's own curmudgeonly personality and are not a reflection on the actual fine work done by those parties during the war.

Aggie's story was inspired by a *Washington Post* article from February 10, 1918, "The German Spy and the Cake with the Hollow Center." The real-life cake-shop spy lived in Québec, not Langres, but I couldn't resist borrowing from those events for my story. Thanks to researcher Alix Barnaud for helping me with French pastries of the era, the realities of food shortages and rationing in France during the war, and translations.

The story of Mon Chou is very closely based on the true story of another pigeon, Cher Ami. Cher Ami actually flew a dozen critical missions, including a friendly fire incident much like the one I described. Unlike Mon Chou, Cher Ami was patched up, survived, and was awarded the French Croix de Guerre. Thanks to the wonders of taxidermy, both Cher Ami and his medal are still on display at the Smithsonian.

A few other notes: Forrest Pike refers to "Emma Gee," which was slang for MG, or machine gun. Norma's complaint to Forrest Pike about the fact that she doesn't hold the rank of lieutenant reflects a real problem for women serving overseas at the time. They fought for "relative rank," the idea that their positions should be assigned ranks equivalent to those given to enlisted men. They were unsuccessful in that effort: women who wore a uniform and served overseas were denied military benefits and honors when they returned home.

The concept of a *filleul de guerre,* or a wartime godson, is described in more detail in *Canteening Overseas, 1917–1919,* by Marian Baldwin. Please see the recommended reading list at the end of these notes for a partial list of the collections of women's wartime letters and diaries I consulted while writing this book.

Fleurette did not, to my knowledge, tour Army camps performing with the real-life May Ward. There is, however, a real-life connection between the Kopp sisters and May Ward. If you're new to the series, read the historical notes in *Miss Kopp's Midnight Confessions* to find out more.

In fact, May Ward did perform at some Army camps, mostly in 1919, after soldiers returned from France but before they were released from active duty. My descriptions of the camps, the Hostess Houses, and the policing of girls' behavior comes from photographs and newspapers of the era. Nancy K. Bristow's *Making Men Moral: Social Engineering During the Great War* describes the work of the Committee on Protective Work for Girls and Maude Miner's role in great detail. Maude Miner's letter to Constance draws from that book, Miner's own memoir, her published letters, and quotes of hers in newspaper articles of the era.

Fleurette's and Bernice's experiences in detention only scratch the surface of what happened to women during World War I and for decades after. Tens of thousands, if not hundreds of thousands, of women suspected of promiscuity or sexually transmitted diseases were locked up with no due process, sometimes for years, under a program called "The American Plan." I recommend Scott W. Stern's book *The Trials of Nina McCall* for more on this mostly forgotten travesty.

Oh, and about that parrot. Fleurette Kopp really did own a parrot named Laura, who was with her from childhood until well into her later years. Fleurette's family tells stories about Fleurette working at her sewing machine while Laura sat on top of her cage and carried on conversations with her all day long. I'm happy to bring Laura into the story at last. Norma's birdkeeping advice comes mostly from *Bishop: The Bird Man's Book*, first published in 1886.

Constance, as I said previously, did some sort of intelligence work during the war, perhaps for a private company called the Sherman Service. I chose instead to put her to work for A. Bruce Bielaski, director of the Bureau of Investigation (later called the FBI). I had an ulterior motive: I wanted to introduce Constance to my great-grandfather, William E. Allen, who worked for Bruce Bielaski and then served as interim director of the Bureau for six months in 1919. One of the four daughters Mr. Allen refers to during his meeting with Constance is my grandmother.

Although there were not, to my knowledge, any women employed as agents for the Bureau during the war, Constance's activities are based on real cases from the era. The case involving David Rogovin at the Curtiss North Elmwood plant in Buffalo happened as described, as did the explosion at the munitions plant in Syracuse. The raid on the "disreputable house" at the St. Regis is loosely based on a real raid that took place there that year. The Wilmington case is fictional, but is a composite of several real sabotage cases from the era.

The American Protective League was both a useful volunteer organization and a thorn in the side of the Bureau. Mr. Bielaski really did have to testify before Congress in December 1918 about the League's activities, and then he resigned. For more on the League, please read Bill Mills's *The League: A True Story of Average Americans on the Hunt for WWI Spies.*

Constance's recipe for a chemical solution that would allow her to steam open envelopes comes from recently declassified CIA documents from World War I. Those documents also revealed some of the government's techniques for developing secret ink. For more on that subject, I highly recommend *Prisoners, Lovers, and Spies: The Story of Invisible Ink from Herodotus to al-Qaeda* by Kristie Macrakis. Mr. Bielaski's story about the German pigeon with holes in its feathers is based on a similar story told by American cryptologist Herbert Yardley.

Bessie's efforts to help with the war—including the fundraiser in which children wrote letters, the librarians' book drive for soldiers, the program to "adopt" French war orphans, and the process of collecting nutshells and fruit pits for gas masks —are all based on real events. Frankie Jr.'s and Lorraine's letters to French children are quoted from actual letters American children wrote at the time. There really was a Tobacco Fund to raise money to send cigarettes and pipe tobacco to soldiers.

For more about the real-life Kopps, please visit my website at www.amystewart.com/bookclubs, where you'll find photos, Q&As, and information about how we can chat about the books on Skype. And stay tuned for the next installment!

WOMEN IN WORLD WAR I: RECOMMENDED READING

Aldrich, Mildred. *A Hilltop on the Marne: Civilian Letters from War-torn France.* 1916. Reprint, London: Hesperus Press, 2014.

Baldwin, Maria T., and Margaret Wade Campbell Deland. *Canteening Overseas, 1917–1919.* New York: Macmillan, 1920.

Boylston, Helen Dore. *"Sister": The War Diary of a Nurse.* New York: Washburn, 1927.

Crewdson, Dorothea. *Dorothea's War: A First World War Nurse Tells Her Story,* edited by Richard Crewdson. London: Phoenix, 2014.

Dent, Olive, and R. M. Savage. *A Volunteer Nurse on the Western Front.* London: Virgin, 2014.

Foxwell, Elizabeth. *In Their Own Words: American Women in World War I.* Waverly, TN: Oconee Spirit Press, 2015.

Hunton, Addie W., and Kathryn M. Johnson. *Two Colored Women in World War I France*. 1920. Reprint, Bellevue, WA: Big Byte Books, 2015.

Janis, Elsie. *The Big Show: My Six Months with the American Expeditionary Forces*. New York: Cosmopolitan Book, 1919.

O'Brien, Alice M. *Alice in France: The World War I Letters of Alice M. O'Brien*, edited by Nancy O'Brien Wagner. St. Paul: Minnesota Historical Society Press, 2017.

Saltonstall, Nora. *"Out Here at the Front": The World War I Letters of Nora Saltonstall*, edited by Judith S. Graham. Boston: Northeastern University Press, 2004.